A Dark and Stormy Knight

Bridget Essex

Rose + Star

Press

Other Books by Bridget Essex

The Protector
Meeting Eternity (The Sullivan Vampires, Vol. 1)
Trusting Eternity (The Sullivan Vampires, Vol. 2)
Wolf Pack
Wolf Heart
Wolf Queen
Falling for Summer
The Guardian Angel
The Vampire Next Door (with Natalie Vivien)
A Wolf for Valentine's Day
A Wolf for the Holidays
The Christmas Wolf
Don't Say Goodbye
Forever and a Knight
A Knight to Remember
Date Knight
Wolf Town
Dark Angel
Big, Bad Wolf

Erotica

Wild
Come Home, I Need You

About the Author

My name is Bridget Essex, and I've been writing about vampires for almost two decades. I'm influenced most by classic vampires– the vision of CARMILLA (it's one of the oldest lesbian novels!) and DRACULA. My vampires have always been kind of traditional (powerful), but with the added self-torture of regret and the human touch of guilt.

I have a vast collection of knitting needles and teacups, and like to listen to classical music when I write. My first date with my wife was strolling in a garden, so it's safe to say I'm a bit old fashioned. I have a black cat I love very much, and two white dogs who actually convince me to go outside. When I'm actually outside, I begin to realize that writing isn't all there is to life. Just most of it! I'm married to the love of my life, author Natalie Vivien.

Find out more about my work at
www.LesbianRomance.org and
http://BridgetEssex.Wordpress.com

Date Knight
Copyright © 2016 Bridget Essex - All Rights Reserved
Published by Rose and Star Press
First edition, June 2016

ISBN: 1519245122
ISBN-13: 978-1519245120

A Dark and

Stormy

Knight

DEDICATION

For my own lady knight in shining armor — you are my universe.

And this book is especially dedicated to my sister, Kitty, who loved my stories enough to get them inked on her skin. Your constant support is the reason I write today. This dark and stormy (k)night is, and always has been, for you.

Chapter 1: The Unexpected Goldfish

"My knight in shining armor!"

I chuckle while toeing the door closed, balancing the five boxes of pizza on my hip and nearly losing my balance as I kick my shoes off. "I wouldn't go *that* far, Iris," I tease, but Iris is already dancing forward, snatching the pizza boxes out of my hands and pirouetting in place as she inhales the delicious aroma wafting from the hole in the top box.

"Mara's back with the 'za!" she shouts at the top of her lungs.

I toss my purse on the floor beside the large pile of shoes, and then I'm on my knees in a split second to avoid being bowled over by Sammie—who bowls me over, anyway, plastering me onto my back. My enthusiastic ("aggressively affectionate" might be a better description) dog slobbers love onto my face.

Love in the form of drool.

When Sammie was adopted, the shelter said he was part husky, part Saint Bernard, part terrier, and part every-other-dog-you-can-think-of. He looks cobbled together, as if a toddler took various dog parts and taped them on top of each other. And he has the zany personality to match.

I love him like crazy.

"Okay, baby," I tell him, squirming beneath his two-hundred-and-fifty-pound bulk until I manage to rise into a sitting position. I ruffle his fluffy brown ears, and then Iris offers me a hand, pulling me up to my feet.

"You've got a little something there," she says helpfully, pointing to my ponytail, and I groan, trotting toward the nearest bathroom to wipe my dog's drool out of my hair.

Unfortunately, the bathroom is locked.

I knock.

"Who *is* it?" Toby sings out from behind the door.

"It's Mara, Tobes—Sammie slimed me," I tell him patiently. "How long are you going to be?"

"I'm practicing my faces!" Toby sings again.

I shake my head and groan, banging my forehead gently on the wooden door. "That's awesome, but can you stop for just a minute while I wash the drool out?"

Toby throws the door open as dramatically as possible. Actually, Toby does *everything* as dramatically as possible, including dressing for the day.

I didn't see Toby before I left to pick up the pizzas; he's a night owl and usually begins his day around six pm. So I'm taking in his appearance for the first time now: he's currently dressed as a mime. Like…an actual mime, with white face paint, a black bodysuit, and a French beret tipped at a jaunty angle on his head.

Keep in mind that Toby is almost seven feet tall, as thin as a sapling, and comprised mostly of elbows and handsome poses. He throws one of said poses at me now, cocking his hip and placing his hand on it, as if he just walked the runway in Milan…in a mime costume.

"How am I going to get that part if I don't practice my *faces,* Mara?" he complains to me; then, without a pause, he turns his white-painted nose toward the kitchen, grinning. "Hey, do I smell *pizza?*"

"I banged on your door before I left and told you I was going to get it," I say as I sneak past him into the bathroom. "But there were some…um…amorous sounds coming from your room, so I didn't push the matter."

"Rod and I were engaged in a lovemaking session that involved a trapeze," says Toby. He starts down the hallway, aiming for the kitchen. "So thanks for the space, Mara!"

"Wait—a *trapeze?*" I shout after him, peeking out of the doorway, my mouth hanging open.

"Cecile said it was okay to install one!" he calls out airily over his shoulder, and then he's rounded the corner and drifted out of sight.

I guess I should pause here to explain my living situation—because it's…kind of unusual.

I live in a grain elevator.

The first question I get asked when I tell people this is—actually, no, there *are* no follow-up questions. Instead, people tend to stare at me as if I've just told them I'm an alien from the planet Venus, so I usually have to clarify the situation quickly.

I live in Buffalo, and if you've watched any show about blizzards on the Weather Channel, you'll know what we're famous for (besides the chicken wings and a really, *really* bad football team). But at the turn of the century, Buffalo was a booming city and one of the biggest grain producers in the world. Weird, I know.

The manufacturers needed somewhere to store all of that grain before they shlubbed it onto the boats on Lake Erie or sent it down the Erie Canal.

So they built the grain elevators.

Unless you're from Buffalo, you've probably never heard of the grain elevators before. Think massive, industrial-looking buildings, all metal, scraping the sky. Now imagine them empty and rusting, like something out of a post-apocalyptic movie. When Buffalo stopped producing so much grain, the elevators were abandoned.

Despite being a blue-collar city, Buffalo has a thriving arts community, and we love to play up the corroding-metal and crumbling-dreams drama of our bygone era. So when a friend of mine, the indomitable Cecile Sanderson, bought an old grain elevator with the intention of transforming it into an artists' residence, I—and several other fellow artists—jumped at the opportunity to live in the rusty building beside the Lake Erie shoreline.

Cecile named the elevator the Ceres, after the Greek goddess of grain, and once the renovations were, more or less, complete, we moved in, and the rest is history. Or herstory, as the case may be.

Admittedly, this is a weird way to live. But if you're keen on cohabitating with a bunch of artistic misfits—which I am—it's a lot of fun. All of that creativity... We bounce ideas off of each other and spend long nights talking about art, life, and everything else. I'm a painter, and being around so many other creative people really fuels my work.

However...living with so many people with their heads positioned firmly in the clouds makes for some, well, interesting situations.

I stare at myself in the mirror and try to see my reflection, but it's difficult with Iris' motivational post-it notes littering the shiny surface. *You are beautiful through and through!* has to come off in order for me to find the strand of drool draped over my ponytail. I pick it up with my finger and pull it off of my hair, letting the sink water wash it away. Toby's mime makeup is all over the counter, and when I take a step backwards to grab one of the hand towels from the shelf, there are, of course, no hand towels left. Instead, there's a silky kimono covered in blue butterflies (which might be Iris' or Cecile's or Miyoko's…or Toby's). I leave that on the shelf and shake my hands in the air, letting little droplets fly. When I glance back at the mirror to make certain that I removed all of the drool, I stare at something that's staring at me with just as much surprise.

On the back of our toilet, and on top of a stack of books that includes the *Kama Sutra*, the first three *Hitchhiker* books, and a Donald Trump biography (with devil horns drawn over his forehead), is a brand-new goldfish bowl. The goldfish inside of it glances up at me dolefully.

For a long moment, I do nothing. It's common for new pets to appear overnight in the Ceres, after all.

But the goldfish bowl is precariously balanced on top of those books, and—as I learned in fifth grade science class—goldfish bowls make goldfish go blind, due to the light reflecting off of the curved glass. I sigh as I stare down at the bowl and its aquatic inhabitant. Then I'm picking the bowl up and exiting the bathroom. Some of the goldfish's water sloshes out of the bowl and onto my shirt as I carry it into the kitchen.

"Hey, do you know whose goldfish this is?" I

ask Toby, who's trying to fit an entire slice of pizza into his mouth. He looks up at me with wide eyes that remind me of a baby owl, and he mumbles something, but around the pizza, it sounds like "mmf, mff, ffm," which isn't very helpful.

I turn to ask Iris next, but she's obviously in the middle of an argument with someone on Facebook. I know that look: she's scowling at her phone as if it's a miniature version of Donald Trump (the doodled-on book in the bathroom is hers), and she's jabbing at the screen while muttering something dangerous under her breath.

"Hey, Iris?" I say, and then I try again three more times before she tears her eyes away from her screen and slams the phone down onto the counter.

"*Ass*hole," she growls, then grabs a slice of cheese pizza, hissing as she burns her fingers on the melty cheese. "Don't they know that racism is—"

"I'm sure they have no idea," I tell her gently, smiling as I set the goldfish bowl down on the counter beside the open box of 'za. "Hey, do you know whose goldfish this is?"

"We have a goldfish now?" squeals Iris, going from "completely pissed about the state of the world" to "there's an adorable animal within my immediate vicinity" in a heartbeat. Characteristic Iris. "Can I name him?! I name him Vladimir Futon! Get it? Get it? Like Vladimir Putin!"

"That doesn't *quite* work," I begin, at the same time that Toby fist-pumps the air—in what I'm assuming is solidarity for the goldfish's new punny name.

"No, Mara, I don't know whose fish that is," says Iris then, taking an enormous bite of pizza. "But you should—mmf, ffm—ask Cecile."

"Okay, thanks—hey, Sammie, *no*!" I groan. I tell my dog *no* about eighteen-thousand times per day, give or take a few, so he doesn't pay me any mind as he jumps up, placing his two massive front paws on the counter as if to grab himself a slice of pizza. Instead, he spots the goldfish bowl and tries to angle his head *just so* in order to lap out of it, his enormous tongue licking the rim of the bowl enthusiastically.

"Iris, will you watch him for me? I'll go ask Cecile about the fish really quickly."

Iris is nodding, affectionately shoving Sammie off of the counter with her hip before grabbing herself another slice.

Sammie sits down at her feet and looks up at her with pure hope, a big doggie grin on his adorable doggie face.

"Tell everyone they'd better come down now, before all of the pizza is gone!" Iris calls out as she drops the rest of her slice into Sammie's waiting maw. I glance at the four as-yet unopened boxes of pizza on the counter; I don't think we're going to run out of slices anytime soon.

Chuckling, I ascend the rickety metal stairs that are hooked to the inside wall of the elevator, and soon I'm standing on the second level of the Ceres, a mezzanine that encircles the lower level. The bedrooms are situated along the curving wall. I knock on the first door—Toby and Rod's room—because Toby said his boyfriend had been by earlier, but there are no sounds from within. Then I skip the next couple of doors, my and Iris' bedrooms respectively, and I'm knocking on the fourth door, winding my way around the mezzanine.

"Yeah?" Miyoko shouts from inside. She opens the door and grins out at me sheepishly. "Oh, great, Mara, it's you. Can you help me with this?" She turns, her elaborate, full-length ballgown sweeping the floor. She gestures to the Elizabethan collar attached to her neckline. "The clasp is stuck, and I can't get this thing off."

"Why are you practicing in full costume?" I ask her, and I unhook the clasp—it had gotten tangled in her glorious blonde hair. Miyoko is an amazing actress, and she's currently starring in the Shakespeare in Delaware Park's rendition of *Macbeth*—as Lady Macbeth.

"Because the thing weighs, like, five hundred pounds, and I had to make sure I could be appropriately dramatic in it. *And* make sure no one could tell that I'm wincing in pain," she says brightly, gesturing to the floor-length mirror behind her, propped up in the corner of her extremely bright room. Her walls are orange, her bedspread is hot pink, and all of her furniture has been painted aqua. It suits her cheerful personality perfectly.

"Okay, so test it out. Act at me," I tell her with a smile.

Miyoko strikes a pose. "Yet here's a spot," she whispers, holding up her hands. In an *instant,* her expression has transformed from happy-go-lucky to one of spine-curdling dread. Her hands are curled into claws. "Out, damned spot!" She begins to rub her hands together feverishly. "Out, I say!—One: two: why, then, 'tis time to do't.—Hell is murky!—Fie, my lord, fie!" She stops and grins at me again, which is a little disconcerting after she just looked so unhinged. "So, whadya think? Good?"

"Great! Actually, you're terrifying," I tell her, darting forward and giving her a congratulatory hug.

"Perfect! I'm going for the unraveling of Lady Macbeth's sanity at that point."

"Well, it was spot on," I promise her, then startle, surprised, when Miyoko steps toward me, gripping my hand with wide eyes.

"You know about the curse of *Macbeth*, right? That there's a curse on the play, and on every opening night, something terrible happens?"

I nod vaguely. "But—"

"I mean," Miyoko goes on, "I'm not usually superstitious—"

I suppress a smile. Miyoko is the most superstitious person I've ever met. She refuses to walk under ladders, and when she spills a bit of salt, she has to toss a pinch of it over her shoulder. Every Friday the thirteenth, she walks around with wide, fearful eyes...

"—but what if this curse isn't just theater lore? I've never been in *Macbeth* before, Mara. What if the play really *is* cursed?"

"I promise you it's not cursed," I assure her. "There's no such thing as curses! And, anyway, the only reason that whole story came to be was because the players wanted to build a controversy, stir up curiosity. It's on the Wikipedia page."

"Wikipedia lies," Miyoko tells me dismissively, waving her hand.

I chuckle, gesturing downstairs. "Maybe so, but in good news, the pizza's here."

"Oh, my God, I'm *starved*," she moans, hitching up her skirts and sweeping past me. "Are you grabbing the others?"

"Yeah—hey," I call after her, and Miyoko turns to glance back at me. "Do you happen to know whose goldfish was in the bathroom?"

"We have a goldfish now?" asks Miyoko wryly, and she shakes her head. "Nope. Anyway, hurry up, or we'll eat all the pizza!" she laughs—it's a familiar threat in the Ceres—and then she's racing down the steps, her fabulous gown trailing behind her.

Miyoko in Elizabethan dress eating pizza: this I've *got* to see.

The second-to-last room belongs to Cecile, and as I knock on her door, I lean back on my heels; the scent of pizza wafts up through the air and assaults my nose. My stomach rumbles, but I wait patiently for Cecile to warble out, "Come in!" Then I open her door and step inside.

Cecile used to be a dancer. We're not sure if that means she was a ballet dancer, a contemporary dancer, or, you know, a stripper. But that's the great thing about Cecile: she has all sorts of mystery about her. Couple that with the perfectly white hair she keeps piled atop her head, the cat-eye glasses dangling from a brightly beaded lanyard around her neck, and her amazing vintage dresses, and she is, easily, one of the most glamorous people I've ever met. Greta Garbo-esque. She reminds me of how Greta Garbo would appear with several decades beneath her belt: gorgeous, wise—and completely cheeky.

"Hey, sweetheart," she says when I usher myself into her quarters. Cecile *should* have a bigger room than the rest of us. Hell, we just pay rent (and sometimes we don't even do that, depending on our monthly artistic successes) to live here, but Cecile owns the place. She turned it into the amazing home that it is, and she didn't even claim an enormous room for herself; her space is just as big as everyone else's.

Sometimes it's hard to remember that, before Cecile got her hands on the Ceres (back before it *was* the Ceres), the building was just an enormous, empty grain elevator. She built all of the rooms within it, brought in electricity, internet, and plumbing—which was no easy feat, considering the fact that our nearest neighbors are other, unoccupied, grain elevators. She is a force of change.

Buffalo's art scene might be pretty robust, but there was no place like the Ceres before Cecile dreamed it up. She told me once that, when she was a kid, she was the weird one out, and it was hard to find people like her, people she could relate to. So, in her old age, she wants to surround herself with fellow artists. Fellow "weirdos" who live together and love each other, like one big happy family.

That's exactly what we've become—family—thanks to Cecile.

"The pizzas are here," I tell her, and she glances up at me with genuine affection, blinking her bright blue eyes as she gestures me to her easel with a paint-spattered hand.

"What do you think, doll?" she asks me, her head tilted to the side as she stares at her painting, brush poised in her fingers. I come beside her and stare at the picture, too.

Cecile's been working on this one for a while. The painting is a complex wash of blues and grays; the colors blend into a fog-like blur. And out of that blur rises a series of soft curves reminiscent of a woman's shape: the swell of breasts, the graceful slope of a neck, of hips.

"It's gorgeous," I tell her, the truth. Cecile looks up at me, her eyes twinkling, and with a satisfied nod, she tosses her brush into a pot of water.

"You humor your old bat," she says, rising with a smile on her lips. "But I have to admit: I do like it, too."

I stand there, chewing on a fingernail until I realize I'm chewing on a fingernail—but it's too late. Cecile caught me.

"You only do that when something's troubling you," she remarks wryly, a brow raised. "Okay, so what's the matter with the painting? Be honest, doll."

"Nothing. *Nothing.* It's beautiful. Really evocative," I promise vehemently, and then I offer her a weak smile. "It just made me feel guilty. I mean, I haven't painted in…three days now, I think," I sigh. "This is how I make my living, and I'm being ridiculous and—"

Cecile raises a hand. Her palm has a wash of blue paint over it, as if she pressed it to the damp paper. "I'm personally acquainted with the starving-artist archetype, my dear," she smiles. "And if you're having a bad month, you know that you don't have to pay me rent. There's no pressure. Don't worry—"

"But that feels rotten, not paying rent." I shake my head. "I *love* living here. The last thing I want to do is take advantage of you."

"How is it taking advantage of me if I'm *telling* you it's all right?" she asks, her brow furrowing deeper. "What's really at the bottom of all of this? What's blocked you? As far as I know, you paint *every* day. It's your…" She searches for the right word, then chuckles. "Well, it's your obsession."

I swirl Cecile's paintbrush in the water pot,

picking it up and looking at the soft blue that's still on the bristles. "I *want* to paint," I tell her, biting my lip.

"But…" Cecile prompts me.

"I just keep painting…her," I whisper with a self-conscious sigh.

Her.

The reason I haven't picked up a brush in three days.

The reason I haven't been sleeping well.

I've had this reoccurring dream my entire life. Always the same dream.

Always…her.

"You're talking about the woman from your dream, I assume."

I nod.

"You've told me the dream before," says Cecile, sitting back down on her stool and folding her arms in front of her, "but my memory just isn't what it used to be." She watches me shrewdly for a moment. "Tell me again, Mara."

I draw in a deep breath, let it out. Then I close my eyes, and I see the dream play out, see it so clearly that it's as if I'm dreaming it right now, even though I'm wide awake.

"It starts with water," I whisper. "Cold, black water. There are stars in the water, and I become aware of them gradually, of their reflection sparkling on the surface. And then I notice that the moon is reflecting in the water, too, but it's so big and round and *real* that, for a moment, I wonder if the moon's *in* the water instead of above me.

"I'm floating, treading my feet, my hands opened up on the surface. And then she's just…there. She's in the water with me. She's naked," I tell Cecile, unashamed. Cecile's seen and done pretty much everything, after all. "And she's reaching out to me. She draws me toward her and holds me tight. And then she's kissing me." I swallow, remembering the sensation of her mouth on mine.

"Her black hair is everywhere. It reminds me of the night sky. The starlight is reflected in it, it's so glossy. That always stands out to me." I pause, biting my lip. "She looks like she has stars in her hair." I inhale, feeling shaky.

"Go on," Cecile coaxes me.

"She...she leans back from me then, and she tells me in this voice...this *voice*," I whisper, closing my eyes, hearing its timbre in my head. I've dreamed this dream so many times, and every time, her deep, growling voice pierces me through. "She says, 'A storm is coming...but I'll keep you safe.'"

Cecile watches me with hooded eyes; I spread my hands, shrug helplessly. "That's it. That's the end of the dream. There's a flash of lightning overhead, a crack of thunder... And then I wake up."

"And you've had that dream for how long?"

"My whole life," I smile. "Since I was a kid." My smile softens as I remember my childhood response to the dream woman in the water. "It's how I knew I was gay."

Cecile nods, rising from her stool, shaking out the sleeves of her flowy cardigan. There's a little tension in the air now that I've mentioned my growing-up years; I wait, anxious, for her to make a comment about my upbringing...

But, blessedly, she doesn't. Because Cecile always knows when to talk about something and when *not* to talk about something...

Growing up gay—in my conservative family, in my conservative neighborhood—was awful. My parents hated me. Our relationship...didn't end well.

Period.

But Cecile is looking at me now, and there's a soft smile on her face. "And why do you keep painting her, do you think?" she asks gently.

"I never *intend* to paint her," I say quickly, narrowing my brows. "I've never set out to paint her, I swear. But somehow, someway...she just shows up in my paintings, anyway. Always," I murmur reflectively, heaving a big sigh.

"Painting's the only thing that's been a constant for me, Cecile. A steady source of pride. And purpose. It makes me feel—I don't know—*calm*. When I pick up a paintbrush..." I take the paintbrush from her water pot, and I turn it carefully in my hand, sweeping the wet bristles over my palm. They leave a faint trace of blue on my skin. "When I pick it up," I begin again, "I start painting the picture that's in my head: water. Always water."

"That's what you're known for," says Cecile, her head tilted to the side.

"But then, in the water, something starts to...rise. Kind of like this," I tell her, gesturing to her painting.

"My figure is deliberate," she says, tracing her fingers in the air about an inch over the paper, indicating the woman's shape.

"And mine never is." I frown in frustration. "I go to all sorts of lengths to avoid painting *anything* that resembles a woman, but she shows up, anyway."

"People love your work," she reminds me gently, and I acknowledge that with a weak smile.

"I'm grateful that I have an audience. That people buy my paintings. I'm really lucky, I know."

Cecile nods again—but she's watching me closely.

"I'm just haunted by this, by...her." My mouth has gone dry. "This woman... She shows up in my work. She shows up in my dreams. I mean, am I crazy, Cecile?" I ask her with a little laugh, though it's a serious question.

"'We're all mad here,'" she quotes *Alice in Wonderland* with a chuckle and a wink. But then she steps forward, wrapping her arms around me in a tight embrace. "You're not crazy, Mara." Her voice is soft, soothing. "Something special is afoot in those dreams of yours."

"Don't say I've got the Gift!" I groan, at the exact same moment that she laughs and tells me, "You've got the Gift!"

"'The Gift,'" I tell her, putting air quotes around the words as she takes a step back, still laughing, "is mumbo-jumbo used by people with tarot cards and crystal balls; they only tell people what they think they want to hear."

Cecile scoffs at that, wagging a finger in my direction. "I'll have you know that I made my living for quite a few years telling people that 'mumbo-jumbo,' dear."

"You did?"

"Mm-hmm. I made my living as a fortuneteller for, oh, decades." She has a faraway look in her eyes as she sighs.

"And did you make it all up?" I persist, but Cecile looks thoughtful now as she turns her gaze on me.

"Never," she says, and it's emphatic. "Not once."

I change the subject a little, leaning back on my heels. "You never told me you used to work as a fortuneteller. Why?"

Cecile shrugs, and with twinkling eyes, she smiles at me. "You never asked, my dear."

I laugh at that. "Fair, fair. Hey, the pizza's getting cold," I say, taking a step back and glancing appreciatively at her painting. "And that's gorgeous. It looks like you'll finish it soon."

"My darling girl," says Cecile, and then she's darting forward much faster than I think any eighty-year-old woman has a right to move, and her fingers are closing warmly around my elbow and giving me a gentle squeeze. "I have a good feeling about things."

"Oh?" I ask her with a small grin.

"About your dream woman," she says, her eyes sparkling with extra mischief now. "Haven't you ever wondered if you dream about her because she's going to appear in your life? Just show up one day, sweep you off your feet?"

I chuckle, too, and I shake my head. "I mean, I thought so once, but—let's face it—I've been having that dream since I was a kid. Don't you think, if she was going to magically appear, she would have done so already? Like...when I was a teenager, and she could've taken me to prom?" I ask with a laugh.

But Cecile isn't letting this go—and she's not letting me go, either. "Honey, if I've told you once, I've told you a million times," she says. "You take care of everyone but yourself. Someday, you'll find a woman who realizes how amazing you are. And she'll be the woman of your dreams. And she'll take care of *you* for a change."

"You're being mushy," I tease her gently, but she only shakes her head.

"Once you reach my age, you're allowed to be as mushy—or as non-mushy—as you like." Then she's raising a brow again and regarding me shrewdly. "When are you going to get rid of this?" she asks in a quiet tone.

I stare at her in surprise. She's waving to my necklace. It's usually hidden beneath my neckline; no one's ever pointed it out before.

No one knows what it is...or why I wear it.

"What...?" I murmur, but Cecile is pinning me to the spot with her gaze, her brows furrowed as she frowns at the pendant that must have pushed its way out of my shirt when I was carrying the goldfish bowl.

It's a vintage gold pendant: small, teardrop-shaped, with a tiny teardrop diamond in the center of it. It was my grandmother's, and then it was my mother's, and now it's mine. I never take it off.

Self-consciously, I pick it up and tuck it beneath my collar.

"Why would I get rid of it?" I ask her, mumbling the words. I stand a little straighter, blood rushing in my head.

"You know you shouldn't wear it, sweetheart," she says then, and the words are so kind that they actually hurt.

I've never told anyone the history of this necklace. And no one's ever asked. I think it's too small to provoke much notice on the rare occasions that it does slip out from beneath my clothes. So how does Cecile know...?

I shift uncomfortably; I'm actually a little

queasy.

We were just talking a moment ago about "gifts." Does Cecile honestly have psychic powers?

She waits for me to answer, and I wait for her to drop the subject—but she doesn't.

"It was my mother's," I finally murmur, and Cecile's eyes start to flash, her lips drawn into a thin line.

"Exactly," she says, and she shakes her head, crossing her arms in front of her. "So I ask you again: when are you going to get rid of it?"

"You don't understand," I begin, and I'm reaching up like I always do, touching the pendant, swirling the pad of my thumb over the back of it. The motion calms me—and has for as long as I can remember.

"It was your *mother's*, doll," Cecile reminds me, as if that's all that needs to be said on the matter.

It was my mother's.

Yeah... Remember earlier when I alluded to my not-so-great upbringing?

Cecile knows all about that.

She steps forward now and rubs my back in slow, circular motions, a gentle touch that radiates warmth. "Sweetheart," she says, and her voice is low, "your mother—"

"I don't want to talk about it," I say too quickly, and she raises a brow at me. "I'm sorry, Cecile." I glance at her cautiously, shaking my head, clearing my throat. "I just... I don't want to talk about it tonight."

She stands there for a moment, still rubbing my back, and then she nods, resigned. "I'm sorry I brought it up, my dear," she says, but I reach out, take her hand and squeeze it.

"You shouldn't be sorry," I insist, and then I offer her a small, wan smile. "I haven't dealt with it yet, obviously. And it's...really hard to talk about."

Cecile gathers me in her arms and gives me a very quick, tight hug. "I love you, you know," she says, taking a step back, her eyes shimmering with kindness. "And you didn't deserve what you went through."

My back stiffens at those words, but then Cecile's grin deepens, and the mood in the room begins to change. "Okay," she tells me with a little sniff, "it's pizza time. I'll kill Toby if he's already eaten the whole veggie explosion pizza. Like he did *last* week."

I chuckle, weak with relief, as we leave her room and make our way downstairs.

It's been years, and I'm still not ready to deal with what happened to me. As I follow Cecile, I reach up and brush the pad of my thumb against the back of my pendant before dropping it beneath my tank top again. Then I breathe a sigh of relief.

I'm just *not* ready. Someday I will be. But...not yet.

We encounter chaos—as expected—when we arrive in the common area.

Miyoko is still in her Elizabethan gown, and she's holding a slice of veggie pizza over Sammie's head; his tail is thumping the floor—hard. Toby's in the middle of a loud argument with Rod—who apparently was here, after all—about which Queen song is the best. It's a halfhearted argument, obviously, because everyone knows the best song is "Bohemian Rhapsody." Iris is standing on the table and singing "New York, New York," for some reason. And the goldfish...

Well, his bowl is now sporting exactly half the

water it had before I went up the stairs.

"Sammie was just really thirsty," says Iris breathlessly, vaulting off the table and standing beside me with a cheesy grin. "And you know I can't say *no* to that gorgeous, fluffy face."

I groan and glance down into the bowl. At least the goldfish looks okay...

"That's Emily's new pet project," says Cecile, nodding toward the fishbowl. The goldfish gives the two of us a long-suffering stare, then starts swimming in tight circles.

"What do you mean 'pet project'?" I ask; my stomach sinks, heavy with dread. "And where *is* Em, anyway? She never misses a Friday night pizza party."

"She'll be here soon. She had to work," sings out Toby.

Emily is the only Ceres resident with a day job, working at Queen City Comics, the huge local comic book store. She bills herself as an up-and-coming comic artist, but she's best known in Buffalo for her performance art pieces which...are pretty weird.

As if we summoned her, Emily chooses that moment to waltz through the front door, and we all turn to greet her warmly.

Emily has purple hair that she teases every morning, and she dresses like Madonna did in the eighties. *This* week, anyway. Next week, she might switch to orange hair and pink fishnets and tutus... It all depends on her mood—and which hair dyes are in stock at Hot Topic.

"Party!" she yells happily, waving her tattooed arms in the air, and she dives onto a still-unopened box of pizza.

"Rough day at work?" I ask her with a grin as

she holds up two pieces of pizza and proceeds to eat from both of them at once.

"I can't complain. Hey, I work at a comic book store. Dream job, right?" She cocks her head thoughtfully. "Though there was this guy today who had no idea that there was any difference between the Marvel and DC universes, and *I* had no idea how he'd *survived* this long on planet Earth." She gulps down a big bite. "Who took Nemo out of the bathroom?" she asks then, nudging the goldfish bowl with her elbow.

"His name is Vladimir Futon now," Iris declares, and Emily shrugs her acceptance.

"Cecile says he's your new, um, pet project..." I begin, raising a worried brow. "What does she mean by that?"

Emily shrugs again and toes off her platform shoes, kicking them under the kitchen island and sighing happily now that her feet are free. "I bought him for a performance art piece," she says dismissively. "Little guy just has to survive until tomorrow, and then he'll die honorably. For a goldfish."

I stare, and Em groans.

"See, I *knew* if you found out about this you were going to be like, 'Em, you can't swallow a goldfish onstage. He's a living being with *feelings.*'"

I blink at her, and then I'm shaking my head slowly, trying to put words to my thoughts. "And...*why* are you going to swallow a live goldfish onstage?"

"Art!" says Em with a wide grin, waggling her purple eyebrows playfully. "*Ob*viously."

"Okay. But *why*?" I press, and Em waves her hand.

I mean, I love Em to death, but sometimes she gives us artists a bad name.

"I figured I'd come up with a reason at the show," she tells me with a little frown. "Do I even *need* a reason? Everyone's going to be like, '*Whoa*, that chick just swallowed a *goldfish*,' and then I'll say something like, 'America!' and give a bow. It'll really screw with them, make 'em think!"

"God." I groan, rocking back on the counter. "First off—wait, I don't even know where to *begin*," I start, flustered.

Toby's leaning beside me on the counter, an exaggerated frown on his mine-painted face. "Seriously, Em, I'm all for art for art's sake," he says, gesturing to his makeup and black bodysuit, "but if you don't have a *reason* for swallowing a goldfish, don't swallow a goldfish. It's common sense."

"Common sense is the bane of all art," pronounces Emily loftily, but Cecile is listening in to our exchange, and she rises up from one of the couches in the living area to come over and grab herself another piece of pizza.

"What's this about swallowing a goldfish?" she asks Em mildly. "You didn't mention that to me earlier, dear."

Emily glares at me and then shakes her head, a petulant expression on her face. "I need a really cool gimmick for the show tomorrow, Cecile," she says, her tone wheedling. "I mean, what's *cooler* than swallowing a goldfish?"

Cecile seems to consider this, and then slowly—and a little dramatically—she points up to the sign welded to the wall in the kitchen above our much-abused oven (I say "abused" because we use the oven for art, like clay work and melting plastic, rather than cooking).

The sign reads: "Do no harm, but take no shit."

"It's the one rule we've got here, honey," Cecile says sympathetically.

Em groans for a solid minute.

"And swallowing a goldfish for no reason," Cecile goes on, "is doing harm."

"But...but...you don't always have to have a *reason* in art," Emily says heatedly, dropping her piece of pizza onto the counter in frustration.

"Were you doing it to be sensational, dear?" asks Cecile sweetly. Em grumbles, crossing her arms, but then—begrudgingly—she nods. "Then that's not really art, dear. That's sensationalism," says Cecile, patting her arm. "Rule of thumb: don't swallow anything onstage that would fight back."

"We should get *that* made up into a sign!" says Iris brightly.

Em is still grumbling, but she's eating her pizza again. "So what *am* I going to do onstage? Last week, it was the American Whore piece, and I've done that one way too many times."

"People love it, though," I smile at her. And it's true—they do. Emily dresses herself as the Statue of Liberty, goes onstage, and recites porn scripts for an hour. It definitely makes a point, although...I'm not sure what that point is.

I'm not even sure that *Emily's* sure.

"Hmm, yeah, they do love it. I got a standing O last performance. Oh, *okay,*" she tells me with a grin. "If you insist, Mara. Hey, now I can even say, 'Back by popular demand!'"

"You do that, honey," says Cecile, patting her arm.

I stare down at the goldfish in the bowl, and the

goldfish stares back at me. He's not thankful—he's a goldfish, after all—but I do feel kind of like I did my good deed for the day, saving the goldfish from Emily's stomach—and saving Emily from the goldfish, too. I've never swallowed a live goldfish (or a live *anything*) before, but that *can't* be a pleasant experience.

"So," I say, clearing my throat and picking up my own slice of pizza; it is, much to my sadness, already cold. "We have a pet goldfish?"

"Vladimir Futon," Iris says, nodding, and I chuckle.

"Em, do you have goldfish food?"

Emily stares at me as if I just asked her if she owns Antarctica. "Why would I buy goldfish food?" she asks, shaking her head. "I was just going to toss a pizza crust in there and call it good. Fish like bread, don't they?"

"That's…um…I don't think they do…" I trail off.

"Whatever!" Em rolls her eyes. "If it's not going in my belly, it is no longer my problem," she says, giving me a wink, grabbing three more slices of pizza, and making her way toward the couch.

Emily isn't a bad person. She just has her priorities, and this goldfish is not on that list.

Vladimir Futon opens and closes his mouth, and a little bubble blows up, rising to the surface.

I'm assuming this is Fish for, "Feed me."

And that is, after all, what I do: I take care of people. And dogs. And fish…I guess. I groan a little, smiling ruefully as I set the cold slice of pizza back in the box and head toward the door. "I'm taking Sammie out to pee," I call over my shoulder, "and I'll pick up some goldfish food at Wiggs."

An errand for a goldfish.

It's a perfectly normal excursion in a "house" like the Ceres.

Chapter 2: The Unexpected Rescue

Wiggs is our corner store—though it's actually several corners away—and you might think that your average corner store wouldn't be well-stocked with fish food. But then you've probably never been to Wiggs.

When I first moved to the Ceres, we were out of toilet paper pretty much right away, and I volunteered to go to the convenience store I'd noticed to pick up some TP. Wiggs, much to my sadness, did not have toilet paper (that first time), but it did have a parrot for sale behind the cash register, hand-poured candles, Halloween masks (two types, werewolf and Frankenstein's monster, even though we moved to the Ceres in *May*), books, fabric (sold by the yard) and homemade brownies—along with all of the normal stuff you'd find in a gas station mart. There's a running joke in the Ceres that when you *really* need something, Wiggs will never have it. But if you go next week, they'll have ten.

I'm really hoping that won't be the case with the fish food. Last I checked, the store had every type of pet food you could imagine, including live crickets. So I hope I'll find a dusty bottle of fish food stuffed somewhere on a back shelf.

"Take the katana!" calls Cecile, as Toby hops over the back of the sofa to sit down next to her. Miyoko is attempting to sit on the other side of Cecile, but her hoop skirt is giving her grief. Every time she tries to sit down, the hoops come rushing up toward her face.

"I don't need to take it—I'm just walking to Wiggs!" I say over my shoulder as I grab Sammie's leash from the hook by the door. The hook is a plastic pirate's hook from one of Toby's old Halloween costumes; he melted it to the wall. "It's not even that dark out yet," I protest, but when I peer into the living room, Cecile is glaring at me over her crossed arms, and I sigh, shaking my head. "Okay, okay. A two-hundred-and-fifty-pound dog clearly isn't enough protection," I chuckle, resigned. "I'll take the katana."

"Good girl," Cecile beams, and then she picks up the ratty pack of playing cards from the coffee table and begins to deal everyone in. They're starting the poker game early tonight, so I'll have to get back quickly if I expect to play a hand or two. We're using M&Ms in the place of cash, and I really, *really* like M&Ms.

I clip the leash to Sammie's collar, and then I scoop my keys up from the floor and deposit them in my purse. On my way out the door, I reach above the door frame and take down the katana from its resting place.

A katana is a Japanese sword. Emily bought ours on eBay about a year ago for a performance art piece; she thought she could teach herself to swallow swords. Turned out she couldn't, and disgusted that her five dollars wasn't being put to better use, she offered the sword up to the Ceres as a weapon we could use to "hunt down corrupt politicians." Ever the diplomat, Cecile came up with a better idea: we could carry the katana with us whenever we needed to walk outside at night. Sort of like pepper spray. But a little more...pointy.

To Cecile's credit, I've taken a bunch of walks alone at night since we got the katana, and I've been jumped exactly zero times. So, hey, it works.

I place the silk ribbon attached to the scabbard over my shoulder, and away Sammie and I go—through the door, down the front cement steps of the grain elevator, and onto the street in front of the river.

The Ceres is located on this little peninsula that juts out into the Buffalo River, which sounds lovely, but the Buffalo River is connected to Lake Erie, and we locals joke that, unless you want to grow an extra head, swimming in Lake Erie isn't a wise idea.

Since the peninsula is home to nothing more than a series of abandoned, rotting grain elevators, the place is a little spooky at night. Our closest neighbors are on the "mainland," and that's where all of the streetlights are, too.

Here, outside of the Ceres, it's practically pitch black.

Cecile keeps promising that she's going to install an outdoor light, if only to make poop pickup easier when I walk Sammie at night, but there are other, more important issues for her to deal with when it comes to building maintenance. Creating an artists' residence inside of a grain elevator is a romantic concept, but it comes along with some logistical and mechanical problems that Cecile always has to keep on top of—despite the fact that about half of the residents aren't even paying her rent on a regular basis. So I would feel like crap if I reminded her about the outdoor light; she's busy enough.

Besides, I've never been afraid in the dark. I've

got Sammie, after all, and no stranger intent on doing me harm would realize that Sammie, big as he is, is the nicest dog they could ever meet. I'm pretty sure Sammie would escort any would-be rapist, serial killer, or corrupt politician into the Ceres enthusiastically, provided there were impending treats for him.

So, Sammie, paired with the katana and my little flashlight keychain, make me feel pretty safe.

I flick the flashlight on now and walk in its tiny beam, Sammie tugging at the leash to go pee on his favorite spot. I let him do his business, and I rock back on my heels, glancing up at the stars with a contented sigh.

Buffalo is bright at night, but we're in a disused area, so we get better stars than the rest of the city folk. Overhead, I can make out the constellation of the Big Dipper—and there's Cassiopeia, that pretty constellation in the shape of a W that ancient peoples thought looked like a queen. Nope. It looks like a W. Whatever the ancient Greeks were on when they decided the letter W resembled a seated queen—well, it must've been some powerful stuff.

I smile as I stare up at the constellations, basking in the glow of the familiar stars. Ever since I was a little kid, I've really loved them. There's something comforting about gazing at millions and millions of years of light. People say that most of the stars we can see right now are already dead, their light long extinguished, exploded. And maybe that's true. When I look up at all of the bright lights, so far away, I like to think that I'm looking at the ghosts of stars. And that, for some reason, gives my heart peace.

If stars have ghosts, after all, maybe we do, too.

"Come *on*, buddy," I tell Sammie, tugging on his

leash after a long moment.   I thought he was still peeing, but I quickly realize that he isn't, not anymore.

Instead, Sammie is staring toward the river.

And his hackles are raised.

I...don't think I've *ever* seen Sammie's hackles raised—he's always so friendly and trusting—and it's disconcerting, so much so that the hair on the back of *my* neck rises as I stare down at the spiked-up hair on his neck. He isn't looking at me, not even when I tug on his leash again. He won't stop staring at the dark river some twenty paces away from us.

And then he starts to growl.

I've had Sammie for two years.   Originally, Toby adopted him after he broke up with his last boyfriend. But then Toby got together with Rod, and he learned that Rod was allergic to dogs... So Toby, after owning Sammie for about a week, decided to return Sammie to the shelter.

However, everyone in the Ceres had already fallen head-over-heels in love with that ungainly pup (he was a couple of months old at the time), and there was no *way* that Sammie was going anywhere.

And no one had fallen deeper in love with Sammie than me.

Side note: this story might make Toby sounds like kind of a jerk, giving up his dog for a boyfriend he'd just met.   And, trust me, I love the guy like a brother, but Toby *can* be a jerk. Still, his heart is usually in the right place. When he met Rod, he had cartoon birds swooping around his head, and he just couldn't acknowledge anything but love—and his libido. Two years later, their relationship is *still* in the cartoon-birds stage, so everything turned out for the best in the end.

After all, I got Sammie out of the deal.   And

Sammie has never, not *once,* growled. Not even for good reasons. He didn't growl when that little Welsh Corgi bit him at the Elmwood Arts Festival. He didn't growl when the kid on the scooter ran into him at the Allentown Arts Festival. He didn't growl when that Pride parade float almost fell on top of him. (Now that I think of it, the local festivals are kind of a peril for my poor dog.)

Sammie is one of the most stoic, most loving, most wonderful dogs on the planet, and there's not a violent or aggressive bone in his body.

So seeing his lips drawn up over his pointed teeth, seeing his hackles raised, hearing that low, deep growl emanate from his throat—it's just *weird.*

And it makes me realize that there is something very, very wrong.

I stare at the river, and I shiver a little, a tiny tremor of fear moving through me. Sammie hasn't finished his walk—he ate a *lot* of pizza—but I've got to be honest: there's a part of me that wants to head back into the Ceres, even though I need to get fish food...

For a moment, I stand frozen in place, wracked with indecision.

I've got a bad feeling, but I shake myself out of it. Honestly, Wiggs isn't that far. And though Sammie has never growled before, there's a first time for everything, right? He probably just smelled a squirrel.

I reach up and nervously tug my pendant out from beneath my shirt, brushing the pad of my thumb over the back of it as I swallow.

Sammie tugs on his leash, still growling, and he pulls me forward about a yard before I dig my heels into the cement and tug back.

"Come on, buddy," I tell him, using my most

soothing voice. "Let's head over to the bridge. There's nothing over that way."

But Sammie isn't in the mood for placation. Again, he tugs me toward the river.

"Sammie, *no*, boy—come on," I tell him, pulling in the opposite direction. I drag him back toward the bridge.

Then everything happens at once. I'm facing away from Sammie, and even though my hands are wrapped tightly in his leash, Sammie is, after all, two hundred and fifty pounds; between the two of us, he kind of has the upper hand in the muscle department.

He *pulls* so hard and so fast, darting away from me in an unexpected direction, that I'm taken by surprise. Sammie backpedals, shrugging out of his collar.

And he dashes toward the river.

I stand there for a split second, my heart in my throat, as I hold the dangling end of the leash. I thought Sammie's collar was tight enough. Granted, I never *imagined* he'd attempt to run away—

"*Sammie!*" I yell at the top of my lungs, but he's not listening to me. His paws hit the cement with frightening speed, and he's running as if the hounds of hell are behind him, aimed for the edge of the river.

There's about a ten-foot drop-off from the "bank" of the river into the river itself. When the Ceres and the rest of the grain elevators were built on the peninsula, the river's edge was shored up with metal walls, so Sammie's racing toward what amounts to, more or less, a cliff. If he doesn't stop, he's going to plunge over the edge and into the water.

I race after him, my heart thundering. From my point of view, it looks as if my dog is going to hurl himself into the river, because he's still growling, and he's running faster than I've ever seen him run before.

But he stops: he skids to a halt right at the edge, his claws skidding on the top of the metal wall.

I run up beside him and loop the collar around his neck in one fast motion before dropping to my knees and throwing my arms around him, heaving a huge sigh of relief. A single tear leaks from my eye as my adrenaline falls, and I squeeze him tightly, kissing the top of his head.

"You *stupid* dog," I whisper. He leans against me, and—for a moment—his growling pauses. "I love you *so much*, and you could have been *so hurt*, buddy," I tell him, burying my face in his fur.

But Sammie is only half-listening to his terrified mother berate him for running away. He's focusing most of his attention on the river.

I make certain that the collar is secure (though not too tight), and I get up. I'm wearing a black skirt, and there are bits of gravel sticking to the skin of my knees. Bent over, brushing a hand over my legs—that's when I see it.

I see what Sammie's been growling at.

I straighten, my brow furrowed, peering down into the dark, flowing waters of the Buffalo River.

I thought I saw…

I gasp, my mouth open, straightening as I peer down into the black.

It couldn't be.

The river is flowing slowly, sluggishly. The moon is dark; there was only a thin crescent earlier, and it has already set. The stars overhead cast little light, so when I lift my mini flashlight and shine it down into the water, I see…

No.

It's a body.

Sammie is growling at a body floating in the water.

For a long moment, I stare at it, really *stare* at it. Because humans think we see ourselves everywhere, right? The trash bag on the side of the road—we think it's a body for that first half a second, before we realize the truth. We see human faces in pieces of toast, in weird wallpaper designs on the walls. We're *trained* to search for a human resemblance in things. Maybe it's instinctual.

So, *it's probably trash* is my initial—and somewhat desperate—thought. The river is, after all, pretty polluted.

But when I stare at the shape longer, I start to face facts: that doesn't look like trash at all. It looks like a body. But...I don't *want* it to be a body. I don't *want* it to be someone who drowned, or someone who was murdered and dumped in the Buffalo River, because that would be *awful*. My heart aches as I stare down at the body-shaped thing. I swallow, trying to make my hand stop shaking as I hold the flashlight higher, trying to make out features...

And then my heart falls out of my chest, or, at least, it *feels* like it does. Because those floaty bits riding the water's surface...are hair. Long strands of hair.

Yeah.

That's a body.

"Oh, God," I moan, my fingers tightening in the fur of Sammie's coat. He leans his shoulder against me, either to comfort me or to comfort himself.

I have to do something, call someone... Should I call 911? I've never called 911 in my life. Is that what you do when you find a dead body? I don't have my cell phone on me, I realize then. It's back in the Ceres. I left it charging in the kitchen.

Sammie and I stare at the body in the water, and I try to decide what to do.

And that's when… Well, I think my eyes are playing tricks on me…

But I could have sworn the body moved.

It's summer, and we haven't had much rain this year. The newscasters have been talking about a drought, so the river is low and sluggish, and the body hasn't drifted far from the place where I first noticed it, bobbing gently on the surface of the dark water.

But as I trained my tiny flashlight beam on it a moment ago, I thought I saw the head move.

I gulp down air, lean over the edge of the escarpment, and squint.

And the body moves again. The right hand comes up, the skin pale white—*cadaverous,* I think. Still, the hand rose from the water vertically, not in any way that a current could pull a limb.

Oh, my God.

The person in the water is alive.

But he or she is floating face-down.

I weigh my options for a split second as I reach up and squeeze my fingers around my gold pendant. And then I'm tossing my purse to the ground, kicking off my flats, looping Sammie's leash around one of the metal poles on the side of the wall…

And I leap into the water.

I wasn't prepared for it to be so *cold.* We haven't had the warmest summer, and it was a cloudy day, with a particularly spectacular thunderstorm earlier. The storm had just been clearing up when I brought the boxes of pizza back to the Ceres. There was no sun today to warm the water.

God, it's *freezing*.

I gasp as my head breaks through the surface; I'm treading water as I glance around madly, trying to place the body now. I'd leapt down with my flashlight, but when I hit the water, the flashlight spun out of my hand,. It's gone. And that means that there's no light for me to see by other than the far-distant shine of the stars.

It's pitch black down here between the metal walls, and—for a brief second—I panic. I can't see a thing; I can't see the body I threw myself into the river to save, and I have no idea how I'm going to climb *out* of here when I reach said person—if I can even find them.

Okay.

Think, Mara.

I take a deep breath, squelching my panic.

First thing's first: find the body.

Or, rather, find the *person*. It's not a body anymore; it's a living person.

But he or she might not live for much longer if I don't act fast.

I glance up to where Sammie is peering over the edge of the escarpment. He isn't staring down at me; he's still staring at the person in the water, his nose is pointed to my left.

So I set off with a strong breaststroke to my left, and after three strokes, I stop, treading water, and I check in with Sammie again. He's still peering to my left, so I swim some more, gasping against the cold.

My hand bumps against something in the water.

I scream—just a little.

But what I hit was soft, and it felt like a person.

I draw in a deep breath.

I didn't expect to run into him or her so suddenly; I thought I'd be able to see them by now, be able to make out *something* when I got close, but the darkness is too absolute to see my hand in front of my face. I reach out, and my hand brushes against something soft again, and then hard: the back of the person's head.

I trail my fingers down the head and toward the shoulder, and I start in confusion as my hand reaches...metal?

What the hell? Why does this person have metal on their shoulders?

It doesn't matter. I spit some water out of my mouth (it tastes just as gross as you'd imagine), and I grimace as I hook my fingers around the metal plate, hauling the person against me. I wrap my arms around their shoulders, and I pause again in surprise.

The person is *completely* covered in metal. For half an instant, I wonder if the cold water is playing tricks on me, numbing my fingers...

But then my confusion evaporates, because the person groans a little, a low sound that's accompanied by a deep cough.

"Hello—are you okay?" I ask, and—obviously—they're *not* okay, but I have no idea what else to say in this situation. The person groans again, and when I listen closely to the sound they make, I begin to think that the person in my arms is a woman.

I kind of suspected that, with the long black hair, but it was impossible to tell anything for sure from the land above, and even now I'm not certain, especially since she's covered in metal.

The problem with being covered with metal?

Yeah, she isn't exactly buoyant.

I grimace as I try to lift her body higher in the water, but even though I'm straining with every muscle, the feat is near-impossible. That's why she was floating face-down: she has a metal back piece and two shoulder pieces, but the majority of her weight is centered on her chest piece, making her top heavy and effectively pulling her face under.

The woman moans again, and she's coughing violently against me; she spits water out, dragging it from her lungs. I glance toward the metal wall closest to me. Sammie is peering over—so, so far above.

I really didn't think this through.

Because what stands between us and dry land is a wall made of ridged metal—no beams, nothing but those vertical ridges that, even if they were horizontal, would be impossible to climb over because of their soft slope.

I kick as hard as I can, but the woman is slipping in my arms, and holding us both above the surface is incredibly difficult even if I'm just treading my legs. If I try to actually *swim*... Well, I move about a foot forward, and she's slipping farther down, her metal-clad front end tilting her head underwater.

"Hello?" I call desperately, trying to shake the woman awake. She's stopped groaning and coughing. She's not fighting at all as her face slips underwater again. That can't be a good sign. "Hello?" My voice cracks with fear as I shake her a little harder, my fingers gripping the slippery metal on her shoulders.

Her face comes up, rising out of the water, and she inhales, struggling for air.

"Please try to stay awake," I beg, kicking with

all of my might, trying to keep us both above the surface. "Can you swim?" I ask her, spitting water out of my mouth, but she doesn't answer me, only groans, and her head lolls to the side.

Her face goes underwater again.

I gasp, my head plunging under, too, as her weight comes onto me, forcing me beneath the water. I remember hearing something once about how sometimes, when swimmers try to save drowning people, they drown themselves—and then I realize that's the *least* useful information right now. Terror seizes me, as cold as the water surrounding us.

I *can't* just let her die. Sure, I could let her go. I could swim to the edge of the wall, feel my way along until I reach *something* like a ladder or a pipe, climb up, and save myself—and only myself. And that would be the shittiest thing imaginable. Without me pulling her out of the water, this woman is going to *die*, and I would be complicit in her death if I don't help her…

She *will* die without me, and there's not a world in which I'm going to let that happen.

Anger inspires my legs to kick harder: anger at the impossible situation, at the stupid metal walls, at the cold, cold water. The anger pumps through me, warming my body and giving me the strength to heft the woman's face out of the water again. I can't tell if she's breathing, but I don't have the time to check.

I've got to get us out of here.

Now.

I just…have no idea how I'm going to do it.

Over the sound of the gentle waves, I hear Sammie on the wall above us. He's whining, a high-pitched, distressed yowl. I listen to him, blinking water out of my eyes, and then I turn my head around to look up at him. He's is peering over the edge, looking terrified. I spit water out of my mouth, and I kick back with my legs, heaving the woman up as high as I can. Her face breaks the surface, and that's going to have to be good enough until...

Until what, Mara?

I reach out with my hand, floundering through the water, but I'm rewarded by the sensation of corroded metal beneath my fingertips.

I've hit the wall.

Sammie begins to bark. Normally, his bark is pretty deep; he's a big dog, after all. But there's an unmistakable note of fear to the sound.

"It's okay, buddy!" I yell up at him, or try to, but my throat is so raw. I'm exhausted, trying to prevent both this woman and myself from drowning. I lean against the metal wall, and I gape up at the faraway night sky, searching for something familiar, something soothing.

And I think about those stars, about the fact that they're ghosts.

I really, *really* don't want to be a ghost. Not yet. Not now.

My hand, trailing along the edge of the metal wall as we're pulled along by the sluggish current of the river, brushes against something I wasn't expecting.

For a moment, I wonder if it's just a pipe attached to the wall, and even if it is, it's something I can hold onto, something I can hook the woman's arm through... But no, it's even *better* than that.

"Yes!" I yell hoarsely, adrenaline surging through me.

It's a rusting metal ladder.

Chapter 3: Do You Believe in Magic?

The ladder is bolted to the side of the metal wall—right *here*, exactly when I need it. A *ladder*. Safety, salvation…whatever you want to call it. I whisper *thank you* to the stars, and then I loop my arm through the bottom rung and heave the woman up as high as I can, maneuvering her arm through the rung, too.

But she's unconscious, so her body sags; her face is still half-submerged.

Okay, just because I found a ladder doesn't mean we're out of hot water yet. Ooh, hot water. I *wish* the water we were in right now was hot. I'm going to take the hottest shower in the world when I get out of this situation, but right now, I have to *focus*.

The woman—because she's covered in metal and waterlogged—is *heavy*, and I'm worn out, but I have to push past my limits. We're so *close* to safety now…

First things first. This isn't like a pool ladder with rungs beneath the water. The bottom rung hangs about an inch above the surface. I'm going to have to heft myself up onto the bottom rung with my arm strength alone.

Good Lord, it's the hardest thing I've ever done, heaving my body up high enough to hook my foot onto that bottom rung. My entire being screams in protest, but somehow—thanks to adrenaline or luck—I manage to do it. Then I'm reaching down and gripping the woman's shoulder plates; I groan in pain as I begin to lift her up toward me.

It's the most excruciating experience of my life, climbing up the ladder and pulling the woman after me. Rung after rung after rung. I'm not sure how I accomplish it, but after an eternity of pain, swearing, and searing, tearing muscles...it's over.

When my hand reaches over the edge of the metal wall and strikes pavement, I let out a gasp of pure, unadulterated joy, and when I drag the woman onto dry land, I collapse beside her, rolling onto my back and staring up at the stars with my heartbeat thundering like a summer storm inside of me.

I did it.

I saved her.

I saved us.

I exhale the longest sigh, and that's all I allow myself before I sit up, rolling the woman onto her back.

Her shoulder thumps against the cement with a dull metallic *clang*. I stare down at her, and I realize a few things all at once: one, she's still unconscious; two, she's no longer breathing...

Shit, shit, shit.

And…

I mean, all of these thoughts occur to me in the same instant, so I don't feel particularly guilty that, when I take in the sight of her face for the very first time in the dim light of the stars...

She's beautiful.

That's…kind of an understatement. She's *gorgeous*. She has a sumptuous, full mouth, and her face is finely sculpted, with high cheekbones and an aristocratic nose. She looks... This is going to sound cheesy, but she looks *noble,* somehow.

Her long dark lashes rest against her too-pale cheeks, and they don't stir.

In this heartbeat, as I stare down at her, as I realize that she's not breathing, that she's beautiful, and that she might already be dead, a fierce pang of determination surges through me.

"Not on my watch," I whisper, and I kneel beside her, pulse pounding in my ears. "You can't quit on me, not yet," I murmur to her, and I search my memory, trying to remember the time that the Red Cross brought someone in to teach my Girl Scout troop how to perform CPR...when I was eleven.

Yeah, that was a while ago. And I don't remember much, other than the fact that the dummy tasted like disinfectant.

Sammie is tugging madly on his leash, trying to come over to me. He's about thirty feet down the bank, and I want to go comfort him, but I don't have time to do anything right now but save this woman.

If she's even savable.

God, I hope she's savable. It would be horrific if she died because I didn't remember how to give mouth-to-mouth.

I take a deep breath. Okay. I'm supposed to tilt the chin up. My fingers are wet and shaking as I place them under her chin. She's so soft beneath my fingers, but her skin is cold—no, freezing.

"Please don't be dead, please don't be dead," I whisper like a mantra as I lean down over her. My heart is beating so hard that I feel lightheaded. I take another deep breath, stars winking at the corners of my vision, as I lower my face to hers.

"Please, please, please," I whisper.

And I kiss her.

It starts out as a kiss, because, save for that CPR lesson when I was eleven, I've never done mouth-to-mouth on anyone before. And in movies and television shows, mouth-to-mouth always looks like it starts out with a kiss and then moves on from there. So I press my mouth to hers, and I'm shocked at the sensations that fill my body.

So…strange. I kiss this stranger, and time is suspended. Everything seems to…stop.

Her mouth is cool against mine, but there's a faint warmth beneath her skin. And I know this sounds weird, but it feels like a spark. As if something ignites between our mouths, like the shock that you get when you rub your socked feet on the carpet and touch someone. It's that bright, that electric…but it's not painful. It's warm. And weird. And unexpected…

But I don't have time to be surprised by anything. Gently, I force her cool, full lips apart with my own, and I breathe into her.

Nothing.

I take another deep breath, and I reach up, carefully pinching her nose closed this time. I exhale again, a little more forcefully, my hot breath rushing between my lips and into her.

Again, nothing.

"God, no, no, no," I whisper, sitting back on my heels. I stare down at the motionless body in front of me, and I reach out, patting my hands over the contours of metal over her breasts. I tap harder, but I can't get through it to pound the water out of her lungs.

I try, anyway. I hit her harder, pushing down

on the metal plating with the heel of my right hand. But it doesn't budge.

"Damn it!" I whisper, my voice catching as I stare at my trembling hands. I'm shaking from the cold of the water, from the exertion of dragging her up the ladder, from the fear of failing to save her. "You can't *die*," I whisper, and in desperation, I take one more deep breath, lean over her, and press my mouth to hers.

I breathe into her, filling her with my air one last time, my mouth hard against her own, that spark shocking me again, leaving me gasping...

The woman convulses beneath me, and I sit back quickly as she coughs up water, rivulets pouring over her face. She turns, coughing more water onto the pavement. Her body is wracked with coughing as she tries to breathe, and I tap her gently on the shoulder, relief flooding my soul.

She's alive.

At last, after a hell of a lot of wheezing, her long, black hair hanging in front of her face, the woman rolls onto her back tiredly, a hand pressed to her stomach as she faces the sky, breathing in and out raggedly.

Her full lips are parted, and when she raises her lashes to gaze up at the stars, I stare into her eyes for the first time.

Her eyes are blue. Bright blue. Ice blue.

Star blue.

She flicks her gaze from the sky...to me. And she watches me for a long moment—silent, just breathing. We stare at one another for a minute, two, as if mesmerized. I can't look away.

And then, finally, she speaks.

"You saved me," she murmurs.

It's not a question.

I blink down at her, the hairs on the back of my neck rising because...her *voice*. It's low and deep, almost a growl. Gruff.

And I... I could *swear* I've heard it before.

But that's impossible. I've never seen this woman before in my life. I'd *remember* if I had. She's striking. It would be impossible to look at her face even once and then forget it. Her features are smooth and chiseled, as if she's a walking statue. People don't spend months of their lives sculpting not-beautiful people. A sculpture is exquisite because an artist pours his or her own desires into it, forming the perfect person.

And that's what she is, lying there with her wet hair spread around her face like a dark halo.

She's...exquisite.

"Yes," I say, and then I cough a little in embarrassment, realizing that there was a long pause between her words and mine. I reach up, brush my fingers against my gold pendant nervously. "Yes—I...I got you out of the water. Are you okay?"

She grimaces a little and flicks her gaze from my eyes back up to the sky. "No," she replies simply, her jaw clenching as she curls her gloved hand upon her middle.

She's wearing leather gloves and, well, *armor*. Those metal pieces on her body are armor, I realize now. But...we don't have a local Renaissance festival (the closest one is a few hours away). And there aren't any other festivals in town right now that somebody would dress up for. No conventions. I would have probably heard of a medieval-style performance art piece going on tonight, if there was one, and we don't

58

even have a big Live Action Role Playing community in the city.

So, why is she wearing armor?

"So...you're not okay?" I ask, sitting back on my heels. "Do you need to go to the hospital?"

She exhales and winces, her brow furrowing deeply as she tries to sit up. I reach out to help her, putting an arm around her shoulders, which feels oddly intimate...though I just lugged her unconscious body up a ladder and put my mouth on hers. There's a small part of me that's recognizing I'm kind of attracted to her, and that makes me feel awkward as I touch her now.

But *most* of me is focused on the fact that this woman is *not* okay.

She slumps forward a little when I help her rise to a seated position, and she groans, pressing her gloved hand even harder against her middle. "I need a healer," she growls, and then she falls against me.

"Wait—a healer?" Maybe she *is* into Live Action Role Playing. Or maybe she's part of a theater troupe.

"I have been stabbed," the woman growls to me, her voice even, calm. "I must be healed, or I will die. I do not have the energy to heal myself."

Stabbed. Healed.

Energy?

What?

"I think you must have hit your head," I venture nervously.

She grips my arm and turns her face toward me; we're practically nose to nose. There's so much pain in her ice blue eyes that they look flat, glassy.

"I need to get back," she whispers, feverish.

And she closes her eyes, her face as white as a ghost.

Get back *where?*

Then I stare down in horror at the place where she held my arm. Because her gloved palm was slick with blood, and blood stains my skin now.

"Oh, my God," I whisper, shifting my gaze to her stomach, where she'd been clenching her hand.

She's bleeding. She's bleeding a *lot*. The acrid scent of blood stings my nose as she sags against me, incapable of holding herself upright.

"*Shit*," I whisper, and then, heart pounding a thousand beats per minute, I ease her gently to the ground, cradling her head until it rests on the pavement, the metal of her back piece making another dull *clang*.

"I'll be… I'll be right back," I croak, my mouth completely dry. I stumble to my feet, and I run to Sammie, feeling the katana bang against the small of my back, thinking vaguely, *Hey, the ribbon held up.*

Sammie is staring up at me with wide eyes, and he starts to sniff me like crazy when I reach him. I unloop his leash from the metal wall, and we both sprint as fast we can (which is, admittedly, not very fast, considering how winded and broken I feel) back to the Ceres.

I left my purse with my keys in it back by the riverfront, so I bang on the locked front door frantically.

"All right, all right. *God*," says Toby, as he swings open the door with a flourish and a distasteful frown. "What…Mara…" And then he trails off as I push past him, running into the building.

"Here—someone take Sammie," I say quickly, and I'm shrugging out of the katana, setting it on the counter before I scoop up the roll of paper towels and find the first aid kit—kept in the kitchen because we're all terrible at using knives—under the sink. I throw open the kit, and then I'm staring down at all of the supplies but not really seeing them as it hits me how terrible this situation is…

The woman *still* might not make it, even though I saved her from drowning and managed to drag her up the ladder by myself and brought her back to consciousness.

After all of that? Yeah, I *refuse* to let her die.

I grab an antiseptic wipe and some gauze as Toby gapes at me, holding onto Sammie's leash. The game of cards in the living area falls silent; Cecile stands up.

"What's wrong, Mara?" she asks firmly, but I'm shaking my head.

"No time—someone's been hurt, I've got to drive her to the hospital," I tell Cecile in one breath, and her expression changes.

"Call an ambulance, sweetheart," she tells me quickly, but I'm racing out the door.

"There's no *time*. She'll die if we wait for an ambulance!" I call over my shoulder.

I run to where I left my purse and car keys and am grateful that, when I look over my shoulder, I see all of the inhabitants of the Ceres spilling out of the building and running with me, taking in the sight of the woman lying on her back on the river's edge.

"Can someone help me get her into the car?" I ask, kneeling beside her and ripping open the antiseptic wipe. It's too dark to see, but I place the wipe against her leather undershirt (she's wearing a *leather* undershirt?), and then I put the gauze on top of that, and I pick up her hand, pressing it down on the wound.

"Please apply pressure here," I tell the woman, whose eyelids flutter. I'm not sure if she heard me or not, but I can only hope that she did.

"You should really call an ambulance, Mara," says Iris, staring down at the woman in shock. "She's in bad shape."

"I would if I thought they'd get here in time," I tell her, glancing up quickly, and I ask again, "Can someone help me lift her into the car?"

"But what if she dies? Will you get in trouble?" asks Iris, her face as white as the woman's now.

"I can't sit here and wait for an ambulance to show up while she bleeds out onto the pavement," I say simply, and Toby comes to stand beside me, his boyfriend Rod right behind him, and Miyoko joins us in her Elizabethan dress.

"We'll help you," says Miyoko quietly, and then I hand the keys, my hands slippery with blood, to Cecile.

"Can you unlock my car door?" I ask her, and Cecile nods, racing over to my car, which is only about twenty feet away, parked in its usual spot. She unlocks the door, and then I'm gesturing to Toby, Rod and Miyoko to take up positions at the woman's shoulders and feet. I'm holding onto her right shoulder. "Okay, we're all going to lift on three and carry her to the passenger side."

"Right," says Miyoko, her skirts ballooning around her as she crouches beside me at the woman's other shoulder.

"One, two, *three*," I say quickly, and we're all lifting the woman at the same time. She weighs a ton with her metal armor—good Lord. But I dragged her up the ladder with only adrenaline on my side, and adrenaline pumps through me again as we carry her to the open passenger door of my vintage VW bug.

I begin to calculate the fastest route to Mercy Hospital in my head.

"Hey, easy, easy," I murmur, as Miyoko and I lift up the front part of her body and Toby and Rod tuck her legs into the car; then we're sort of pushing her to a seated position on her side.

"Just be careful," Cecile says to me, ducking forward to give me a tight hug before pressing my keys back into my hand. She hands me my purse, too, and I nod my thanks, glancing around at the worried faces.

"I'll call soon," I promise, and then I'm in my seat and slamming the door, peeling out of the parking lot with the tires screeching and my head racing.

Maybe Cecile was right. Maybe I should have called an ambulance. But the woman beside me is fading fast, and what if she'd died while we were waiting, or what if she died while they were transporting her to the hospital? All I know is that she's bleeding from a wound in her stomach—where she was stabbed, I assume—and I couldn't imagine waiting a moment longer…

This *felt* like the best decision, to drive her to the hospital myself.

I really hope I made the right choice.

Thankfully, there aren't many people heading to South Buffalo on a Friday night, so I arrive at Mercy Hospital without any traffic issues, rolling onto the Emergency ramp so quickly that I almost forget to throw the car into park, something that hasn't happened to me since my learner's permit days.

I run to open the passenger side door.

It took four people to lift the woman into the

car, but there's only me now, so I take her by her shoulders and sort of roll her toward me, trying to help her out of the seat. A bored-looking orderly is smoking a cigarette right beside a "no smoking on hospital grounds" sign, and he stubs out the cigarette against the side of the building before pushing off of the wall and trotting over.

"Hey, you need some help?" he asks, and I nod, and somehow, even with his assistance, it still takes a solid minute for us to pull her out of the car.

"Shit, what's she wearing? It's so heavy," the orderly mutters, but I don't have the energy to reply. We carry her between us, one of her arms slung around each of our shoulders, into the hospital waiting room.

The orderly helps me set her down onto an empty seat. I'm surprised to see how many people are sitting around waiting for medical attention... There are probably about twenty people waiting to be seen. I rush up to the nurse behind the desk; she doesn't look at me when I approach her.

"Hey, someone needs help," I gasp, licking my dry lips. Only then does she glance up at me, probably because of my frazzled tone. She raises a brow, and she sweeps her gaze over me. I probably look pretty scary, considering the fact that I climbed out of the Buffalo River minutes ago.

"Sign in here," she says in a bored tone, handing me a clipboard and looking back down at her computer monitor.

"I'm sorry. I don't think this can wait," I tell her, all in a rush. She glances at me again and sighs for a moment.

"What's the nature of your injury?" she says, taking a pen from behind her ear and setting it down on the clipboard.

"It's not me. It's that woman over there," I say, gesturing behind me. "She nearly drowned, and I think she was…um…stabbed?"

The nurse appears slightly more interested. "Did *you* stab her?" she asks.

"What? God, *no*," I say hoarsely, staring at the nurse in shock. "I found her in the river. She was dumped in there by someone after getting stabbed…I guess." I lean over the desk. "Look, she's hardly conscious, and she's losing a lot of blood—"

"So is that guy," snaps the nurse, pointing to a man holding a towel tightly over his right eye, slouching back in his seat, his upper body curled forward with pain. "And so is she." The nurse points to a woman with a piece of clothing—a shirt, I think—wrapped around her right thigh, her knuckles white and her hand bloody as she presses the shirt to her leg.

Then the nurse crosses her arms, shaking her head sharply. "I'm sorry, but this is a busy hour for us. We're two doctors and three nurses short, and we've just taken in five critically injured people from a collision on the 33. So if she's not at death's door—"

"I'm pretty sure she *is*," I insist, staring the nurse down. My heart's in my throat, but I try to remain as calm as possible while I think about the woman bleeding to death in the chair behind me as I argue with this unresponsive nurse. "Can someone just please come look at her quickly, make sure she's *not* going to die while we're waiting?" I lick my lips. "*Please?*"

For a long moment, I think the nurse is going to tell me no—but then, miraculously, she's nodding. "Sign in, and I'll get someone out onto the floor."

I scribble my name onto the clipboard, adding "stab wound," beside the "reason for your visit" space. And then I turn around and head back toward the woman in armor slumped in one of the blue chairs in the far corner of the waiting room.

God, it's so surreal to see her sitting in that chair. Now that we're under the florescent lights, it's apparent that she's wearing the kind of armor you see on fantasy movies. The metal is jet black, and there are a lot of separate pieces to it. It completely encases her shoulders, her chest—with a sculpted breast plate straight out of *Xena*—her hips, thighs, and knees, with a black leather shirt and pants beneath the armored pieces. There are black-armored bits on her forearms and her calves, and black *spikes* on her shoulders. Her long hair is already drying: it spills over her shoulders in unbound waves, the color blue-black.

Her skin, too, is practically blue, and there are deep gray circles around her eyes.

The blood spilling from her stomach and over her gloved hand is starting to drip onto the white floor tiles, a bright, ugly red in the disinfected space.

"Hey," I tell her, my voice soft as I sit down beside her and grab a box of tissues from a little table. I take out a bunch of the tissues, and then I place them on the floor beside her boot to absorb the blood. "Can I see?" I ask her quietly, pointing to the hand clamped down firmly on top of the gauze.

The woman is barely conscious, but she nods slowly, letting her hand relax and fall open beside her as she breathes out, long and low.

"I will die soon," she tells me, her voice almost a whisper. She licks her dry lips, shakes her head from side to side, her eyes closed, her brow deeply furrowed with pain. "Is there no healer here who can help me?"

"I...I hope there is." Her voice is faintly accented... Maybe she's from a different country, where doctors are called healers? "They're sending someone out to look at you. The, um, healers are kind of busy right now, so we have to wait our turn," I tell her. I lean forward, reaching out, my fingers curled into a fist because I don't want to hurt her; I'm unsure of what to do: the gauze is soaked, blood dripping over her leather shirt.

"I will die, then," she says softly, with a small shrug. She opens her eyes, and she gazes at the fluorescent lights overhead calmly. "I have done what I should have done, and there is no shame in my death." Her voice is low and rasping. She glances at me, blue eyes bright with pain and...something more.

Something *electric* pulses between us.

She breathes in, and she breathes out, and then she shuts her eyes and squeezes them tight, making a low moan as she grips her wound harder. "I only wish..." She shakes her head from side to side, and a single tear traces its way out of her eye and along the side of her face, etching a pattern over her pale skin.

"I'm sorry. Please hang on. They're going to get someone to treat you as soon as they can," I say, desperate, swallowing and glancing at the front desk again, but the nurse has turned away, isn't looking. I wonder if she really did send for someone at all. I've been to this hospital before, and they've always been really awesome. They must be severely understaffed...

"Look, just...just hang on. Please. Just hang on," I tell her again, grabbing a few tissues out of the box and wiping them over her black leather shirt to try to sop up the blood.

The woman opens her eyes again and stares at me. She looks feverish now, her eyes much too bright, as if there's a fire burning somewhere inside of her. "I do not fear death," she whispers to me, her full lips forming the words with surety. I stare at her mouth, and then I wrench my gaze up, look into her eyes. She leans forward just a little more, and then she's reaching out with her gloved hand, and she's gripping my forearm with surprisingly strong fingers. "But...can you do something for me?" she asks, her voice low, urgent.

"Yes," I tell her, swallowing the lump in my throat. I wrap my fingers around my little gold pendant, anxiety racing through me, in time to the beat of my blood. "Of course. What do you need?"

The woman regards me for a long moment, her blue eyes practically sparking as she weighs something internally. Then she lifts her chin, she takes a deep breath, and she whispers softly, "Can you get a message to my queen?"

I stare at her, and I whisper, "Your...queen."

"Queen Calla. She's not from... She's not from this world, this...this Earth." It's hard for her to speak for a moment, so she swallows, drops of sweat appearing on her brow as she struggles with the pain. "Queen Calla is from my world, Agrotera. And it is far..." She winces, letting me go and covering the wound again with her gloved hand. "But you must get the message to her. Please."

Not from this world.

I lick my lips again, feeling sick inside.

She's mentally ill.

Pain washes over me; I hurt so much for her...because this woman's last moments alive are going to be spent trying to give me a message for a queen from another world who doesn't exist. She's so confused. She thinks she's from another world—and she's in so much pain...

I don't know what to do. I feel so terrible that she's suffering, so confused, unaware of what's really going on, pain lancing through her. This is the worst way to die, and I don't know how to make things easier for her, more soothing...except to play along. That's what I did with my grandmother before she died. She had dementia, didn't know who I was, thought I was her sister who was long gone from this world. But I played along when I went to visit her. It made her so happy to talk to her "sister" that I couldn't deny her that simple joy.

And it's the least I can do for this woman now, this woman in immeasurable pain, whose blood is dripping on the floor, who I promised to help...and who isn't getting the help she needs.

"Sure. Sure, I can get a message to her," I tell the woman in the most pacifying tone I can conjure. I lean forward, holding the woman's gaze. "What do you want me to tell her?"

She watches me closely, her forehead creased, still staring out of fevered eyes...but her brow is raised. For a long moment, we look at one another, and then she shakes her head slowly.

"Do not patronize me," she murmurs, her voice low as she growls out the words. "You do not believe me."

I stare at her, blinking. "Believe...what?" I hazard.

"You do not believe that I am from another world," she tells me bitterly.

I clear my throat, sighing for a long moment as I gaze down at my ballet flats...and her big black leather boots.

"I believe you," I tell her then, mustering up the strength to lie. Of course I don't believe her. She's delusional, but she's also dying, and she deserves respect, kindness, a listening ear...

But the woman leans forward now, and she's gripping my upper arm with her strong hand, her leather-gloved fingers pressing into my skin. "I am from Agrotera," she tells me, her voice heated now, her other hand clenched hard against her wound, but the blood is pumping faster; it's cascading over her hand. "I am the vice queen of Arktos City. I serve Queen Calla of Arktos."

But as soon as she finishes this litany, the light leaves her eyes, and she slumps back in the chair, her face anguished. "You must think me a madwoman, muttering rantings of no truth."

My heart is aching. At this point, I'm moments away from running into the hallway, grabbing a doctor by the collar of his lab coat, and hauling him out here to help this woman. "I'm really sorry," I whisper softly, but the woman grips my arm harder, so hard that I wince as she pulls herself forward again, locking her eyes on mine.

This close, her eyes are breathtakingly clear, like blue crystal.

"What," she growls softly to me, searching my gaze, "is your name?"

"Mara." I place my hand over her hand. "What's yours?"

"Charaxus," she tells me, and when she speaks her name, her voice takes on a stronger accent. "If," she says then, her face tight with pain and concentration, her voice low, "there is no healer coming, I will die; I cannot heal myself yet. I'm too weak." Her jaw clenches as she looks at me. "But…but I think I *could* heal myself…if you gave me some of your energy for the spell."

"Um…" I have no idea what that means, and I have no idea how to respond to her.

"Knights should never ask for something for themselves. It is our code. We help others; we do not ask them to help us," she says, shaking her head. "But…now is a desperate time. I must return to Queen Calla. She needs me."

"What…what do *you* need?" I ask her, feeling my throat tighten. I glance back up at the nurse's desk, but there's no one behind it now. Where the hell is the doctor? This woman needs help, and she needs help *immediately*. The blood is pouring through her fingers; it's excruciating to watch someone bleed to death in front of you. My heart is tight in my chest as I look at her, as I gaze into her bright blue eyes…

"What do you need?" I repeat when she closes her eyes, when she vacillates in her seat a little, shifting from side to side because she's too weak to hold herself up.

"I…I do not know. I have not done this before, taken energy from another," she says, licking her lips. Her eyes are still closed, and her face is pained, as if she's thinking very, very hard about a solution to a problem. But then her brow's furrow smooths, and she opens her eyes, pinning her gaze to me. "Are you willing to try this, Mara?"

The way she says my name… Her voice is low already, but when she speaks those two simple syllables, it sounds as if we're sharing a secret. I watch her, and suddenly my heart is beating a little faster—but not for the reasons you'd think. Yeah, I'm in an emergency room. Yeah, I just saved a woman from drowning…

But there's something I've never experienced before pulsing between us.

"Yes," I tell her, and then I clear my throat. "I'm…willing." My voice cracks, and that makes me feel a little strange, but Charaxus is already nodding.

"All right, then. Please stay still."

I sit there, feeling more helpless than I've ever felt in my life as a bleeding, dying woman grips my arm tightly and concentrates on something only she is aware of, or believes in. These could be the last moments of her life; I'll do anything within my power to alleviate her pain.

You take care of everyone but yourself. Cecile's words come back to me unbidden, and I close my eyes, shaking my head slightly as I hold the woman's hand.

She needs my help. And I'm going to give it to her.

Time passes, and nothing happens. I can only imagine what she was hoping for, can only assume she believes she's doing magic… Maybe she expected her wound to magically heal itself. I watch her carefully now, see concentration etched on her beautiful face, her brow breaking out into a glimmering sheen of sweat.

Anxious, I glance back up at the nurse's desk. Still, no one is there. No doctor is coming. The blood drips down onto the floor. People moan all around me in pain, terrible pain.

This is one of the worst moments in my life.

And, trust me, I've had a lot of bad moments.

But I have to do whatever I can to make it

better. So I sit, still and quiet, as the woman continues to concentrate...

And then...

This is impossible.

Something...changes.

At first, I think it's my imagination. I'm exhausted, after all. Maybe exhaustion is just making me see things.

Making me see *light* traveling over my skin.

That's the only way I can describe it. Beneath the florescent bulbs of the hospital, a flicker of white and blue and green starts to appear, like a mist, over my skin. It's hazy, but then the colors solidify, spiral... I'm wearing a black skirt with a black tank top, my arms and lower legs uncovered, and the colors spiral over my limbs, about an inch above my skin, as if I'm a sun and a miniature galaxy is spinning around me. The colors are transparent, a light show dancing across my body.

A few moments later, and the colors parade along the arm that Charaxus is holding.

"What's happening?" I whisper, as the colors spiral faster and faster; they pulse over Charaxus, too, over her gloved hand, her arm, her body, as if she's drawing the colors from me to her.

Charaxus doesn't reply, but the creases in her forehead deepen, a single trickle of sweat trailing over her face. Open-mouthed, I stare at the colors, mesmerized and disbelieving but unable to look away, unwilling to even blink.

I do blink eventually; my eyes are watering from holding them open. And when I open my eyes again, the colors are still there, still moving over my body and hers—faster, faster...

I look up, gaze around me, but no one is paying

attention to us.

Suddenly, there's a bright flash of light. It's like the flash of a camera, and I close my eyes against it instinctively. When I part my eyelids, the flash of light has grown brighter, brighter... I shield my eyes with my other arm, but all I can see right now are colored spots, blinding me.

It takes a long moment before I can see again clearly. My breathing is shallow; Charaxus has released my arm. I blink away the spots, and then I'm looking at the woman in front of me, the woman who—a moment before—was slumped in the chair, her face so pallid that she almost looked dead, blood pouring over her leather shirt, dripping onto the floor below.

I stare.

She's sitting up in the seat, her back poker-straight. Her long, black hair falls in waves down her back, shining in the overhead florescent lights. Her skin is still pale—I think she's just naturally pale—but now there's a rosy glow to her cheeks. Her eyes are no longer feverish but bright with energy, the blue of them so brilliant that I blink again, taken aback by their clarity.

There is no more blood on her shirt, only a hole, the leather torn over her stomach...

And there is no wound.

I stare at her smooth stomach, and then I lift my gaze to take in her relaxed posture; she's calm, at ease, when a moment before she was making her final requests.

I open my mouth. I shut my mouth.

I...have no idea what to say.

Charaxus looks to me, and she nods her head. She's no longer panting with pain, her mouth a thin, hard line. Instead, she's breathing evenly, and her lips are softly parted. She leans forward in the chair now, toward me, lifting her chin.

"Thank you for helping me, Mara," she says, and then she's standing smoothly. "How are you? Do you feel all right?"

I stare up at her, shocked.

I mean, I know I dragged her out of the river, but I've never seen her standing before: she's *really* tall. Like, a whole head and shoulders above me, and I'm not short myself. She towers over me, and when I find myself tongue-tied, unable to reply to her question, her brow furrows, and she offers me a gloved hand, palm up and open.

"Are you all right?" she repeats, her voice low, her bright blue gaze piercing me through. I notice so many things at once, like how her full lips are parted, how her metal-clad chest rises and falls with each breath, how her hand—once I take it—is firm and gentle as it closes around mine, the soft leather of her glove supple as she holds my hand.

There's a spell on this moment, I realize, as we touch for the first time since the magic. There's something potent crackling where our hands come together…

Something electric.

But, as I watch her, as my own breathing starts to come faster, as I open my mouth to speak…that's when the spell is broken.

Because I hear the first scream.

Chapter 4: A Surprising Development

I stand, Charaxus assisting me to my feet as she casts a glance behind her. With her free hand, she's reaching over her shoulder, as if for a weapon, but her fingers grasp at air. There's nothing there.

The scream continues, echoing through the halls of the hospital, and it isn't the sort of scream I'm used to hearing—like a kid's scream when they're in the middle of playing with their friends, or the short scream of someone who was just startled.

No, this is the kind of bloodcurdling scream that I'm not sure I've ever heard before in real life. A terrible, bone-chilling sound that seems to come from everywhere and nowhere as it echoes off of the walls. Charaxus and I are both on guard as we try to figure out where that scream is coming from and, more importantly, *why*.

Everyone else around us is standing, too, instinctively turning their heads this way and that…

And that's when I begin to realize that things have become really, really...well, *strange*.

Because all around us, the people have leaped up from their seats—they're *standing*, even though they were hurting or injured, awaiting medical attention in the emergency room. These were people who were bleeding, collapsed in the blue waiting room chairs bonelessly, and they're on their feet now. Even the woman who had been holding a bunched-up piece of clothing tightly to her thigh, looking as if she wasn't going to be standing without medical attention anytime soon, is standing by herself, that piece of clothing now crumpled on the floor at her feet. I can see her thigh through a hole in her jeans, and her copper skin is unblemished, smooth, no wound in sight.

She's *fine*.

The man who was holding a towel over his eye? He's standing there with his mouth gaping open, both brown eyes gazing around the room in shock, his hands hanging limply at his sides.

His eye looks fine: he's staring around at everyone else.

And everyone else…looks fine, too.

They're looking at their hands and their legs as if they're in some sort of daze. A man who had been cradling his hand, a red bandanna wrapped tightly around it, is unwinding that bandanna, taking in his whole, albeit grubby, hand. There appears to be nothing wrong with it. A woman who was seated closest to the emergency room doors wearing a silver formal dress, formerly doubled over in pain, is standing with a surprised smile on her face, patting her much-hairsprayed updo with her hands, looking perfectly well.

That scream isn't coming from the waiting room, not from any of the people gathered here, looking around at one another in wonder. The scream is coming from somewhere deeper inside the hospital.

I see that the nurse is behind the front desk again, and she's wearing a disgruntled expression as she peers around the corner, as if she's waiting for someone to come clear things up, someone to explain what all this fuss is about...but that someone just isn't coming.

That's when her phone starts to ring, the sound of it startling as the scream—at last—dies away.

Hand over her heart, the nurse snatches up the phone from its cradle and asks the caller, testily, "What do you want?" The caller says something, and then the nurse behind the desk, the nurse who—I'd assumed—had seen and heard everything in her years at the hospital, blanches as white as a sheet.

"That's...not possible," she whispers, a whisper I can hear in the near-silent room. Then, with a shaking hand, she sets the phone back down in its cradle.

She looks around at all of us, and she stands still for a long moment before she bolts from the front desk, and then she's shuffling quickly down the corridor, away from the waiting room, until she disappears from sight.

The lady by the waiting room doors in the silver dress is now whispering something to herself, but then she lifts her face up at that moment, and she looks so happy, so joyful, that I'm stricken speechless as I stare at her.

"I'm better," the woman keeps saying over and over again, each word louder than the last. "It... I mean, it doesn't *hurt* anymore!"

"Me, too!" mutters the guy with the bandanna, holding up his hand in awe. "I cut my fingers with a hacksaw blade," he's saying in a thick, southern drawl, "and they were bleeding pretty badly—but I don't even have cuts no more! They're all gone!"

People are starting to exclaim to one another, and Charaxus, towering over me, folds her arms, regarding the people in the waiting room with a soft, thoughtful frown. Overwhelmed, I fall back into my chair, and then Charaxus is crouching smoothly in front of me. She searches my face.

"What did you *do?*" she asks me, arching a single brow. The words aren't soft, aren't kind; rather, they're pretty sharp. I stare at her in shock.

"Me? *Do?*" I repeat, and then the adrenaline finally catches up with me. "I didn't do anything," I reply quickly, and—if I'm being honest—my voice is a little sharp, too. "There were colors...and then..." I gesture to her stomach. "This is all *really* weird. I mean, what happened?" I ask her, point blank. "What just *happened?*"

There's another scream from a distant area of the hospital, a woman's scream, high-pitched and prolonged, and while the scream is still going on, a male doctor starts backing out of the swinging doors that are used to discharge patients. He looks just as pale as the nurse did earlier, and his mouth is sagging open, slack-jawed.

"The people...in the morgue," he whispers, and he's turning around to stare wildly at all of us as he raises his hands. "They're... I think this is *the* zombie apocalypse. Like, the actual fucking *zombie apocalypse,*" he whispers now, his eyes glazed, and he starts to move as quickly as he can toward the front doors.

"Wait a second, doc," says the guy with the bandanna, gripping the doctor as he tries to sprint past him. "Whadya mean? Zombies? You playin' a cheap trick on us?" He laughs a little, though the laugh sounds uncertain to my ears.

"Everyone in the morgue came *back,*" says the doctor, rolling his eyes so that the whites are showing.

"They're... I mean, they're all *alive*. They came back from the *dead*. They slid out of the... I mean, they *literally* slid out of the drawers. They were dead, and then they just..." He laughs, bewildered. "They just *weren't*. All of them," he gulps. "Even the guy in the bus accident. The one who lost his head. *It's back on him.*"

Charaxus lets go of my arm, and she's stepping forward, gripping the doctor on his other side now, her eyes as hard as stone. "Explain yourself," she says, her voice gruff. When the doctor looks up at her, he seems to quake in fear. She *is* a little intimidating: a tall, gorgeous woman wearing spectacularly spiky armor, demanding something of him in a cool, commanding tone.

As we all wait for the doctor to say something, *anything,* I realize how surreal all of this is. None of this is possible, from Charaxus' wound disappearing, to the other patients' injuries vanishing, to the *corpses* rising from the dead...

But...it looks it's happening, anyway. Right now. To us.

Or it could all be a really spectacular dream. I latch onto that idea, swallowing the lump in my throat. Yeah, maybe it's a dream... I mean, it *has* to be a dream...

I pinch the skin of my arm. Hard. And it hurts. Okay.

This isn't a dream.

I step forward then, and I place my hand on Charaxus' hand, the same one that's gripping the doctor, her leather-gloved fingers making indents in his lab coat. When she glances my way, I shake my head warningly once, twice, and—surprising no one more than me—she releases the doctor, allowing her hands to fall to her sides, though they're clenched into tight fists.

"Lady, I don't know anything," the doctor mutters, and quick as a flash, he's running past us, making his hurried escape through the automatic doors.

"Zombies, huh?" asks the bandanna guy; he folds his arms over his expansive, plaid-covered chest. "I always figured that's how we'd go. It's 'cause of all them liberals, of course. Am I right?"

I stare at the guy long and hard, and then I realize that, though I *want* to challenge his prejudices, now's really not the time. "Come on," I whisper to Charaxus, and then I'm tugging her after me, curling my fingers under one of the metal plates on her arm. With quick steps, I guide her through the doors and toward my car, which is still parked right in front of the hospital.

Charaxus follows me, and she doesn't protest until we're outside of the hospital. Then she lifts her nose to the air, a worried expression crossing her face. "But something's gone..." It seems as if Charaxus is about to say "wrong," but she stops herself at the last moment. "Something's...strange," she begins again, and then she pauses on the sidewalk near my car, and with all of that metal and height and muscle, no amount of my tugging is going to move her.

She looks down at me, seemingly exasperated: she breathes out a curt sigh. I watch her expectantly as more screams filter out of the hospital. I would, personally, like to get the hell out of Dodge. But I wait.

Finally, Charaxus frowns deeply, and she says, "I do not know why the spell worked as it did. It was only supposed to heal *me*. Not all of the other people in there. And it was supposed to exhaust *you*." She rakes her blue eyes over me, brow furrowed, her expression perplexed. "But you appear…well," she settles on, her mouth drawn into a thin line as her eyes flash, and, again, her gaze roves over me.

There's a sizzling moment of connection as she searches my eyes…

But that might just be the adrenaline coursing through my veins. It's a little hard to figure out *what* I'm feeling right now.

I open my mouth, and words start to spill out: "I'm well, yeah, but I *am* kind of tired. Well, exhausted. I did just lug you out of the river," I smile weakly, but her expression remains still and severe. "Look," I sigh, "I have no idea what just happened in there, but whatever it is, it spooked a doctor into running away. And there's all sorts of screaming. Dead people coming back to life… And, I mean, you're…apparently okay now. When you were dying before." I blink and wave my arms in the air. "None of this makes sense."

"No," she says, and she sighs again, arms crossed, her feet hip-width apart. It's a strong stance, and with the wind blowing, cool and soft, through the streets, her hair moves, soft tendrils of black gusting over her shoulders.

I shiver a little. "Okay, one of my top-ten fears is a zombie apocalypse. So…" I glance toward the hospital doors nervously. "Can we just go back home and figure stuff out there?"

"Zombies?" Charaxus asks, her head angled to one side, but then her voice lowers. "…home?"

"Yeah. My place. I live near the river, where I rescued you," I say, pointing my chin in the general direction of the Ceres.

"Oh. Yes, take me there," she says, her voice sounding weary. "I need to go back there. I need to find it."

"Find what?" I ask, mystified.

She lifts her chin, her eyes bright. "Something important."

"Okay, okay." I place my hands at the small of her back and urge her to fold herself into my Beetle's passenger seat. "Sure. *Don't* tell me," I say in a soft huff to myself as I walk around behind the car.

I glance back at the hospital through the automatic doors, and there's a guy walking, dazed, out of the corridor leading into the surgery area. He's wearing a hospital gown, and he's close enough that I can see that there's something attached to the big toe of his bare foot…

"Oh, my God," I mutter to myself as I stare at the morgue tag.

The guy peers out through the automatic doors, his eyes wide, his mouth formed into an O of astonishment, while the people in the waiting room start to shriek and move away from him, knocking over chairs.

"Oooookay," I tell myself hoarsely, drawing in a deep breath. "Okay. Okay. Okay…" My hands are shaking as I open my car door and slam it, sitting down in the driver's seat and stabbing the key into the ignition. "Buckle up," I tell my armored co-pilot, and then I'm peeling out of the emergency room loop, tires screeching.

"Buckle what?" asks the woman seated beside me, eyebrow raised.

"Um…" At the stoplight, I reach across her, pulling out the seat belt from the passenger side and drawing it over her chest. It's only when I'm buckling it into place that I realize how close we are, our heads bent together, nearly touching. My cheeks flush.

The light changes, and after a moment of driving, I risk a sidelong glance at her, but she's already staring out the window, up at the few stars peeking through the cloud cover overhead.

We might be in for another storm tonight.

Chapter 5: Starry, Starry Night

I pull into the parking lot of the Ceres and shut the car off before turning in my seat to face my passenger.

"Okay," I say, clearing my throat, voice low. "Who are you? I mean, *really*?"

The woman I rescued, the woman I pulled from the Buffalo River, the woman wearing full, spiky armor turns to look at me, her pale face grave. There isn't enough light to fully illuminate her expression, but my vision has adjusted enough to see that her eyes are enormous in the dark, and I know she's looking at me.

"I am Charaxus," she tells me in that low growl, "and I am the vice queen of Arktos, which is on Agrotera."

I'm silent for a long moment as I muddle through the unfamiliar words. "Agrotera," I repeat. "It's... You're telling me that's another world. That you're from another world." I'm hoping, desperately, that this is *not* what she's telling me. It's a thin hope...and it's dashed in the next heartbeat.

"Yes," she replies simply, no hesitation.

Another world.

Another *world*.

"How..." I begin, but then I start over, shaking my head. "Okay, what happened..." My voice cracks, though I'm trying to keep it calm and steady. "What happened at the hospital?" I lick my lips, shift my gaze. "What happened when you touched me? All those colors? And then—"

"Mara." Charaxus is silent for a full minute before she unbuckles her seat belt expertly and shifts her shoulders to look out the front window of the car. Her jaw is firm, set. "You were kind to save me from the river," she says gravely, "but you need have nothing more to do with me. I will disappear, and you will never see me again." She turns to look at me, her eyes softer now, and she breathes out into the stillness, a soft sigh. "Thank you, Mara, for your kindness."

We stare at one another in the cramped confines of my Beetle. The car is ready-made for intimate moments, but this moment in particular is so strange, so unexpected. Charaxus is close, right beside me, and after everything that we've gone through together, confronting death itself...

I'm a little confused.

Yeah, I'm attracted to her, and I think she might be attracted to me. The way she's looking at me... The way her eyes trace the curve of my cheek, my chin, down to my shoulders, my breasts... She's giving me the once over, and though her eyes are still soft, there's a fire within them, burning low.

"Wait," I tell her, and I place my fingertips on the metal plate over her forearm. She stares down at my fingers, and I stare too, because in that moment...

There was a spark. Like, an honest-to-goodness, genuine *spark*. Like static shock. Like electricity.

Overhead, lightning explodes.

The stars are lost. Another storm is brewing.

"What's going on, Charaxus?" I ask her quietly,

but her jaw is tight, and she's glancing sidelong at the door, her brow furrowing as she stares at the door handle.

I'm about to say something else, but then Charaxus is lifting her hand, is placing it against the car door as if she's bracing herself for something, her palm flat, her eyes closed.

And though she wasn't touching the door's handle at all…the door opens.

I sit there, my mouth open as Charaxus pushes the door wide, and she steps out of my car, into the night, where ominous clouds build overhead and another rumble of thunder growls along the horizon.

I grab my purse from the backseat, and then I'm vaulting out of the car and running after her. Charaxus has very long legs, so when she walks, she covers distances a basketball player would probably be jealous of. I race to catch up, and I manage to by the time we reach the edge of the river.

"Hey, where are you going?" I call after her as she aims right for the escarpment.

"Home," she snaps back over her shoulder. "I must go home."

"But you can't just—" I begin, and then my words are cut off when I run into Charaxus. Literally. She suddenly froze in place, and because I wasn't looking where I was going, I ran into her, slamming into her metal-clad back. She hardly seems to feel the impact: she's too tall and muscular to budge an inch, and with the laws of physics working like they do, that means I start to fall backward. I'm falling a little like a cartoon character who just ran into a brick wall, arms flailing at my sides.

But Charaxus turns, and with a single, graceful

movement—a pivot on the balls of her feet, wrapping an arm around my waist with a gentleness and strength that leaves me breathless—she catches me.

I still can't breathe as I stare up at her; the moment stands, suspended. She holds me in her arms, gazing at me with eyes so blue that they seem to glow in the dark.

We remain this way as her lips, so subtly, turn up at the corners.

"You find it hard to believe that I'm from another world?" she asks, and her voice is surprisingly soft as she helps me stand upright.

Flustered, shaky on my feet, I draw in a deep breath—and then I opt for honesty. "Yes," I tell her. "It can't be true."

"Why not?"

"People appearing from other worlds..." I gesture helplessly. "That only happens in stories. Not in real life."

She arches a brow. "But your mind does not know how to explain what you've experienced. What you saw when I, and the others—including the deceased—were healed." She indicates the hole in her leather shirt.

The light is dim, but Charaxus has such pale skin she could probably be seen glowing from outer space. So it's fairly easy to see her skin through the hole in her shirt and—wait. Does she have a *six-pack?* Like, the kind of abs you only see in fitness magazines?

That's...pretty damn hot.

I wrench my gaze away, force myself to meet her eyes. She's standing there with her arms crossed, and she almost looks smug, her small smile slanted after she caught me staring.

"My mind," I say, clearing my throat, "has no idea who you are or what you're doing here. I saved your life, and then…" I rock back on my heels a little, frowning. "It's just been a weird night," I finish, breathing out.

"For you," she murmurs, one dark brow raised, "and me, too." She turns on her heel again, and she stalks the rest of the way to the edge of the escarpment and the metal wall lining the river.

"Okay. So you're from another world," I say flatly, not a question. I stand there, trying to breathe evenly—trying and failing—before I follow after her again. I want her to turn around and yell, "Just kidding!" with a mischievous grin. I want cameramen to pop up out from the shadows. I want Charaxus to tell me that they've been filming a pilot for a new fantasy/reality show, and I've been duped into believing (with super-fancy, state-of-the-art special effects) that magic is real, that this woman is a vice queen—whatever the hell that is—from another world.

But that's not what happens at all.

Instead, Charaxus turns to face me, and I stop running just in time to avoid colliding with her chest plate. We stare at one another. My breathing is labored, my legs are weak, and, suddenly, a couple of things happen all at once.

One: Again, I feel as if I've met her before. There's this nagging feeling in my heart that she's familiar to me, that I know her from somewhere…but where?

Two: She reaches for me. I stand there, perfectly still, as she reaches up with her gloved hand and brushes her leather-clad fingers over the outside of my right ear, the soft *shush* of her caress enough to make me shiver. It's such a surprising gesture, and such an intimate one, that I stand speechless as she caresses me.

But just as quickly, her warm fingers leave my skin, and now she's holding something up in front of her right eye.

It's a small glittering star, as silver as the real ones far, far above our heads, hiding on the other side of the cloud cover.

"What—" I begin, but she shakes her head, holds the star out to me, and I let her drop it into my palm. I stare down at the glittering thing, a little spellbound.

"I took it from your ear," she tells me companionably, and then, when I wrinkle my brow at her, she shakes her head a little ruefully. "I used to do that trick for…for my little brother," she says, her jaw tight. "It amazed him. It was the first magic I ever learned." She rakes her fingers back through her hair as she shakes her head, sighs. "I wanted to prove myself to you," she says then, and her words come out frustrated.

"But that's just a simple trick," I tell her, my voice hollow as my fingers curl over the glittery star in my palm, feeling the sharpness against my skin. "Anyone can do that. Use a little misdirection, slide the star out of your sleeve…or glove," I say, waving to her hand. "My grandfather used to do this trick when I was a kid. He'd take coins out of my ears, make me laugh." I lick my lips, swallow. "It's not real magic," I say flatly.

Charaxus raises a brow, says nothing in reply. When the silence has gone on almost *too* long, she lifts her chin, her eyes sparkling in the dark as she holds my gaze. "Look in your hand, Mara," she whispers to me then.

I lift up my hand, uncurl my fingers. The same glittery star is still lying in my palm.

But as I watch…it becomes something else.

That tiny, glitter-covered star starts to ascend from my hand. I stare at it, my mouth open, because the star rises until it's about six inches above my hand. I don't move a muscle: I stand there, transfixed, staring at the star hovering in midair.

Slowly, the star stands up straight on its two little star legs, and it begins to rotate as if it's in a display case at a Swarovski store, sparkling like crazy. And then it begins to glow.

It looks as if it's about to catch fire.

The star spins, glows, hovers above my palm… And then it begins to ascend until it's about ten feet above our heads.

Quickly, brightly, it shoots up into the sky: a reverse shooting star aiming for the heavens.

I gape as the star hits the cloud cover overhead. And instantly, everywhere, there is a shower of stars— little shooting stars sprinkling down over us. They float to the ground softly, slowly, almost like snowflakes, trailing light behind them until they hit the ground… And one by one, they each wink out and disappear.

All of the light is gone, the star is gone, and through the afterlight streaking my vision, I stare up at Charaxus…enchanted.

"I am who I say I am," she tells me simply, her eyes hooded, her mouth downturned. For a long moment, she says nothing more. And then she murmurs to me, her voice low, smooth: "Do you believe me?"

"Yes," I whisper. I don't even think about it; I

give her the word immediately.

Yes. Yes, I believe her.

We're standing close together. If I reached up, I could brush the black hair out of her eye again, could trail my fingers over her face. Why am I thinking this? Why is this feeling stirring inside of me, so deep, so primal?

I haven't felt like this in a long time.

Something is waking up inside of me. And, if I'm honest, it's been waking up for hours. Ever since I rescued her from the river.

I was attracted to Charaxus from the first moment I saw her. And now, standing so near to her...

No, I need to focus. She's from another *world*. I need to understand what that means. My whole universe has to reshape itself around this new piece of information.

But I stare up at her, and I see the curve of her cheek, her jaw, her mouth...and I just want to kiss her.

I want to kiss her *fiercely*.

So, for a long minute, two minutes, three minutes...neither of us says a word. We stare at one another beneath the afterlight of the falling stars. Charaxus' mouth is open, and as she leans toward me, I'm surprised (or am I?) that she's curling her gloved fingers around my wrist gently, as if she's touching something fragile...or as if she's uncertain as to whether she should be doing this. The leather warms my skin, and my heart rate skyrockets, and then she's leaning toward me, her eyes sparking with something raw, real: every bone in my body responds to her, every muscle, every tendon, every drop of blood racing through me...

But at that moment, when I think our mouths are about to meet, when I think we're about to share the most mind-blowing kiss of my life...the expectation crumbles away into nothingness. Charaxus shifts uncomfortably on her heels, releases my wrist, and she gazes away from me, working her jaw as if she's suddenly uncomfortable with the tension radiating between us. She takes a single step back, and the spell that was spun just a moment ago is broken.

What...happened?

"I should not have wasted my energy. I have nothing to prove to you," Charaxus murmurs, her voice stiff. "I must... I must go," she tells me, and then she's turning, and within a few short steps, I realize that she's begun to climb down the metal ladder, aiming for the cold waters of the Buffalo River.

"Wait. Please wait..." I crouch down, reaching out and placing my hand over her gloved one, still gripping the top rung.

She stares up at me from the ladder, her bright blue eyes narrowed.

"Where are you going?" I ask her, gesturing toward the river. I feel dizzy, breathless.

She frowns at me, her jaw still set.

"I came through a portal," she tells me gruffly, leaning against the ladder. "And I must..." She sighs. "I must find the thing that created the portal, so that I may return to Agrotera. At once."

"And what created the portal?" I ask her, perplexed.

"It was a shard of glass," she says, her voice low.

I glance over her shoulder at the water rolling sluggishly past. "Okay. So how big is this shard?"

"Smaller than that star I pulled from your ear."

I blink.

Then, after a pause, I clear my throat. "Look," I begin awkwardly. "I… I mean, you're free to do whatever you want. Obviously. But I...don't think this is the best approach. You just came through a portal. And I just rescued you from drowning. And you just nearly died of blood loss…and then cast a spell that not only healed you but brought people back from the *dead*. Don't you think that's enough excitement for one night?" I ask weakly, sitting back on my heels.

I'm surprised that this question wins a smile from her—though it's a very small one. "Knights," she says, glancing up at me with a raised brow, "do not get tired."

So she's a *knight*? The black armor…

Okay.

Yeah, I can see it.

I guess that makes as much sense as any of this.

I watch her thoughtfully. "You say that, but is it really true, or is it just something you tell yourself?" My mouth turns up at the corners softly. "Why don't you…" I draw in a deep breath. "Why don't you come with me? Back to my place? There's probably still some pizza left. You can eat, rest, and then in the morning, we'll figure out what to do next."

"We?" she asks, her head tilted to one side as she gazes up at me. Her jaw is tight again, and the ghost of a smile has disappeared from her lips. In fact, her expression is suddenly taut and guarded. Wary. It's a surprising change, and it happens in a heartbeat.

Despite my exhaustion, I remain crouched on the pavement, trying to talk this woman down—or, rather, up—from the ladder. I press the pad of my thumb to the back of my gold pendant as I try my best to bring back her earlier warmth.

"It's been a long night, Charaxus." My tone is gentle, but the tiredness comes through. "You *must* need to rest."

"Knights don't—"

"I can tell you're tired," I say, and my throat tightens—I'm going for broke here. The truth is...I don't want her to disappear. I don't want the woman who materialized from another world, who made a star appear out of thin air, who I feel such an intense connection with...to vanish.

There's something nagging at me. Something that's growing stronger by the moment. She's familiar, but I still can't place her. It's as if there's a cloud in my mind's eye, obscuring something vitally important from me.

All I know is that she can't go. Not yet.

Not tonight.

Charaxus pauses, her hands gripping the rung of the ladder tightly as she stares up at me. And then, slowly, rung by rung, she ascends, climbing until her boots are back on land; she's standing in front of me once more. Her jaw is still tense, her eyes are narrowed and distrustful—but she listened to me.

I rise to stand beside her.

"I don't need your help," she tells me quickly. Her voice is low, and the words are flippant, but there's quite a lot of pain beneath them.

I stare up at her, confused.

"I know you don't," I tell her, rubbing at my arms. The night has gotten chilly. Or maybe I'm shivering for a different reason. When she stands this close, I'm not sure what happens to me... Something shifts, deep inside. It feels like… Well, it feels like an unfurling.

I'm attracted to her.

But I've never felt attraction like this before.

I hold her eyes, and I clear my throat again. "I know you don't need my help. I'm only…concerned," I say, offering her a small smile. "I pulled you out of that river, and you weren't breathing." Goosebumps break out over my skin as I remember the many and varied terrors of the evening. "I don't want you endangering yourself again. At least, not *right* away. And heading down to the river without a plan… That's dangerous. I mean, you *didn't* have a plan, did you?" I ask gently.

A flicker of sheepishness passes over her face, telling me all that I need to know. But the sheepishness doesn't last long. Charaxus huffs, gazing over the escarpment to the river flowing slowly below. "That river is no danger," she tells me imperiously.

"It may not look like it is. But it nearly took your life." My words are soft, my head tilted to the side as I gaze at her solemnly. "No reason to give it two chances in one night, okay?"

Charaxus' whole body stiffens, and for a moment, I think she's going to argue with me. Her eyes flash dangerously, her mouth drawn in a thin, hard line, but then…she doesn't argue at all. She sighs, nods stiffly, and her shoulders curl forward as if she's defeated.

"Some food, a soft place to sleep—I would not begrudge these things," she says gruffly, her tone still very formal, but there's a detectable softness in her body language that wasn't there a moment ago.

"Good," I tell her with a nod, and then I'm taking a few steps toward the Ceres, glancing over my shoulder to make certain she's following me. Charaxus stands in place, look toward the river uncertainly.

"Are you coming?" I ask her.

Charaxus' jaw tightens. "The shard," she begins, and she clears her throat. "It's how I got here. It's how the portal was formed... The portal is my only way to get back home," she tells me. "What if..." Her hands curl into fists. "What if it's lost forever?" she whispers.

I raise my eyebrows, staring at this woman wearing thick black armor who is, all of the sudden, exposing her vulnerability to me, as if her sharp, commanding mask slipped, just for a moment, out of place. She seems young now, even though she must be thirty-something, around my age.

She almost looks fragile. My heart hurts, seeing her like this.

"Look, you said the shard of glass is small, right?" I step toward her, offering her an uncertain smile, my chin tilted upward. "There's no way you're going to be able to find it tonight. Tomorrow morning, with fresh eyes and sunlight, you'll be able to search more productively. Maybe you'll find it right away. And then what?"

"Then I'll go back home," says Charaxus, almost wistfully.

My stomach turns over inside of me. I shake my head, nodding quickly. "Sure. You'll do that. I don't doubt it. But right now, it's dinnertime. Past dinnertime. Come on... Do you guys have pizza on Agrotera?"

"Pizza?" she asks with a raised brow as she begins to follow me. We walk, taking slow steps, toward the Ceres. "No, I don't think so," she says thoughtfully, her hands folded behind her back. She casts me a sidelong glance. "What is it?"

"The best food our planet has to offer." I smile. "Come on in and meet everyone." I ascend the concrete steps in front of the Ceres, and I rummage through my purse as I search for my keys, peering down into my dark purse.

Charaxus waits quietly behind me. When I turn to glance at her over my shoulder, my throat constricts.

She looks so beautiful. That's a simple way to put it, but that's how simple it feels. My eyes have adjusted—as much as possible—to the darkness, but her skin is so pale that she almost shines. She is gazing up at the heavy cloud cover, and her brow is furrowed, as if she's considering something of great importance.

As if she's thinking of home.

Her expression is pensive and guarded. When she catches me looking, her gaze shifts from the heavens to me.

We stand there on the steps—Charaxus two steps down from me, making her equal to my height.

Somewhere far away, a cat hisses and yowls, followed by a small metallic bang, as if something tumbled from an overly full dumpster. There's the distant, mournful siren-song of a train's whistle.

A soft wind blows through the parking lot in front of the Ceres, stirring Charaxus' hair softly over her shoulders.

She stares at me, and her bright blue eyes burn. She narrows her gaze a little, her head poised to one side.

"Why do you think I appeared here?" she asks me then, her gruff voice surprisingly soft in the stillness. "With…you?" The last word is so low that, for a moment, I wonder if I heard her correctly.

I watch her, my lips parted, my breathing shallow, because she looked as if she was about to place her hands on me. I *know* she was. Maybe she would have fit her hands around my waist, her fingers curling over my curves there. But she drew back, stopped herself stiffly, as if there were an invisible wall between us, keeping us apart.

Separating us by more than two steps.

She fists her hands, and there's a war fleeting over her face.

Tension crackles between us, electric, and a heat slides over my skin. I rub at my bare forearms a little, trying to settle myself.

"I don't know why you ended up here," I whisper then, and my brow furrows as I look at her, really *look* at her.

Why does she seem so familiar?

And why does my heart *ache* at the sight of her? I feel as if it's obvious, as if the truth is crying out to me, and I just can't hear it…

Charaxus turns to glance up at the sky again, and my breath catches in my throat as I watch her face turn in profile, as I watch a hole in the cloud cover open overhead, allowing a million stars to shine through…

I swear, at this moment, the starlight is reflected in her glorious black mane…

And it looks like…

It looks…like…

I breathe out.

I know her. I know her as if I've known her my entire life.

Because I *have.*

"You…" I whisper, and Charaxus stares at me in confusion. "You…" I whisper again, and then I'm reaching out to her, my hands moving unbidden, and I can't stop them; I can't stop myself from moving toward her like a gravity, as if she's the sun and I'm a simple planet, pulled inexorably toward her light.

My fingers brush across her right cheek, her high cheekbone, her warm, soft skin. She remains perfectly still, her blue eyes wide for a moment, but then she surprises me. As I trace my fingers over her cheek, lightly, lightly, as if I'm tracing the contours of a painting, she closes her eyes, and she breathes out, her breath hot against my palm.

"You look like you have stars in your hair," I whisper to her, watching the light of the faraway stars somehow, impossibly, reflect in the glossy blackness of her hair.

Her eyes snap open, and she stares at me wonderingly.

"What did you say?" she asks, her voice low, a growl.

I stand there, very still, and I lean closer. "You look like you have stars in your hair," I tell her urgently. It's important. She needs to know this, because I've dreamed of this, of her… I've dreamed of her so many times that she became an integral part of my life long before I met her, knew her.

My dream girl. That's who Charaxus is. The woman who has haunted my dreams since I was small, since before I knew what a dream was or what a dream could do. All of my life, she has haunted my sleeping hours, and, awake, I know her now.

I stare at her in the darkness.

I don't know how this is possible.

But it's real.

She's real.

The woman of my dreams is standing in front of me. And I'm touching her.

She's warm and soft and *real*.

Something prevented me from recognizing her until now. Maybe I didn't believe it. Couldn't. Maybe I didn't want to see the truth. But the foggy woman in all of my dreams, the woman I knew I loved with all of my heart... This is her. I know it like I know who I am: I'm Mara, and I've had a hard life. I'm an artist. And I *really* love pizza. These things make up part of my identity.

And so does Charaxus.

She takes a step up, standing closer, a little higher than me now, her gloved fingers—finally— curling around my waist. "Say it again," she whispers.

"Say what?" I ask, as Charaxus searches my face.

"About..." Her voice cracks, but she shakes her head, clears her voice, lifts her chin, blue eyes flashing. "About the stars."

I swallow. "You look like you have stars in your hair," I tell her one last time, and as I watch, a single tear leaks from the corner of her right eye, tracing all the way down her cheek, the curve of her chin; the tear glitters, suspended in the air for half a heartbeat, before falling down to her black breastplate.

"I know you," she whispers then, gripping me, and her voice is breaking. "I've dreamed of you."

I stare at her, my mouth open. "*You've* dreamed of *me?*"

"Yes," she says, nodding, and she wraps her arms tightly around me, as if she'll never let go, as if she's drowning and I'm the only sure, real thing to hold onto in a storm at sea. "Yes," she murmurs again, and I'm reaching up, touching her face as she stares down at me, eyes shining.

I draw her face to mine. And I kiss her.

At first, she's surprised, and she makes no movement. Her mouth is soft, warm, gentle, as I kiss her. But then her surprise evaporates, and she devours me, her mouth suddenly ferocious as she kisses me deeply, passionately, with so much strength and fervor that I lose my breath. She tastes of cinnamon, of fire, of hot, spicy things. I wrap my arms so tightly around her neck that, when she lifts me up at my waist, I rise from the ground.

She sets me back down gently, and we both break from the kiss, taking a step away—my back colliding with the door of the Ceres, her feet finding pavement once more. She stares up at me as I stare down at her; my heart is knocking so hard at my ribs that she must be able to hear its rhythm.

"What the hell is going on here?" I gasp, heat surging through me, want following on its heels as I watch the woman of my dreams, see the lust in her too-blue eyes.

"I don't know," she says, her voice gruff, tense, as she fists her hands, her lips drawn into a line as she tries to gain control of her breath. "I don't know," she repeats, and in frustration, she rakes a gloved hand back through her hair. She glances up at me as if unsure of who I am for a moment, and then she ascends the steps slowly, until she's staring down at me, her brow furrowed.

Then Charaxus threads her fingers through my hair.

"I didn't know you until this moment," she says, and her eyes find mine, burn into mine. "But I've dreamed of you since I was a small child. I've dreamed of a woman with red-gold hair, like a lioness," she murmurs, her eyes soft, sparking now as she gazes past me, to her hand in my hair, her fingertips at the back of my neck as she takes a step closer, the leather grazing my skin and causing a tremor to move through me. "A woman who said my hair looked like stars. Who wore a star about her throat..." And then she reaches out, and she's touching the gold pendant at the hollow of my neck.

I stare at her in wonder as I touch the pendant, too.

She dreamed about my mother's pendant?

Charaxus locks eyes with me, her gaze simmering. "Who kissed me as if I were the only woman in the world for her," she whispers.

"How is this possible?" I whisper back, but when she's this close, the heat of her burning through me, her hand against my skin, I can't really think straight.

"I don't know," she says again, and there's a particular growl to her voice now; when she looks down, when she gazes into my eyes, I'm panting against her.

"How..." I begin again, but I don't get very far. She's capturing my mouth with a kiss, and it's profoundly soft, the way her lips graze mine, the way her tongue finds its way into my mouth. The leather of her right hand is curled around my neck, and her fingers are delicate against my skin, but wherever she touches me, I burn with want.

I can't take much more of this.

She's pressing me against the door now, and I hiss out into the darkness as her mouth leaves mine, trailing heat over the skin of my cheek, my jaw, trailing a pattern of kisses to my neck. I arch my back a little, and though there's confusion in the corners of my mind, assaulting me with a constant, consistent "what-the-hell-am-I-doing, what-the-hell-am-I-doing" loop, I ignore it. I ignore everything except for her.

Until the door that I'm leaning against, the door that's bearing all of my weight, opens.

I fall through, and Charaxus falls on top of me.

Chapter 6: The Knight of My Dreams

"You're not the pizza dude," says Toby reproachfully as he stares at the pile of limbs comprised of Charaxus and me.

"Good observation, Mr. Obvious," I groan from the floor, and then I'm struggling to a sitting position beside Charaxus. I peer up at Toby with narrowed eyes. "Wait a second—why the hell did I go pick up pizza earlier if you were just going to have *more* delivered *later*?"

Toby, still a mime but now also wearing an Uncle Sam hat, stares down at me with his hands on his hips.

"We ate all of your pizzas, and we were still hungry, so Cecile offered to get us more. She said that you'd be sad that there wasn't any left for you, so…" He pauses then, blinks, gazing down at Charaxus as if noticing her for the first time. "Hold *on. Mara.* Is this the lady you dragged out of the river? The one with the *stab* wound? Wait." He holds up a hand. "Were you just *making out* with her against the front door, or am I hallucinating?"

"Fewer questions and more helping up," I say, raising a brow, and Toby rolls his eyes before offering a reluctant hand to Charaxus. She's leaning against the wall, and she gazes at him with uncertainty; he does look pretty weird with all the mime makeup, not to mention that oversized hat. I give her a tired smile.

"Charaxus, this is Toby. Toby, this is Charaxus," I say, and after a moment's consideration, Charaxus accepts Toby's hand and rises to her feet.

"Were you stabbed?" Toby asks her excitedly, and Charaxus stares at him, her expression flat.

"No, no, she wasn't *stabbed*," I say quickly—maybe too quickly—as I scrabble to my feet. Both Charaxus and Toby stare at me as if I've suddenly grown another head: Charaxus because I'm lying through my teeth, and Toby because my cheerfulness is, even to my ears, unconvincing.

"Sorry," I tell Toby, clearing my throat as I shrug my shoulders and shake my head. "It's just… It's been a long night. Charaxus nearly drowned." I start babbling a little faster. "But she got checked out at the emergency room, and she's in tiptop shape, as good as new," I say, smiling inanely, and then I'm looping my arm around Charaxus' waist and steering her down the hallway, toward the living room of the Ceres.

"Why are you acting this way?" she asks me, her voice low as she murmurs in my ear, but I shake my head, offer her a little grimace.

"I'll tell you in a minute."

When we reach the living room, I'm surprised to see that nearly everyone has already gone upstairs, either to bed or back to work. Sammie is conked out on the sofa, and Rod, Toby's boyfriend, is the only person left in the living room, and he's eating the very last slice of pizza. The empty pizza boxes lie open on the counter, sad bits of cheese glued to waxed paper all that remains of my once vast pizza empire.

"Oh, hey, Mara!" says Rod, saluting me with the half-eaten slice in his hand. "Cecile ordered more pizza, so don't panic or anything," he says, with a slightly worried smile.

My love of pizza is kind of legendary.

"Actually," I say, and I have both of my hands at Charaxus' back now, aiming her toward the stairs, "I'm not hungry."

Rod stares at me from the couch, his eyes round, as Toby comes in behind us, hands still on his hips; he gazes at me in suspicion.

"Did the pizza queen really just say she wasn't *hungry*?" Toby asks Rod in a hallowed whisper.

"There was free pizza at the emergency room!" I call back over my shoulder, and as Toby is asking Rod if that's even possible, insisting, "They never had free pizza on *ER*," Charaxus and I mount the stairs, and then I'm opening the door to my bedroom, pushing the black-clad knight gently over the threshold.

Charaxus and I stand in my room with the door shut behind us, the sounds of the Ceres fading away.

We're alone.

I sigh with relief as I lean against the wall, gazing lazily at Charaxus in all of her armored glory. She's watching me with a quizzical expression, as if she's not quite certain what just happened; her arms hang loosely at her sides, and her head angles to the right as she awaits my explanation.

"So…" I clear my throat, trail off, searching her eyes as I shrug my shoulders weakly. "I just thought that maybe we shouldn't bring up the whole 'from another world thing' to the guys down there. Or, you know, anyone else who lives here…"

Charaxus crosses her arms, raising a single brow. "Why? You think they would have doubts, as you did? I could prove it—" But I step forward, wrap my fingers around her metal-plated forearm, and stare deeply into her eyes, licking my lips.

"Charaxus," I begin softly. "We don't have magic on this planet. I mean, we do, but it's not really *magic*. I mean, it's not *real* magic…" I trail off, waiting to see if she understands. And apparently she does: she nods curtly, pressing her lips into a thin line as she observes me closely. "That's why I didn't believe you earlier," I tell her, raking my fingers back through my hair. "That's why you had to prove to me that you could actually *do* magic. And…it still sounds really weird to me, saying it out loud." I sigh. "I'd like to think that I took the revelation pretty well, but other people might freak out. Like, *really* freak out, because magic… It's make-believe. It doesn't exist. Period. And if they find out that it *does* exist… Well, they'll have to reorder the whole universe in their heads."

Like I'm having to do right now.

She's still staring at me, and as I gaze into her bright blue eyes, I realize how strange this moment is. I've been dreaming about Charaxus since I was a kid. Since I was a *kid*, I've had the powerful, charged dream of being with this woman, the same flesh-and-blood woman standing in front of me. I dreamed that we were in the water, our mouths meeting, merging, our hearts touching, my soul soaring...

It was a dream; *she* was a dream.

And now…this is reality.

I've recounted the dream to my therapist because it's so weird that, throughout my whole life, no detail of the dream has ever shifted. I've asked her why

I have this recurring dream, and she has always chalked it up to my being a lesbian, that it was a way for my subconscious to "sort out feelings and longings for women." I guess I believed her when she told me that, because people don't dream about their ideal woman and then find her in real, waking life.

It doesn't happen. Ever.

But magic doesn't exist, either, and there aren't other worlds. And yet, just a little while ago, I discovered magic is real, that other worlds are, in fact, out there...

It's been an eye-opening evening, to say the least.

Charaxus' gaze isn't locked on mine anymore. Instead, she's trailing her eyes over the curve of my jaw, my neck, my shoulders, my breasts...roving over every inch of me. She's not touching me, but the weight of her gaze is enough to leave me breathless.

My heart pounds inside of me, the roar of my pulse loud in my ears as my body leans toward her of its own accord. We stand there, electricity pulsing between us, and we watch one another, paused, uncertain.

"This is...strange," she says finally, her voice gruff.

There's about a foot of space between us, and when she speaks, her last word breaks, her breath coming out in a shallow pant. I shift beneath her scrutiny, beneath her burning gaze, and I place my purse on the ground, needing to do something with my hands—but I can't reach out and touch her. It doesn't feel right. Not in this moment. So I cross my arms over my chest, turning my gold pendant over and over at my throat.

"Yeah, strange," I force myself to say. Then I'm nervously babbling: "Nobody... I mean, nobody understood when I told them about you. About the dream. About you being in the dream." I wave my hand toward her. "They said it was no big deal, nothing significant. It didn't *mean* anything aside from my being attracted to women. But that made no sense to me, you know? Why would I have the same dream over and over again, a dream about a woman I never met? I knew there was something more to it, but it just..." I trail off, clear my throat. "It just made me feel crazy."

Charaxus sighs, stiffening a little beneath my searching gaze. "I never told anyone about you," she finally says, her voice so low, I can hardly hear it. She growls out the words. "It was my secret. It was... The dream was the only thing that was...that was all mine."

I stare at her in surprise, and then, reflexively, I close my eyes. I'm overwhelmed. Still, my body leans toward her, drawn toward her; I could take that final step toward her right this minute, could close the distance between us.

But the reality of the situation is something that I just can't ignore.

"We don't really know anything about one another," I tell her quietly, bracing myself at the pain in those words. I open my eyes, and Charaxus is watching me, her face solemn. "You're from another world."

"As are you," she murmurs.

"We're so...so *different*," I tell her, gazing up at her smooth, pale face. I step forward, then, and I lift my hand tentatively. She continues to gaze at me, her eyes soft, and then I press my palm to the curve of her jaw and her cheek.

Her skin is warm against me, and the shape of

her feels familiar against my hand. As if I've done this a hundred times before.

I still have difficulty wrapping my head around the fact that she's from another world. *Lord of the Rings* happens on another world. *Star Wars* happens on a bunch of different worlds. They aren't real worlds, though; they're *fiction*. But Charaxus is real, built of metal and muscle and bone and blood.

I trace my thumb across the line of her jaw, the silkiness of her skin making me shiver.

I take a step back; I'm trembling. "I mean…" I'm blushing before I realize what I'm saying. "In the dream you had about me, were we… Um…*where* were we?"

"In the water," she says, and her eyes go dark as her gaze traces down, over my chin, my neck, and to my breasts again. "And we were naked."

"See, that's…" I cross the room, sitting down on the edge of my bed and raking my fingers back through my hair. "It's uncanny. I don't know what to think."

Her jaw clenches, and her hands curl into fists at her sides—a habit I've noticed she falls into whenever she's uncomfortable. Her words are so soft now that I barely hear them: "Are you glad that this has happened, Mara?"

I sink back onto my hands, propping myself up on the bed as I let my feet swing against the mattress.

A long time ago, longer than I can remember, I began to dream about the woman standing in front of me. She—or her dream self—got me through some pretty rough times, times that, well, I'd like to forget.

But she doesn't know that about me.

She doesn't know *anything* about me.

"I'm sorry," I finally whisper, and I lean forward, elbows on my knees, spreading my skirt out over my legs and tugging my shirt down a little so that I can reach up, press the pad of my thumb against my gold pendant. I take a few deep breaths, trying to calm my racing heart. "I've…" I stop, frown. I was about to say, "I've had a hard life," but why would I tell her that? As proof that I'm having a difficult time dealing with this?

As proof that I'm messed up?

I stand quickly, and I smooth my sweaty palms against my skirted thighs. "Sorry," I say again, and I give her a quick smile, a fake smile. I clear my throat, shaking my head. "This is just…hard."

You were there for me when no one else was.

You were my dream. You knew the deepest parts of me.

But you *don't*, not really.

You were real, all this time, with your own dream, your own life.

You *weren't there with me at all…*

The thought is unfair, ludicrous, but it springs to my mind, anyway, and then there's no going back. I dreamed about Charaxus, and I clung to that dream my whole life, through all of the darkness, all of the hardships. And somewhere in this great, big universe, Charaxus was living, breathing. She existed.

So she wasn't *really* with me, wasn't ever part of my life…

I swallow around the lump in my throat.

I feel so alone.

Charaxus crosses the space between us, and she sinks down in front of me, crouching back on one heel, resting her elbow on her knee as she watches me from beneath a swoop of dark mane in front of her right eye.

"Where did you go?" she murmurs, and her voice is so surprisingly gentle that it guts me.

"I...I didn't go anywhere," I tell her, but her blue eyes stare deeply into me, burning with brightness.

"I know that look."

I watch her, surprised. "How could you know it?"

"Because I've had it myself," she says, and then she changes position: it's graceful, the way she crosses her long legs in front of her. She gestures to me. "I've...often had it myself." Her hand hovers above my knee before she places her palm down gently on top of my skirt.

I rest my hand on hers, and we sit that way for a long moment.

"I didn't have the best life," I admit then, my mouth suddenly dry. "Dreaming about you... Honestly, it was the *best* part of my life."

Charaxus gazes at me, her eyes softening. "What happened to you?"

My throat tightens; I can't breathe. "It's...it's not important," I say hastily, and then I'm smiling at her, shoving all of my feelings back into the deep, dark recesses of my heart, squishing them down. I change the subject. "Can you tell me what brought you here? You said you came through a portal."

Charaxus nods, but she doesn't remove her hand from my leg. It's a gentle, reassuring weight, and I love it. I press down on her hand as she works her jaw, as she glances at the floor with a small frown.

"Well," she says, and then she lifts her gaze toward me. "I am the vice queen of Arktos. And...my queen was in danger."

"You have queens?" I ask her, suddenly very interested. "Queens and magic."

She nods, and there's the ghost of a smile on her lips. "Queen Calla. I am her vice queen, next in succession to the crown. But my...my brother wants to overtake Arktos. He is the king of Furo. It is another country," she says, waving her hand airily, dismissively, "to the north of Arktos. And he is bloodthirsty, and he has been trying to get back at me for years for leaving Furo. So he wants to gain control of the kingdom and rule it."

I stare at her. "Wait. You're vice queen of Arktos, which is a country."

"Yes," she replies.

"And your brother is...king of Furo, which is another country?"

"Yes," she nods.

"Then how did you become the vice queen of *Arktos*? Isn't that stuff, like, inherited through bloodlines? That's how I thought monarchies worked..."

"Not in Arktos. If you work hard enough and are loyal enough, you can become anything. Even queen," she says simply, with a little shrug.

"And your brother...hates you," I murmur to her. She glances up at me—and in this moment, her eyes are full of so much pain, I'm stricken speechless.

"Yes," she answers simply.

I squeeze her hand, swallowing. "So, what happened to bring you here?"

"My brother and I were battling. There were other knights, the queen... We were all battling," she says, and her voice is soft, her throat tight. "I was stabbed by my brother. And I opened a portal, trying to trap him…but I was taken into it, too. Along with my brother and his own knights. They are somewhere nearby," she says, her voice urgent. "And I must find the shard before *they* find it. If they find the shard that can open a portal anywhere…they would be invincible. Unstoppable."

"That's a problem." I sigh and watch her thoughtfully. "Okay. So…how bloodthirsty is your brother, exactly?"

"He has killed so many," she whispers to me, "and he enjoys it."

Reeling, I shake my head. "And you think he's here? In Buffalo?"

"Is that where I am?"

I nod.

Charaxus pauses, looking thoughtful. "I do not think that the shard's portal would have deposited us far apart. I do think he is here, yes. And he will be looking for the shard right now. I shouldn't rest…" She rises, and she begins to pace in front of me, walking back and forth, back and forth across the tight confines of my room.

I get up, setting my laptop on my desk to play some light classical music that will muffle our conversation. The first soft strains of a Brahms melody filter out of the speakers, and her shoulders relax a little.

"You're no good to anyone if you're exhausted," I remind her. "I don't know how hard it's going to be to find that shard," I say with a little shrug, "but I don't think you can do anything in pitch blackness, and when it's threatening to storm again." I wave to the only window in my room, cut into the side of the metal walls of the grain elevator. Outside, it's starting to sprinkle lightly against the window.

Lightning flickers along the dark clouds of the horizon.

"I don't know if my queen is safe," she says quietly. "Everything happened so quickly." Her jaw tightens. "I am loyal to her. I am her vice queen. If anything happened to her…" She grimaces, trailing off.

When she spoke the words "my queen," her voice was soft, in the reverent tone one might use to recite a prayer. Emotion passes over her face quickly, but it's there for a heartbeat, and I see it.

My lips part in surprise, and my heart sinks.

Oh.

Charaxus is in love with her queen.

It feels as if the ground is opening up beneath me, and I'm falling, falling…

Sure, I've slept with a lot of women over the years, and I've dated quite a few. But I've never been in love with anyone.

Well…

That's not entirely true.

I've been in love with her. My dream woman.

Charaxus.

"I'm… I'm sure that your queen is fine. You said that your brother came through the portal with you," I say, and the words don't sound right coming out of my mouth. They sound too stiff, forced. I clear my throat, and I'm suddenly feeling lightheaded. "Um, if you'll excuse me," I say, and I move past Charaxus, heading toward my bathroom.

Cecile, in her infinite wisdom, decided that every bedroom of the Ceres needed a bathroom to go along with it, if only to avoid the morning rush. What's funny is that artists operate on different schedules, and we probably would have rarely been getting prepared for the day at the same time—but the thoughtfulness was still deeply appreciated by everyone. I step into my own little bathroom, and I'm shutting the door quietly behind me, leaning against it as I try to calm my breathing.

A single tear squeezes out of my eye and leaks down my cheek.

"Mara?" asks Charaxus, her voice low on the other side of the door. A soft knock makes the old wood reverberate a little. "Mara, are you all right?"

She's in love with her queen.

And I kissed her.

I slide down the door a little, and I thread my fingers through my hair. God, I feel so stupid right now. I clear my throat, lift my chin a little. "Yeah. I'll be out in a minute," I manage, and the words sound strained but normal enough. I wait until I hear her boots cross the room, and then I'm standing, staring at myself in the mirror above my salvaged sink.

To put it succinctly, I look like hell.

I turn on the water, let the coldness rush over my fingers, and then I splash a little of it onto my face, allowing the water to drip off of my chin. I wipe my face with my wet fingers and pat myself dry with a hand towel before I step out of the bathroom.

"Are you all right?" asks Charaxus immediately, and I glance in her direction...and I stop.

The metal parts of her armor are all piled neatly at the foot of the bed, and she's sitting on the side of the bed, on top of the tapestry woven in bright hues of orange, purple, red and gold.

She looks out of place.

She's so pale in the soft light of my bedroom, as pale as a ghost. And with her armor removed, she's wearing only leather pants, leather boots and a leather shirt, all in black.

The effect is…striking.

The leather clings to her curves, molded to her body like a glove. I stand there, my hands open at my sides, my chest rising and falling as I gaze at her.

She's lounging back on her hands on the mattress, a small smile turning her mouth up at the corners. She watches me with carefully hooded blue eyes, and my own gaze follows the contours of her body: over her breasts, high and round, and her abs, and the gorgeous swell of her hips and thighs. She leans back languidly, her right leg tapping the bed, and she shifts her head to the side, inky black hair falling over her shoulder with a soft whisper, trailing to her wrists because it's so long.

"I hope you don't mind that I got comfortable. It's been a long day." Her voice sounds almost teasing, but there's a genuine question hanging in the syllables.

"Yeah," I tell her, licking my lips. "That's…fine. So, where do you want to sleep? I can… I can sleep downstairs on the couch, if you'd rather sleep in a bed. You must be very tired after, you know, nearly dying in another world." Wow, Mara. That sounded so very, very stupid.

She raises her brows, and she stands easily, the muscles of her thighs flexing; I can't help but notice them. She is as lean and languid as a panther as she prowls across the floor to me, her blue eyes searching mine.

"I was hoping that we might sleep together," she says softly, the words unfolding in front of us.

I look at her, and the pain from a moment ago bursts through my heart again. I try to stifle it, shove it down, but it's hard. I'm *used* to shoving all of my pain away, pushing it deeply inside of myself. This pain is new, though, still raw, and I'm not quite certain how to soothe it.

"What's wrong?" she asks, and there's tension in her shoulders as she leans toward me, raising her hand—but she doesn't touch me. She lets her hand drop beside her hip again, her jaw working.

"We've dreamed about each other all of our lives." I wrap my arms around myself, trying to shield my heart, but it's already been hurt. It's already been wounded. And there's nothing I can do to fix it.

I'm already broken, broken before she, the woman of my dreams, ever even met me.

She's come too late.

"Yes," says Charaxus gruffly, and she finds my gaze, drawing it up from the floor and holding it in place, staring down at me with soft blue eyes. "I've dreamed of you my whole life. And we are finally together. And do you know what I think?"

I shake my head, watching her.

"I think we've wasted enough time."

And then she's stepping forward, and she's kissing me.

It's a soft kiss, a kiss of wonder. Wondering if I want this, too. If I want her to be kissing me. And I do. God, I do. I wrap my arms around her neck, and she's wrapping her arms around my waist, drawing me toward her. She lifts me up to my toes, and I'm in the air, being held by her tightly as she kisses me. She tastes of cinnamon; her mouth is so hot now, and so soft against my own, but urgent.

Effortlessly, she takes me in her arms and carries me to the bed.

"Wait, wait," I say, and she stiffens against me,

her arms softening, letting me drop down to my tiptoes again as she takes a step back, as she searches my face.

"What is it?" she asks, her voice soft, gruff, questioning.

"You're… Charaxus, you're in love with your queen." My voice sounds miserable, even to me.

Charaxus stares down at me, perplexed, her brow furrowed. Then she shakes her head. "I have served my queen for many years," she says with a soft shrug. "And, yes, I loved her. But," she sighs, "she does not love me, and she will never love me. I knew my feelings could never be requited.

"It was a love that was pure and true and good…and that prevented me from connecting with other women. I knew that I would never be able to love her. All of my life," she says with certainty, holding my gaze, "I have been waiting for you."

It's everything that I wanted to hear, but my throat is tight as I stare up at her. "We don't know anything about each other," I remind her.

"We can learn," she whispers, reaching across the space between us and stroking my cheek softly. Her leather gloves and their metal cuffs are laid neatly on top of the pile of armor, so this is the first time that I've felt her hand against my skin.

And, God, it feels so good, so right. Her skin is soft, warm, and she smells like the leather of her gloves, the good earthiness of it filling me with lust, need roaring through me whether I welcome it or not.

"You want to go back home, Charaxus. To your world," I say, and my voice is thick with want as she takes another step closer, the heat of her body emanating through the leather of her shirt, through the thin fabric of my tank top, our bodies so close, so close, with so little separating them.

"I must go back home," she whispers, and I gaze up at her, pain evident in my expression. Again, she shakes her head. "But I am not going back at this moment. At this moment," she murmurs, locking her gaze on mine, "we are here. Together."

"But—"

"Mara," she says, and the sound of my name is like a caress.

I shiver against her touch, and I breathe out, closing my eyes, listening to her speak. "Mara," she repeats, and then our bodies are melting together as she wraps her arms around my waist, drawing me against her.

"Mara," she whispers again, and she leans close, her breath hot against my ear. "We have dreamed for too long. This is real—here, now. Let us think tomorrow."

"Hmm." I wrap my arms around her neck. "And what are you going to do tonight?"

Her eyes are as dark as a starlit night as she stares down at me, mouth parted, wet. "You," she growls, her head tilted to the side, the shock of that single word moving through me. "If you will have me," she adds, but I hardly hear her, because my panties are already on the other side of the room (metaphorically speaking—I'm not *that* fast), and I'm standing on my tiptoes, drawing her down to me for a kiss.

The woman of my dreams is in my arms, is real, is leaning into the kiss, literally sweeping me off of my feet as she wraps her arms around me again and lifts me up from the floor. She kisses me fiercely, the cinnamon of her kiss burning me up until all I am is fire, fire, fire, a roaring need that must be quenched, or it might burn me to cinders.

Charaxus knows this, because my kiss is desperate, longing, and she turns, carrying me to my bed.

The backs of my calves brush against the mattress, and then I'm tumbling backward as she lets me go. I bounce on the mattress as she slides easily between my open legs, going down into a kneel between them. I rest back on my hands, panting.

"This is all right?" asks Charaxus, her brow furrowed as she pushes me down, her fingers on my shoulders first, then tracing patterns to the hem of my t-shirt and shoving it over my stomach, revealing bare skin.

"God, yes, hurry," I mutter, rocking my head back as she shoves the t-shirt over my breasts, her fingers at the wire of my bra before she stops, gazing down with a perplexed look on her face.

"There is metal in this cloth?" she asks curiously, but I have my hands on top of her hands, pushing her fingers up under the cups.

"Yeah, it's a bra. They don't have those on your world?"

She pushes the cups up over my breasts. "No," she says with a small smile as she leans over me, her inky black hair falling over her shoulder and trailing over my sides.

"I'll…get you up to speed on them later," I whisper, shivering as she bends down, her warm breath causing my nipples to ache, already hard and peaked.

I twist my fingers into her hair, over her scalp, and I arch my back beneath her, trying to pull her head down, down, trying to make her mouth meet my breast. But she's not having any of it. She reaches up, and she takes my hands, and then my wrists are pinned to the bed as she towers over me, blue eyes flashing.

"Still all right?" she growls, and I nod, my breath coming so fast I'm almost hyperventilating.

"God, yes, whatever you want, yes, yes," I say in one big rush of syllables, and that's when she pins my hands above my head hard and bends down for a kiss.

She bites my lower lip, a bright sharpness of teeth that makes me moan into her mouth, and then her tongue is questing past my lips, and all I taste is cinnamon, is her smile as she grins against me. She holds my wrists now with one hand and traces the fingers of her right hand down, over the side of my face, my neck, my bunched-up bra and t-shirt, and, God, yes, they finally reach my left breast.

She pulls my nipple gently at first, twisting it with a soft caress that's absolutely maddening. She chuckles against me, a low growl of a laugh, and then she's tracing kisses down my jaw, my neck, and she's capturing my left nipple in her mouth.

"Yes," I mutter, bucking my hips, trying to find some sort of friction, *anything*, but she remains crouched over me, still pinning my hands above my head but now trailing her fingers down over my stomach as she bites on my nipple, the bright pain so pleasurable that I mutter, "Fuck, *yes*," into the darkness of the room. Her fingers are over my skirt, then on my thigh, her skin hot against mine.

Now Charaxus lowers herself, lowers her hips against my hips, and I cry out from the weight of her against my center, the ache that blossoms between my legs something that fills every part of me with a need so acute I can hardly breathe. I'm pulsing my hips against her own leather-clad hips. She lets go of my hands, and then she's gripping my hips with strong fingers, so hard that I'm probably going to have bruises tomorrow, but it's a delicious sensation now, so perfect; I reach up with my legs, wrapping them around her middle, asking with every inch of my body for more.

Her hands release my hips, and then she's grasping the edges of my skirt and panties, tugging them over my bottom and down my thighs, pulling them off before tossing them aside. She lowers her head, takes my right nipple into her mouth, flicking her tongue across it before scraping her teeth so gently against it that I groan, arching my back, pushing my breast further into her mouth. I need her to bite it; I can't take the want building through me. Her teeth surround my nipple again, biting down, making me hiss out, making me grind my head against the mattress as I twine my fingers through her hair again, scratching her scalp. And she lets me: she lets me push, and she moves her teeth against my nipple now, gently enough that the pain is exquisite pleasure. I moan as she reaches up, pulling the other nipple with her hand, twisting it, plumping it, before tracing a path of kisses across my skin.

Then she takes my other nipple in her mouth, biting down with no warning.

I moan, and she rests her leather-clad hips on my naked center. My clit aches as she pulses her hips against mine, my center throbbing with such intensity that I think I'm going to come from some simple nipple play. Am I really that turned on?

She traces her fingers over my thigh, brushing the pad of her thumb against my clit just once, just for a second, and a shudder of an orgasm moves through me. But I don't actually come. Her fingers trail a line

126

down into my center, moving through my wetness.

What is she *doing* that makes my body respond so instantly?

There's something about the way that Charaxus looks at me as she pushes her fingers inside of me; I'm open and wanting, my mouth open, too, as I moan out and pull her down for another kiss. But Charaxus hovers over my open mouth, and she watches me carefully, her brow furrowed, her bright blue eyes flashing with such a deep, abiding fire that the simple act of holding her gaze is enough for my core to pulse around her fingers.

That's when she reaches up and gently brushes the pad of her thumb against my clit again. Once, twice, and then in soft, practiced circles as she slowly pumps her fingers in and out of me. The heat of her hips and her thigh against my skin, the muscles of her stomach sliding against mine, her gaze locked on me, and suddenly my body is pulsing like a supernova, and I'm coming quickly, quickly, the orgasm moving through me as fast and as bright as a shooting star.

"Yes," I whisper, the syllable sliding through me with the ecstasy. The rhythm of the waves of pleasure merges with the movements of the woman over me, inside of me, and my own body moves with her, and I have no idea where I end and she begins, and it's good, so good, as she presses her mouth to my own, as she captures me with a kiss and we merge as if we were always meant to be one, not two.

It's profound, as I feel that completion flower inside of me. I lie open beneath her, our bodies moving together. Everything feels right in this moment; nothing can be wrong. I pump my hips against her hand, and I whisper her name into the stillness as the last strains of melody fade away from my laptop and silence descends into the room, silence apart from our movements, from the slick slide of her fingers inside of me, the soft quiet of her breath, coming fast from her lungs. She kisses me again, and there's the shush of my fingers in her hair, the gentle creak of the leather on her hips, the hush of our bodies moving together.

I reach up, and I trail my nails down the back of her neck, over the leather. My fingers are at the hem of her shirt now as she draws wet, shining streaks with her fingertips over my thigh.

I push my hand beneath her shirt, under the waistband of her leather pants, but suddenly—surprisingly—Charaxus' hand is gripping my wrist.

It's gentle but firm, the pressure of her fingers on my skin.

"No," she whispers, and I gaze up at her in concern as I realize that she doesn't want me to touch her.

"But..." I lick my lips, trail off. I'm still wobbly from the orgasm, good feelings cresting through me, but this sudden refusal... I don't understand it. "Can't I... Don't you want me to?" I ask her, my voice soft.

Charaxus gazes down at me, and there's a gentleness in her expression, her bright blue eyes satisfied. "Yes," she says, and she leans down, brushing her soft mouth against my own. "I want you to. But not tonight. Tonight, I just want to touch you."

I exhale, nodding. Though I want to make her feel good, just as good as she made me feel, she said no, and I really don't need to understand why. I just need to listen.

Charaxus' mouth curls up at the corners again as she rises over me.

"I want you to say my name," she breathes into my ear, and as she trails kisses down my stomach, her lips hot against my skin, I curl my fingers into her hair, gasping out into the stillness as I arch my back, my hips rising to meet her.

"Charaxus," I cry out into the dark. And I can feel her smile against me as the pleasure rises, potent and powerful.

The night moves around us as she tastes me.

Chapter 7: Her Body's Art

Last night was…

Wow.

I'm lying in bed, breathing evenly as I stare at my blue-painted ceiling, remembering everything that happened between Charaxus and me last night. *Everything.* I'm blushing as I reach up, brushing fingertips over my swollen lips. Our kissing got pretty...intense.

Hell, *everything* got pretty intense.

I hear Charaxus in the bathroom: she's whistling something, a tune I don't recognize. It's pretty, with a lot of trills; it sounds a little like a folk song. The shower is running. I guess she catches on quickly... Someone from another world figured out how to turn on the faucets. Fast learner.

I rest on my pillow, listening to the water, to the whistling, and the sound does something to me.

It makes me *happy.*

I'm highly aware that this moment won't last. I'm highly aware that last night passed by much too quickly, that I already wish I could go back in time and relive it, relive her kisses, her body rising over mine in the dark, her inky black mane sweeping over my shoulders...

I take a deep breath as my insides clench, as I close my eyes, rest my hand on my chest.

The memories will have to be enough.

I turn over, lying on my side now as I twist my fingers into my hair idly and listen to Charaxus whistle. I'm naked beneath the sheets, and my body is deliciously sore all over. Charaxus tasted every inch of me, and she did things, made me *feel* things, that no other woman has ever done before.

Is this what it's *supposed* to be like? Every single second of our lovemaking was *perfect*. Exquisite.

It was almost…too good to be true.

But the one frustrating thing that kept happening, throughout all of it, was that Charaxus stopped me if I tried to initiate physical contact with *her*. It was always a polite halting: if I attempted anything more than kissing her or embracing her, she'd check me gently. I have to be honest... It was kind of nice to just lie there and be ravished, but I also ached to touch her, *taste* her…

I don't know if I'll ever have that opportunity. I don't know what's going to happen today. Charaxus is determined to search for the shard and for her brother. And, obviously, the fate of the universe is a bit more important than my love life. From the brief conversation that we shared about her brother last night, he sounds like a sociopath—at best—and he's running loose in Buffalo with his crazy cohorts.

We have to find him; we have to find the shard before he does.

I close my eyes and breathe out.

Okay, it's probably presumptuous of me to use the word *we*. Charaxus might refuse to let me help her. I don't know if I *should* help her.

I have a good life here. I have my Ceres family. And we both know—are acutely aware of the fact—

that Charaxus is going to return to Agrotera.

Last night was lovely...but it's over. And now we have to face cold, harsh reality.

Charaxus' whistling takes on a bittersweet tone in the shower, as if to reflect my mood...

Is last night all we're ever going to have? Were all of those dreams leading up to one single night of intense and indescribable bliss? Just one?

That hurts.

But I need to talk to Charaxus before I commit myself to this sad, dark path of no return. I prepare myself to rise out of bed at the same moment that I hear the water in the shower turn off. Then I lie there and take deep breaths; my heart starts to pound. And my heart pounds a whole *hell* of a lot faster when Charaxus comes out of bathroom and regards me from the doorway, toweling off her long, black hair.

She's completely nude.

I didn't get to see her nude last night. She remained in her leather clothes while we had sex, and even afterwards, when we curled up together, she was still wearing them. I could *feel* the muscles of her thighs when I wrapped myself around her, but I couldn't see them, couldn't touch or taste them. Maddening.

And now she's standing there in the bathroom doorway...

And....just...*wow*.

It was obvious that, under those leather clothes, Charaxus was well-muscled, but I had no idea *how* muscled. She's pale, probably the palest person I've ever seen, and the paleness of her skin is in deep contrast to her dark mane of hair. But the shadows, slopes and contours of the muscles of her belly, her thighs, her upper arms, her calves, her rear as she turns, shaking out her hair, droplets spattering down onto the old, reclaimed barn wood floor…they steal my breath.

Or, rather, I *forget* to breathe, because I'm staring at her so intently. I have to cough a little, rolling over to my side and swallowing as she watches me, a sly smile turning her mouth up at the corners, her blue eyes glittering.

"Good morrow," she growls, her head to the side as she takes the towel and runs it over her right shoulder. "You slept well?"

"What little I got," I say, voice hoarse, one brow raised. I roll onto my stomach, the tangled sheets falling away as I watch her watching me. Her eyes drift over my shoulders, my back, my ass, and her mouth opens a little as the towel trails gently down her arm, as if she's forgotten what she's doing. And then she's standing there, the towel in her hand at her side, as she leans against the door frame and raises a brow, too.

We don't say anything for a long moment. Sometimes, that's awkward: a long silence between two people who have just met. But right now, it isn't. At all. There's still that shimmering tension between us, bright and silver, like a live wire. Even though we moved together for hours last night, even though she traced her tongue over every last atom of my body, my desire for her isn't sated.

A fire burns inside of my belly, hot and pulsing, as I stare at her.

Her eyes are dark now, stormy, and she flicks her gaze back up to my face as she turns and tosses the towel lightly onto the edge of the tub, prowling over to me, her body still slick and glistening with the water from her shower. She stands in front of me, and I lift my chin as I stare up at her.

Charaxus bends forward then, and she captures my mouth with a kiss.

Her fingers are tangled in my hair, and when she tastes me, the bright burst of cinnamon, of fire, ignites in my mouth. She pushes me over gently, onto my back, and then she's rising above me again, finding her place between my legs, her hands steadying her on either side of my shoulders as I wrap my arms around her, drawing her down to me, holding her tightly, wanting, wishing, hoping this moment will last forever.

I gaze up at her, at the sweeping mane of black that veils around us, falling down over me like night. The water on the ends of her long strands collects and starts to bead over my skin.

My breath catching in my throat, I have an odd thought: she is a storm—as electrifying as lightning, as powerful as thunder...an awe-inspiring force of nature.

She bends down, traces her mouth over my throat, over my hot skin, her own skin hotter yet from the shower. My back is arching beneath her, and I can feel the wetness of her center between my legs, mingling with my own wetness.

She is achingly beautiful—her body shimmering and muscled, the droplets collecting upon her pale skin like gems... Exquisite. I want to capture this, *her*...

I want to paint.

No.

I *need* to paint.

"Wait..." I tell her then, emotion rushing through me. And Charaxus does wait, mouth parted, panting, as she stares down at me, her blue eyes as dark as the sea.

"What is it?" The muscles of her arms harden as she remains over me, her hands resting on either side of my shoulders. She waits for my words, patient and still.

"I…" I lick my lips. I don't quite know how to tell her this, so I opt for blunt honesty. "I've been painting you. All of my life." Yeah, it's an odd time to make this confession, with her hips hard between my legs, the wetness of her center pressed against mine, but I feel an urgency to voice this truth aloud.

"And I really want to paint you now," I tell her, all in a rush. I curl my fingers around her hips. "In the flesh…as it were." I stare deeply into her eyes. "Please?"

Charaxus gazes down at me steadily. "You…wish to paint my portrait."

Well, when she phrases it like that, it sounds a little ridiculous, but I nod, and she nods, too, slowly, as if in understanding, and then she pushes off of me, lying on her side and raising herself up onto her elbow. She rakes her hand through her wet hair as she ducks her head.

"If that is what you wish, Mara, that is what we must do." She watches me, her eyes soft, the blue brilliant. God, she makes me so breathless, I may have to see my doctor about an inhaler.

There's a lot left unspoken between us. She must be anxious to get started on her quest, wondering whether her brother has found the shard, whether she has been beaten in the race. Whether she's already too late.

But this moment feels languid, luxurious, *stolen*. It's *our* moment.

Our time isn't over, not yet.

I slide off of the bed and wrap my sheet around me like a makeshift toga. Then I'm choosing a canvas, one I've already prepped with gesso, from the metal cabinet beside the door and drag it to the easel. I set up, adjusting the position of the canvas as I secure the sheet around my shoulders.

Charaxus stands behind me easily, comfortably, though she remains naked, her hands on her hips, her feet hip-width apart, her chin up, commanding. Her shoulders are relaxed, as if she does this sort of thing all the time: posing naked, without a hint of self-consciousness.

She doesn't ask any questions about my earlier statement, about how I've painted her all of my life. She doesn't speak about the fact that I must have been entranced utterly, thought her inordinately beautiful, to feel inspired to paint her over and over again, trying to clumsily capture something exquisite in such an imperfect, subjective medium.

She doesn't say a word, in fact, only watches me curiously as I bring out my paints and my brushes, my hands shaking as I realize that she'll soon be standing before me in flesh and blood, *real*, willing and waiting to be captured by my brush.

I don't have to try to summon the fleeting image from a dream: she's *here*.

With me.

When everything is ready, I turn to face her. It's dark outside, strangely dark for morning—maybe another storm is brewing—so I flick on the overhead light, letting the softness of the bulb shine down on Charaxus, illuminating her from above like someone from a religious painting; gold shines on her jet black hair.

"Yes," I tell her simply, watching her, my gaze roving over every curve of her gorgeous body.

"That's…that's perfect."

"What would you have me do?" she asks me, her voice low as her eyes search mine. I watch her for a heated moment, taking in her muscled form, the slopes of her arms and thighs, and then I'm gazing around the room, trying to figure out which position to put her in, which position would be my dream to paint.

And then it dawns on me, the light bulb moment.

I know exactly what to do.

"Just…stand there…" I tell her, pointing to the center of the room, directly beneath the bare bulb shining above her. "I'll be right back, okay?" I don't wait for her to answer before I race out of the room, closing the door behind me and running down the stairs. Sure, I'm only wearing a sheet, but I've seen the other inhabitants of the Ceres in fewer "clothes" before. Such is the carefree nature of the artist, I guess. Or the exhibitionist, when it comes to Toby (and which he's emphatically *not* denied).

The katana is lying on the kitchen counter, exactly where I left it after our strange adventures last night. I pick it up, and then I'm racing back upstairs, shutting my bedroom door behind me.

Charaxus stands with her back to me, and I realize she's gazing at the paintings stacked against the wall in the corner of my room. There are a million (give or take) better ways to store art, but I don't want to clutter up the common spaces of the Ceres with my canvases, so I have them arranged along the wall, stacked deeply. I'd argue they're there to get my creative juices flowing again, but I just have no other place to put them.

As I gaze at her—at those long fingers curled

over her hips, at her hair hanging down in half-dry waves over her back—I realize that I already know what I'm going to call my show, my show that will be nothing but paintings of Charaxus.

It could have no other name than *She was the storm*.

Because that's what Charaxus has been, all this time. I just didn't know it.

In my dreams, she is never angry, never speaks with hostility. She treats me with adoration. Every second of that well-worn, perfect dream gleams with tenderness and—frankly—sexiness. Still, I knew there was something powerful pulsing within my dream woman. She tempered it out of love for me, as she moved with me in the water, but somewhere, deep inside of her, thunder roared and lightning flashed, a dormant storm that could burst at any moment, wreaking devastation to all that lay within her path.

I knew that Charaxus was powerful, potent, long before I knew her name.

I knew her heart, and within it rose a storm.

So that's what I painted.

Charaxus is now examining the closest painting of herself, the first one in the nearest stack along the wall. This one is all purples—deep, dark purples, like a bruise—and her face rises out of the storm cloud: her high cheekbones, her unwavering blue eyes, fierce and wild. The woman in the painting gazes triumphantly at the real-life woman who inspired this likeness.

I clear my throat, and Charaxus lifts her chin, regarding me as if she were a million miles away and just now floated back down to earth.

"I am sorry," she says, inclining her head, her gaze flicking back to the painting as she waves a hand toward it, "but I was captivated."

Captivated.

I swallow.

Objectively, I know that I'm a good artist. This is my calling, what I'm meant to do while I'm here on earth. And I can take a compliment. I worked hard to get to where I am today, so when people tell me something nice about my art, I thank them graciously and accept their flattering words.

But with Charaxus... There's this *fervor* in her voice, and when she looks at me, I see awe in her bright blue eyes.

And that's a little unnerving.

This is the woman who has captivated *me* for my whole life. This is the woman of my deepest fantasies. And now she's impressed by something I created. She's impressed...by me.

"That's not my best one. There's one in the back that's kind of..." I begin to argue, but Charaxus shakes her head, silences me with a glance.

"It is beautiful," she tells me simply, eyes shining, her voice rich and low. "As are you."

And she's stepping forward, placing her hands on the sheet draped over my skin, her fingers curving around my waist as she dips her beautiful face to mine, brushing her lips against my lips, her kiss soft, gentle. "I am honored to be the subject of your art," she tells me, searching my gaze. "I am, to be frank, undone by the sentiment of it."

My heart skips a beat as I stare up at her, and suddenly, I feel as if I'm standing on a tightrope. As long as I keep my balance, as long as I don't look down, I can accomplish any sort of death-defying trick that I want to. But the moment I waver, start to doubt myself...it becomes impossibly hard to walk that wire.

All I can think about is falling.

The moment I start to think about who this person is in my arms, and what she's meant to me throughout my life...I begin to lose my nerve. But I can't afford to lose it. Charaxus is standing here with me, and no matter what happens *later* today, no matter the decisions we make, I have time now. And I can't waste it.

I need to paint her.

Before it's too late.

I swallow around the lump in my throat, and I cough a little, staring up at Charaxus, her eyes glittering, a soft smile on her lips. I relax against her, and it's easier than I thought it would be, my form melting against hers.

I can do this. I can walk the wire. So long as I don't look down.

"What would you have of me?" Charaxus repeats, holding my gaze with her blazing eyes, and I step away from her regretfully, the heat of her naked body leaving mine as I pick up the katana from the floor.

"I wish I had a medieval-type sword for you," I tell her with a weak smile, "but I do have this, and I think it will work."

"What weapon is this?" she asks with interest, gazing down at the katana in my hands.

"It's a katana, from a country called Japan," I say, passing the katana to her. "Do you think you can pose with this?"

Charaxus gazes at me, resting the tip of the blade against the floor as she shifts the weight of the weapon in her hand, testing it, before picking it up again, her hand wrapped expertly around the hilt.

"It would be my honor," she tells me, and she salutes me with the katana blade held over her heart, the hilt of it pressed against her chest before she raises the tip to the heavens.

"Whatever pose you want… Just move your body, figure out what feels good to you. Find the pose, and then hold it. I'm afraid you'll have to hold it for about an hour, so make sure you're comfortable," I tell her, like so many artists' models have been told across the years.

I turn my back to Charaxus as I start mixing colors on my palette, the familiar scent of the paint filling my nostrils, the strong yet comforting odor of the pain thinner rising into the air as I move my brushes and blades across the surface of my palette, mixing the colors that I need, that my heart needs, to put on this canvas.

But when I turn back toward Charaxus, my brush poised in my hand, I pause, heart in my throat.

Because she's standing there easily—not a bit of strain in any of her muscles, the katana raised in her right hand at an angle, slicing dynamically in front of her. Her head is tilted to the side, and she's gazing at me with flashing blue eyes, her chin lifted, so much strength and power in her stance that you might (might, *might*) forget she's naked when you first glimpse her. Her nakedness is something that I recognize by degrees: her gorgeous breasts, the swell of her hips and belly, the dark, soft curls at her center an anchor for my eyes… But it's her stance that makes my heart stop inside of my chest.

Charaxus is pure power as she poses, proud and raw and real, her bright blue eyes flashing with light.

Motionless, she lifts the katana in a salutation to the sky, as if parrying with an imaginary opponent, a moment perfectly frozen in time. She stands without moving, without shaking, her footing sure and steady.

"All right," I murmur, mouth dry.

I lift my paintbrush—and I start to paint her: not from memory, not from the fragile filaments of a dream, but from real life.

Charaxus holds the katana with authority, her chin lifted, her eyes flickering with an inner fire that stokes the embers deep within me. But I have to concentrate on painting, and so I do. We both know this moment is fleeting, this slice of time where it is only me and her and the canvas and katana. That's why we made love all night: we knew that every moment, every touch, every taste was so precious.

I move the brush over the canvas now, and I push that feeling into the painting. I couldn't tell you how it happens, how that desire, that craving, manifests on the canvas, merging with the saturated hues of purple, of blue, the colors blending until they create a galaxy.

And that's when Charaxus herself starts to rise within the swirls of paint.

I always begin with the background, and then I draw out the focus of the piece, the subject, coaxing it to life brushstroke by brushstroke. My gaze flits from Charaxus—standing strong, the katana pointed toward the stars—to the canvas, and the Charaxus who is shaping herself there. She's rising, and I paint faster, faster, knowing that our time is drawing short, desperately trying to convey, in the fewest brushstrokes possible, the most beautiful creature I've ever known.

I am fevered, frenzied, as I paint. Blue and

purple stain the sheet I'm wearing, and—gradually—I let the thing fall, crumpling into a heap at my feet. Nude myself, I paint: purple and blue, gold and black. The colors speckle themselves upon my skin, thrown off from my brush. Charaxus stands, watching me, her breath slow, steady, her breasts rising and falling as she holds the blade in her strong hand.

I feel as if I'm racing against time, against inevitability. I am racing, forever racing, because I'm never going to get this moment back.

Charaxus, a creature of storm and star, overtakes the painting. There are stars in her hair, glittering like her eyes, and there are storms rising around her: angry, billowing clouds that could consume a world, lightning licking along her skin as if she channels the power herself. The blade of the katana has been transformed, and it is, itself, a shaft of pure, electric power, a lightning bolt both potent and dazzling, white hot.

Her skin is coated with the stuff of galaxies—bits of stars and suns, moons and milky ways spangling her arms, her breasts. Darkness and the absence of darkness—pure, molten light—burns along her limbs, the sloped muscles of her stomach, the angles of her jaw and collarbones.

I stand back, the brush poised in my hand as I regard the canvas. I ache to see the painting I've created. It is raw and sure and perfect, and I know, undoubtedly, that it is the best thing I've ever done. There's something empty inside of me now, because I've put so much of myself on the canvas. It's part of myself, and it is part of her—and, in this painting, the two of us are joined together forever, in a single moment cut from time.

The painting is finished.

The spell is broken.

But maybe…maybe there's some time left. Just a little, before the rest of life moves on. Before everything changes.

I turn to Charaxus, and I drop the paintbrush into the jar of paint thinner, stepping toward her, stumbling toward her, as if I'm drunk on fumes, but I'm not. Not at all.

I don't think I've ever been more clear-headed in my life.

I reach Charaxus, and I stand in front of her. I'm spattered with paint, and when she glances down at my arms, my stomach, my thighs, my face, I wonder what she sees. I painted galaxies on the canvas, and I wonder if that's reflected in my arms, speckles of gold paint, of purple hues and brilliant blues, melting into my skin.

She is the subject that I have spent my whole life perfecting, my whole life painting. And here she stands before me, the metal in her hand the only thing truly sharp about her. Her hair falls over her shoulders, dry now, an ink-black mane that contains stars. There are storms in her eyes, reflecting the thunderheads outside, as she gazes at me, licking her lips, the scent of cinnamon, of spice, rising around her, drawing me to her, ever to her.

I've spent my life drawing closer to her...

"What—" she begins, questioning, but I raise my finger, and I press it against her full mouth. She sighs against my skin, but she falls silent, watching me, her bright blue eyes unreadable.

"You tasted me last night," I tell her, the heat rising in my body, in my cheeks. We're both naked, but it's not just that. Looking at her, holding her gaze, having just brought her to life on my canvas...I've never felt more open, more vulnerable, more exposed.

And it's electric, the shimmer of power radiating between us, as I press my finger against the softness of her mouth, as I feel her hot breath upon my skin.

I can't breathe, can't think, can only feel as I step forward, as Charaxus lets the tip of the katana sink to the floor, stepping forward, too, and then the paint across my breasts, my hips, my thighs, smears over her skin as we move together, the katana falling, metal clanging dully against the floor, forgotten.

"You tasted me last night," I repeat, licking my lips as I stare up at her, as my voice falters, breaks, the need so raw I can hardly breathe. "Please," I whisper, gazing from one eye to another, "let me taste you."

Charaxus hesitates, pauses, her jaw tightening as her fingers curl at my elbows. She lowers her face to mine, and she presses her forehead against my own, her eyes tightly closed.

"I'm sorry," she murmurs to me, voice tight. "But no."

My heart catches in my throat, and I close my eyes, too, feeling the warmth of the skin of her forehead against mine. It's so tender how we stand, pressed together, and it is diametrically opposed to what she just told me.

No is no, and I must respect it. But as I'm nodding, as I'm pulling away, the euphoria of painting fading fast, knowing that this moment is about to end, knowing that Charaxus must start her quest, knowing that everything is about to shatter...she stops me.

"I'm sorry," she whispers, and there is such

exquisite anguish on her face as she stares down at me that I'm not sure what's wrong. I press my fingers over her heart.

"Don't be sorry," I tell her, shaking my head. "It's all right if—" But she interrupts me, raising her hand, cupping my cheek, staring down at me.

"No one has ever been that close to me," she says simply then. "And you... You must know that you are the woman of my dreams, Mara. I cannot risk ruining that."

"Wait...what?" I ask, but her jaw is tightening, and she shakes her head again, lifting her chin.

"I have dreamed of you all of my life." Her voice is formal now, as if injecting formality into her tone will somehow distance her from the emotion of the moment. But her bright blue eyes are brimming with tears that she refuses to shed, and her jaw is so tense, she's almost grinding her teeth. She breathes out, tries to relax—fails. "If you touch me...it will all be over," she whispers. "Don't you see? I won't be what you wanted, and the dream... The dream will fall apart."

"Hold on," I tell her, and I soften my voice, my heart breaking as I stare up at this beautiful knight...this beautiful knight who stands before me, afraid. "Are you worried that I'd...that I wouldn't like you? That I wouldn't enjoy having sex with you?"

"I have never let a woman touch me," admits Charaxus softly. "I have been..." She inhales deeply. "I do not wish to be that hurt. To let someone touch me, caress me, know my deepest parts...and then leave me... It is too vulnerable. If I touch them..." she whispers, bending her head, brushing her mouth across my shoulder. I sigh at the heat of her lips on my skin.

"If I touch them," she repeats, straightening, holding my gaze, "I can make them feel good. Glorious, maybe. But they will never get close to me."

"You're afraid of getting hurt," I whisper, staring up at her. "You're afraid to let any woman get too close to you, because she'll break your heart."

"My heart," whispers Charaxus, her voice raw, "has already been broken by my family. I cannot allow it to break again."

I raise a paint-splattered hand and delicately, oh-so-delicately, like one would reach out and brush fingers over the broken wingtip of a bird, I place my hand again over Charaxus' heart, pressing my warm palm against her skin.

"I don't know what's going to happen after we leave this room. I don't know what plans you've made. I don't know where I factor into them. I know," I tell her, raising a finger as she starts to speak, "that you must find the shard and your brother. And that you must go home, back to your world. I understand that. But, right now, this moment... Can it be enough? I won't hurt you, Charaxus. I've loved you too long to hurt you," I whisper.

And then I say it: I whisper the words that are true, even though it takes every last bit of courage within me to voice them. "I've loved you forever. Since I was a little girl. You've always been the one I was looking for, my whole life spent looking...and now here you are. If...if you let me touch you, taste you," I whisper, shivering, my cheeks red, my legs trembling, "if you let me in, I will be gentle. I will be loving. And I will *not* break your heart."

Charaxus breathes out, and a single tear traces itself down her alabaster cheek. "Oh, Mara," she murmurs, her voice thick with pain. "You already have."

I don't know what to say—so I say nothing. For a long moment, we hold one another's gaze, my heart aching for her, my eyes traveling the lines of pain on her face, in the slope of her shoulders as she bends toward me.

But then Charaxus is nodding, almost imperceptibly, her jaw relaxing as she steps forward. There's something completely unreadable in her eyes, an emotion I can't identify—that is, until she takes my wrist, curling her fingers over my palm.

Holding my gaze, her blue eyes dark, deep, she moves my hand slowly, slowly, over her breast, my fingertips tracing her skin, following a line down to her belly.

I'm gasping as I touch her; the heat between us is electric. I gulp down air, feel the heat rising in me, the need, the desire burning so strongly that I have to ask her again—I have to know for sure, yes, definitely.

"Is this all right? Do you want this?" I whisper as she lets go of my wrist, as my hand pauses against her belly, feeling the sculpted muscles beneath my fingertips, cherishing the heat of her body.

She is silent for a full minute, wrestling with something deep inside of herself, something buried, secret. But then she comes back to me, comes back here, to this moment, and her attention is latched on me as she leans forward, tension crackling between us like a live wire.

And she whispers a single word, her entire body pulsing with the syllable: "Yes," she growls, and she says it again as I lick my lips, as—heart pounding—I sink down to my knees in front of her. Charaxus watches me, and she reaches out tentatively, curling her fingers in my hair, gazing down with darkening eyes.

"Yes," she murmurs, and her voice breaks. And then: "Please."

It's the *please* that does me in.

I lift my chin, lean forward as Charaxus moves, spreading her legs hip width apart now, breathing out softly in the stillness as I curl my fingers over her lean hips. I can feel the muscles rippling beneath my palms when she stiffens at my touch, but I look up at her again, my eyes wide, watching her, gauging her, making sure that, yes, this is still okay.

And it is, because Charaxus presses her fingers a little harder against the back of my head, encouraging me. She's tall, and her legs are long, but when I rise on my knees, my mouth is at the perfect height to lean forward, to press a kiss against her jet black curls.

She just came from the shower, and the normal, sweet scent of my vanilla soap, merging with the scent of *her*—her spice, her musk—is utterly electrifying. I inhale deeply, gazing up at her again before lifting my chin a little higher, bending forward a little more, curling my fingers tighter against her hips and drawing her toward me. She gasps as my tongue quests between her folds, the sound of her voice low in the stillness. I breathe out, breathe in again, inhaling her as I taste her.

She is so sweet, and as I press my fingers harder against her hips, resting my nails against her skin, I realize…she tastes familiar. Of course, that's impossible—I've never met her before, only in my dreams. Still, the taste of her answers a craving, a taste I know I will crave for the rest of my life. As I trace my tongue over her clit, as I dip my head lower, drawing my tongue lower across her slit, I moan out, tasting her wetness there, the wetness that is already shining against her inner thighs.

She's familiar, and at the same time, so wholly unexpected. Charaxus rises over me, curving forward, her fingers tight in the hair at the back of my head. I move my tongue over her, find the perfect rhythm, one that we both respond to, and I can't believe I'm doing this, can't believe that my hands are gripping the hips of the woman of my dreams.

But the moment is fragile; I can't think too hard about this, or it will all disappear. So I don't think. I taste, I touch, I worship, and I drink her deeply, my tongue drawing her wetness up to her clit, flicking teasingly across it at first, then harder, letting my lips drift over it, drawing it into my mouth gently, applying pressure.

Charaxus moans, long and low, her fingers curling tighter into my hair, and I think about what she said, that she's never let another woman touch her. So I slow down, though everything in me is aching to press my fingers between her folds, to feel her center spasm around my fingers, to taste her deeper, my tongue questing into her slit and savoring every inch of her.

I'm gentle, soft, as I trace my fingers across her center, but I don't press up and in like I want to. I caress her, drawing the wetness of her across her folds, soft, softer still, making her groan again above me, making her fingers curl reflexively against my scalp, making her push me harder against her hot center.

"Yes," she growls to me, and she bucks her hips against my face, the motion gentled, stifled, because I can tell she wants more. "Yes," she repeats, and that's when I glance up at her, over her mound, watching her move above me, and I push my fingers through her folds into the tightness, the wetness.

And it is so tight, so very tight—I'm terrified of hurting her—but I don't, and every motion she's making over me, above me, is one of surrender, of want, of "more." So I push up; I push up until my knuckles press against her center, until I am deep inside of her, and she is hissing out, bucking her hips harder against my mouth, against my hand.

I moan again, and she grits her teeth, gasping, her whole body quivering. Her body becomes slick with a thin sheen of sweat—mine, too—as I pant against her, wanting, more than anything, to make her feel just as good as she made me feel last night. Lust roars through me, the taste of her awakening something deep inside of me, something so primal, so wild, that, as I gaze up at her, as I taste her, as I bring her closer and closer to orgasm, I realize that we're, impossibly, merging, like two stars that collide in a spangled sky, the light coalescing until it's impossible to tell where I end and she begins.

And that's when she comes, the orgasm pushing through her so quickly, so intensely, that her wetness drips down over my chin, leaking to the floorboards beneath my knees. I close my eyes, feeling her muscles move against me, tasting her, drinking her until I gasp for air. Euphoria is cresting through me, too, and Charaxus' fingers, deep in my hair, flex a little. Then she's groaning, her body shivering against me as she presses my face to her center, her hands softening against my head.

I draw out the orgasm for a good long while, moving my fingers in and out of her, slowing my pace until, finally, her entire body curves over me, and she sinks down, down to her knees. She gathers my face in her hands, and she lovingly kisses me, tasting herself on my lips, her tongue in my mouth, her warm fingers cupping my face so gently. Her knees rest on either side of mine, my fingers still deep inside of her.

I kiss her, and I push my fingers into her. She gasps against my mouth, and I don't want this moment to end.

But all moments end eventually. And as I start to move inside of her again, as I kiss her hard, deep…that's when it happens.

The knock at the door.

Our stolen moment is over.

Chapter 8: A Goldfish Breakfast

Charaxus stiffens against me, and she stares into my eyes, her own wide and achingly blue.

I hold her gaze, my heart hurting so terribly, I resist the urge to double over in pain.

"Hey, Mara?" calls Iris from the other side of the door, "Sammie's whining... Should I let him out?"

I blink a little, and then I glance at the wall clock beside my bedroom door.

How is that *possible*?

It's *noon*.

"Oh, crap, yeah, Iris. That'd be great!" I call to her, and then I move my fingers out of Charaxus a little awkwardly as we both sink onto our heels. I draw in a deep breath, gazing at Charaxus, and there's so much regret moving through me...

Slowly, Charaxus composes herself, shoving her hair over her shoulders, a mask of serenity descending over her features. She sits back on her heels, and she places her hands on her thighs, seeking my gaze.

"Mara... I didn't know how much I needed that. How much I needed you," she tells me, and that perfect, gracious mask of serenity almost cracks as she looks at me, as something fleeting passes over her face: true pain. It's quickly replaced by stillness. She sighs. "Mara..."

I lick my lips as her voice trails off. We both

know that she has to go.

"It's…late," she murmurs then, clearing her throat, sadness in her voice. But then she sighs, and she attempts to lighten her tone just a little, though the words break at the end: "I…I must find the shard." I watch unhappily as a few expressions flit over Charaxus' face, finally ending on broken-heartedness. And, yeah, that last one stays.

"I am sorry. Truly, I am sorry," she whispers to me then, and her voice is hoarse. She leans forward on her knees, and she presses a kiss to my cheek. It's pretty chaste, and in its chasteness, it's shattering. She leans back onto her heels, and then she's standing, raking her fingers through her hair in frustration before offering a hand down to me.

I take her hand, and she pulls me up gently, her arms flexing. We keep a careful gap between us, not that it matters. Her sex still gleams on my mouth, along her thighs, on my fingers, and the electricity crackles between us. Keeping our distance from one another isn't going to change anything— but it's all we know how to do.

"The circumstances that brought us together… It seems as if an ill star follows us," she says flatly, glancing at me. "I have wanted…" Emotion makes her voice tremble, and she clears her voice again, leaning away, her dark hair sweeping in front of her face. She's hiding herself from me; I can't see her profile anymore. But she draws in a deep breath, and then she's saying, "Mara, I have waited for you. I have looked for you. And now you come to me in my darkest hour. I wish that you had come sooner."

I am utterly gutted.

My longing for Charaxus is something that's

alive inside of me, this insistent need. I lick my lips, tasting her again, and I feel so broken. I pad over to the easel and, leaning down, scoop up my sheet. I wrap it around myself, hiding my nakedness from her, because—in this moment—I feel too vulnerable, and I hurt too much.

I lift my hand reflexively, pressing my thumb against my gold pendant. "I wish you'd come to me sooner, too."

Oh, how much truth lies in those few words.

Charaxus looks at me, pain etched into the lines of her face. We stand a few feet apart, and the heavy silence hovers until she clears her throat, until she says, with her soft, broken voice, "What do we do?"

There's no right answer. No clear answer. No answer that makes any sense.

She could leave the Ceres right now, go on her way, find the shard, her brother... Open a portal back to her world. And I'd never see her again.

I don't have any doubt that she'll be successful in finding her brother. Finding the shard seems less likely. It's a small piece of glass that could be hidden anywhere in the city of Buffalo. But what do I know? Maybe the thing is magic; maybe she can sense it, feel its presence somehow.

And if she's successful in finding both her brother and the shard, that means she's going home. Back to Agrotera.

And I'll stay here. On Earth.

After all of this, after lifelong dreams of each other, after waiting and watching for one another, after *finding* each other, is that how this story really ends?

Yes, we have a deep connection, a connection that pulses, sparks, radiates—there's no denying that.

But I have to be honest, realistic, even as I stand here, even as I feel my heart breaking. Charaxus and I just met each other last night. We don't *know* each other, don't know each other deeply—our likes and dislikes, what makes us laugh or weep. And there's no time for discovering any of that. Charaxus has important things to do.

"I don't know what's next," I tell her, my voice quavering. I want it to be strong, to be steady, but it's not. I'm not. I grip the sheet around my breasts, and I take a deep breath, releasing it in a sigh. "Well—take a look at the painting, at least." I step back, gesture to the canvas I'm standing in front of, the canvas that Charaxus hasn't yet seen.

She takes a step forward, and then another, her muscles rippling under her pale skin. When she reaches me, she places her hands on her hips, her breath exhaling in one long, low sound.

"What do you think?" I ask her, suddenly nervous, my fingers tightening in the sheet over my breasts. I know that art is subjective—that one painting will make someone cry, while another person might jeer at it. No one piece of art is meant for everyone. But I'm hoping, hoping against hope, that Charaxus likes the painting I made of her.

I watch her, and then I realize that my mouth is hanging open, because a single silver tear is tracing along Charaxus' cheek, and she's staring at the painting as if utterly bewitched, her bright blue eyes wide, her breathing labored.

She looks at me, then, reaches for me. Every motion is slow, measured, as she takes my hips in her hands and draws me to her, kissing me deeply, softly, tenderly. She backs away a little, peering down into my eyes, hers suddenly uncertain.

"Is that... Is that how you see me?"

I nod, glancing at the painting before returning my gaze to her. "From the very first dream," I tell her, offer a small smile as I lift my hand, as I drift my fingers through her jet black strands, "I saw the stars in your hair."

Again, she presses her mouth to mine, but this time it's harder, more urgent.

There's desperation in the way we hold one another: she wraps her arms tightly about my body, and I grip her just as tightly, letting the sheet fall from my fingers, though it remains in place, pinned between us.

And when we back up, her mouth swollen from my kisses, her eyes dark, she repeats the question again, her voice low, breaking: "What do we do?"

I know how difficult this must be for her, because it's excruciatingly difficult for me. So I clear my throat, take a step back from her, and I snatch up the sheet before it drifts to the floor.

"Well," I say, and take another deep breath, "I think we should have breakfast." I smile at her softly.

She regards me as if I just told her dragons are real—hell, maybe they *are* real on Agrotera. There's pain in her expression, but she softens it, just like I'm softening the pain that's rising deep inside of me.

"Breakfast?" she says, her voice cracking, and then she nods, letting out a small chuckle as she watches me uncertainly. "It...it is true," she says with a short nod, "that when I joined the knights, I was told that breakfast was the most important meal of the day."

We're both trying so hard. I'm kind of failing, but I need to stay strong, and I nod, raking my fingers back through my hair, shrugging a little. "Well, that's one thing that's the same on both worlds." I tighten the sheet around myself, folding my arms in front of me. And then I blurt out, "So, um…you're going to look a little conspicuous if you gallivant around Buffalo in your armor. I think it might be best if you wear, well, Earth clothes."

Charaxus watches me, her eyes hooded, and—for a long moment—she says nothing. Because there was something unspoken in my words, and we both heard it, loud and clear.

I'm staying here.

And she's leaving.

And that's…that's how it has to be.

Charaxus doesn't put up a fight. Instead, she sighs, nods, resigned, her shoulders swooping forward a little before she shakes herself, standing straight and tall then, placing a hand on her right hip. "And where might I get, as you so cleverly call them, Earth clothes?" she asks, her voice still hoarse.

I shrug a little, don't look at her, instead gaze at the floor. "I'm assuming that Toby is still fast asleep—he doesn't wake up until around two, usually. Let me take a shower, and I'll go borrow some clothes from him. He's about your height," I say, but I don't glance at her, because if I do…her beauty will break my heart into even tinier pieces. "So…that should work. Will that work?" I ask her, and that's when I look at her again.

She holds my gaze, and she nods, her jaw tightening, resolve smoothing through her features.

"As you wish, m'lady," Charaxus growls to me.

It takes every last bit of willpower inside of me to take a step back from her, to move away.

It takes every last bit of willpower to wait until

I'm inside my bathroom, the door tightly shut behind me, before I start to weep.

Toby is, unsurprisingly, still sleeping when I reach his bedroom, but he mumbles something like, "Sure, sure take whatever you need and leave me alone," before he places his pillow firmly on top of his head and keeps snoring. The image of him, buried under blankets, is so comfortingly *normal* in the midst of all of this not-so-normal stuff going on that I lean down, pat his shoulder affectionately, sniffling, before turning toward his closet.

"Hey…" Toby mutters, sticking his disheveled head out from underneath the pillow, "are you okay?" He's still partially asleep, but I think he heard my sniffle.

"Yeah, yeah," I murmur to him, gentling my voice, making sure that it doesn't give me away. I wipe my tears with the corner of my peasant blouse sleeve, breathe out. "Hey, go back to sleep. I'm okay."

"Are you sure?" he asks, but he's already resting his head back on the pillow, his eyes drifting closed.

Poor guy can't help it: he keeps a really bad sleeping schedule, and whenever he can catch a little shut-eye, he has to take it.

Inside of Toby and Rod's *massively* disorganized closet—well, technically Rod's side is very neat, and Toby's side is an utter disaster—I find a black t-shirt and black sweatpants. Compared to Charaxus' other clothes, this outfit is kind of sad, but I'm not sure if Toby's jeans will fit her, and she'll be able to make a pair of black sweatpants look sexy, anyway.

When I get back to the room and show Charaxus the clothes, she rises easily from her languid sprawl on the bed, her muscles still rippling beneath her pale white skin. She stretches overhead, avoiding my gaze as she pulls the black sweatpants on, tugging the t-shirt over her head. She pulls her hair up through the neckline, and then she's standing there, hands on her hips, a wry smile tugging at her lips, her eyes gazing out the little porthole window cut into the side of the metal wall.

"So, how do I look in these Earth clothes?" she asks me, her voice low.

I clear my throat. "Hot," I tell her simply: it's the truth. Sweatpants were designed for long, uncomplicated Saturday afternoons involving a television and a tub of ice cream.

And yet, somehow, impossibly, Charaxus manages to transform that most unflattering of garments into something absolutely smoking.

The waistband is a little loose, so it hangs around her toned hips as a reminder of what sexiness lies beneath. The t-shirt is actually small on her, and her muscled stomach shows through quite well.

And her breasts... Her breasts show through well, too, the perfect curve of them, the peaks of her nipples... She catches me looking at her chest, and then she's smiling a little—a soft, sad smile—as she ducks her head and threads her fingers back through her hair in what is *possibly* the most adorable gesture I've ever seen.

The sight of her, looking so soft, cuts me deeper than a knife twisted between my ribs. I swallow a little, averting my gaze, and then she's stepping forward. Charaxus is going to say something to me as

162

she curls her fingers around my elbow, her face brooding, her eyes flashing and intense…but her words are left unsaid. Instead, she smooths her features, straightens, and inclines her head toward the door.

"Are you hungry?" she asks me.

I nod, licking my lips, pocketing my cell phone, and then we're out the door and aiming for the Ceres' common area.

It's around twelve-thirty in the afternoon, and there is not a single soul around. "They must have been partying hard last night, or working hard," I tell Charaxus by way of explanation, and she raises her brows questioningly.

"You live with your family?" she asks, her head to the side as I grab some bowls from one of the cupboards and take the soy milk out of the fridge.

"Yeah, sort of," I tell her with a little smile. I drag down a box of some generic, super-sugary cereal named Box o' Magic!!!! Yes, the name of the cereal ends in four exclamation marks. Iris and I were in charge of doing the grocery shopping for the Ceres this week, and when we saw this box in the cereal aisle, we cracked up for five minutes and had to, in the end, put it in our cart. Which means, I guess, that their marketing worked, exclamation points and all.

"The people here aren't my biological family," I tell her, dumping cereal into the two chipped bowls, "but they're the family of my heart." I pour some soy milk on top of the cereal, and I'm rewarded by snapping, crackling and popping—something the box didn't tell me to expect. I push a bowl over to Charaxus and hand her a spoon.

She stares down at the cereal dubiously.

"It's good!" I tell her, and take a big spoonful of

the stuff to demonstrate, shoving it into my mouth. And it *is* good, if you consider pure sugar to be tasty. Okay, so maybe buying the cereal based on its use of exclamation marks might not have been the best—or healthiest—idea. I grimace a little and swallow my sugar—I mean, cereal—and, to my surprise, when I glance over at Charaxus, she's digging in.

"This *is* quite good," she tells me after a big spoonful.

"I'm glad you like it," I chuckle, leaving my bowl on the counter and popping a bagel into the toaster.

Sammie suddenly bounds in through the front door (Iris doesn't follow him, meaning she's late for something), and my dog comes barreling into the kitchen, sitting down on my feet and wagging his bushy tail hopefully.

"Sorry, buddy, I'm the worst momma! I'm late giving you your breakfast." I ruffle his ears before I empty dog food into his bowl.

I'm surprised when Sammie doesn't devour the food right away, like usual, and when I look at him, I'm also surprised to see that he's not at my side...

And that's because he and Charaxus are having a standoff.

I wouldn't expect my dog to have a standoff with a *bunny*, let alone one of the most commanding and powerful presences I've ever encountered...yet he's managing to do just that, his big brown eyes wide as he stares up at Charaxus, black nose pointed directly at her face.

She stares back at him, her blue eyes narrowed.

"Uh...Charaxus?" I murmur, and she startles a little, glancing at me and removing her attention from

Sammie.

My dog chooses that moment to waddle on over to me, pressing his shoulder against my legs and staring up at me reproachfully.

"What was that?" I ask Charaxus gently, and she shakes her head a little, as if she's waking from a spell.

"I apologize," she says, and she takes a deep breath. "I do not much like dogs."

"How—" I'm about to ask how anyone in the world—or on any other world—could *dis*like dogs, but I stop myself. Okay, for one, it's true: as much as it pains me, some people do dislike dogs, and for all I know, a traumatic experience may have happened to her involving dogs in the past. She really does look uneasy right now, placing her half-finished cereal bowl on the counter and pushing it away, as if she's lost her appetite.

"Um, does Sammie make you uncomfortable?" I ask her, grabbing Sammie by the collar before he can jump up and put his paws on the counter in an effort to relieve her of her cereal.

"No," she murmurs, though she folds her arms so that his nose can't uproot under her hand. "I am sorry," she says, and then she clears her throat. "I was…attacked by a…dog…once."

"Sammie, go sit on the couch," I tell him gently, and—surprisingly—he actually listens, trotting over to the couch and sitting on it, thumping the couch cushions with his massive tail as he stares at me in adoration, then casts another suspicious glance at Charaxus.

Charaxus and I stand together at the counter, staring as if we're seeing one another for the first time.

We know so little about each other: that's pretty clear right now. Charaxus' eyes are hooded, her arms crossed in front of her, her feet apart, her body arranged in a strong stance. I watch her from across the small countertop, so little separating us...but so much more coming between us.

It's normal when you begin a relationship to learn the other person's likes and dislikes, their favorite songs, whether they like mushrooms on their pizza or think they're just gross fungus. What Charaxus and I have—it's not a relationship. We made love last night; we made love this morning... And that's it. Case closed.

But...we also dreamed of each other for decades, and that's not something that can easily be ignored.

"So..." I clear my throat, stand up a little taller and tilt my chin up. "What are your plans? For today?"

When Charaxus regards me with furrowed brows, I try again. "Are you going to try to find the shard? And your brother?" I ask weakly.

She sighs, and then she glances down at the countertop, a frown making her full lips downturn. "I must," she murmurs. And her words are tinged with sorrow; I ache to hear them.

I guess this is where we tell each other that last night was great, thanks for all the sweet dreams, but we both have lives to live, shards to find, paintings to paint...

There was a real, honest connection between us. And now it must be severed.

My chest hurts, and my throat hurts, and my head hurts. There's so much pain—physical and emotional—that I'm startled by the severity of it. I'd be stupid to deny the fact that I'd been waiting for this woman my whole life. But she has a mission. A quest. And I can't stand in her way.

Sure, I could go along with her today, play the bumbling sidekick to her heroic warrior. But we both know that, at the end of her journey, we're going to have to part ways.

I've been falling in love with her my whole life. I know that I love her. I know that I know nothing about her. So, really, what's better: learning her heart, her loves and hates, her dreams, her longings, and then having that all of ripped away from me...or ending this now, before any more feelings can grow, before this separation becomes any more excruciating?

I'm damned if I do, damned if I don't.

Charaxus is watching me across the counter, and I know she's thinking similar thoughts; her features contort for a long moment into a grimace of agony. Her jaw flexes, and she cocks her head to the side, placing her hands on the counter, her fingers pressed hard against the surface, her knuckles white.

"Mara," she murmurs, and the way my name drifts over her tongue—it's absolutely erotic. I shiver a little, close my eyes, bite my lip.

I don't want her to go.

"Mara," she repeats, and she's moving around the corner toward me, putting one foot in front of the other with guarded slowness, as if she's trying to edge closer to a prey animal without spooking them. But I don't spook. I stand still, perfectly still, when she reaches me, when she trails her pale fingers over my neck, gently pushing my hair over my shoulder, and then tugging on the sleeve of my t-shirt so that my shoulder is revealed to her.

It's there that she places a perfect kiss, a soft kiss, a warm kiss, her lips brushing against my skin as if she's claiming a treasure.

"I don't know what to do, Charaxus," I tell her, my voice anguished. "This already this hurts so much."

"Yes," she agrees, and her voice is tentative. Hopeful. "But I was still hoping that you would come with me. Come with me," she repeats, but now there's a magnetic quality to the words, as if she's weaving a spell. "Please?" This *please*…there's a question in it. A questing hope.

A low, shivering note of despair.

I glance sidelong at her, my brow furrowed, my breath coming fast as I reach up, as I place a hand over my heart, as if that could possibly quell the pain there (it doesn't). "You know what's going to happen," I whisper to her.

"And what is that?" she asks, voice low.

"I don't know about you," I say with a shake of my head, "but it's…" My throat constricts, yet I keep pushing through, keep talking. "It's very hard for me to love anyone. I've…been through a lot," I say, summarizing my past with that stupid little phrase, as if it could somehow convey the severity of my formative years.

I gulp down another lungful of air. "Somehow, I managed to love you through it all, anyway. All this time, my whole life, I've loved you. And now here you are. And you're going to leave soon. And…if I go with you now, help you find the shard, your brother…" I glance up, hold her gaze, her bright blue eyes flashing, her mouth forming a soft frown as she listens to me intently. "If I go with you now," I repeat, licking my lips, "it's going to hurt *so much more*, that I don't honestly know how I could recover. It will... It would disintegrate my heart."

For a long moment, nothing happens. We stand there, her hand at the small of my back, warm and inviting and heavy, the ultimate comfort. But then Charaxus nods, taking a step back, her hand leaving me.

I can see deep pain written on her face.

I can't breathe.

"If...if only we were from the same world," she says, shaking her head, her hair shifting over her shoulders, the soft shush of it filling me with longing. That same hair trailed across my body last night, moving over my skin like dark water. Those same lips found mine again and again, a hundred times. A thousand times. She tastes like cinnamon, like heat, like longings fulfilled, like answers found.

I will not, cannot, ever forget the way she tastes.

"If only," I agree, and my voice cracks at the end of that last word. "I...I wish you a lot of luck, Charaxus." I'm babbling, trying to find the right words. "I hope...everything works out. And..." My voice cracks again, and I take a deep breath, try to calm down. "I hope you can forgive me for not coming with you now."

"There is nothing to forgive," says Charaxus immediately, simply. "You are right. I feel it, too. There is something profound between us," she says, gesturing toward the empty air with a graceful shrug. "I have felt it my whole life, and last night...this morning..." she whispers, her voice hoarse, "our time together awakened something even deeper and stronger." She frowns, straightening her shoulders. "To feed that desire would be self-sabotaging. We are from different worlds. And you have a good life here."

She glances around the Ceres appreciatively. "You must be a queen to live in such a castle." Her voice sounds almost wistful.

"Oh, I'm not a queen," I say quickly, but when Charaxus looks at me again, her eyes are bright, and her expression is sober. I grow quiet.

"I know a queen when I see one," she tells me, her voice low, husky. "And that is what you are."

I am stricken speechless, and I can tell you this: through all of the pain in my life, all of the suffering I have endured...no moment has hurt me more than this one, right here and right now.

We're saying goodbye to each other. I'm saying goodbye to the woman who has haunted my dreams—and my heart.

This feels so wrong. But I don't know how to make it right.

"It was so good to meet you, Charaxus," I tell her, and my voice breaks on every damn word, but I don't care. It's the truth, and she needs to know it. "I'm so glad I met you," I tell her, and then tears are leaking down my cheeks, and she steps forward, enfolding me in her arms and pressing my face to her shoulder. I weep—openly, uncontrollably—clinging to her as if *I'm* the drowning woman, and she's the only one who can save me.

Quickly, I break away from her, grab a paper towel, and dry my eyes. The real world is crashing down around me, and I need to make certain that Charaxus is as well-equipped as possible to deal with what she's about to face—i.e., heading out into a strange world she has no experience with.

Besides, I need a distraction.

I snap my fingers, and Sammie—good dog that

he is—follows me obediently up to my bedroom as Charaxus finishes the last of the cereal, not because she wants to—I can tell she's lost her appetite—but because she's going to need energy for the road.

I make my way upstairs with my dog, and I take every piece of her armor and place it inside of a really big canvas bag that I got on vacation down in Virginia Beach. It's the only thing large enough to hold all of the pieces, and it bulges, but at least it's something that she can carry pretty easily, and it'll keep her from walking around Buffalo in the armor, which would draw way too much attention.

Then I rummage around in my bathroom. I don't know what she'll need, and I'm kind of blinded by my tears, but I try to anticipate every possible situation, including the likelihood that she might be looking for her brother for a few days. I throw a deodorant into the canvas bag and a small, airline-approved tube of toothpaste with a new toothbrush, a little bottle of shampoo and conditioner and some samples of soap from when Iris took up soapmaking (for an afternoon). I grab a box of protein bars from under my bed and toss it in, too, and then add a big water bottle that she can refill at a water fountain.

I pull open the drawer in my bedside table, and I open up what I've always called my treasure box. It's from my eighties-era childhood, and it has this magnificent flying horse on the top, and I pull out a wad of twenties. Cecile taught me, a long time ago, that if you have a wad of twenties saved "just in case," you'll feel safe, knowing you have the means to make any rainy day just a bit better. So I take the wad of cash— it's really not as thick as I'd like, but then, it was never as thick as I'd like, and there have been a couple of rainy days recently—and I stuff the money into the back pocket of my jeans.

I rise, hefting the canvas bag onto my shoulder (wow, is it heavy), and, after grabbing the katana, I leave Sammie lounging in my room as I pad quietly downstairs.

Charaxus has placed her bowl in the sink. I'm assuming she decided to do that because the sink is full of dirty dishes—a very common sight in the Ceres, dirty plates nearly stacked to the ceiling. *Nearly,* but not quite. She's standing with her back to me, leaning against the kitchen island, her arms crossed and her head bent. When I round the island and set the canvas bag beside my feet, she still hasn't opened her eyes or lifted her chin. Her head remains ducked, her inky black mane sweeping down around her shoulders, her lips pursed.

For half of a second…I think she's praying.

Charaxus glances up at me then, her mouth drawn into a thin, tight line, her eyes pained. "I am ready."

"Um…"

I'm not. I'm not ready to let her go.

But she *has* to go.

I pick up the canvas bag, hold it in an outstretched hand, my arm shaking because the contents are so heavy. "Here," I tell her, voice quiet. "I packed your armor, some things you might need. And, um, here…" When she takes the bag, I reach into my back pocket and bring out the wad of twenty-dollar bills. I press it into her other hand. "This is…just in case. Just in case you need it," I tell her, swallowing.

She glances down at the money, perplexed. "What is this?"

"Oh. It's money. See?" I take the wad of bills from her hand, unroll the first twenty, hold it up for her. "Do you have money on Agrotera?" I ask her, a little mystified as she takes the bill, examining it closely.

"Of course," she says with a slight shrug, "but it is all coins. This is only paper." She hands it back to me.

"Well…" I stand there in the kitchen, the lights glaring down brightly on us, my heart breaking as I try to figure out how to explain our monetary system to her, and I realize it's not really that important, considering the circumstances. "It's paper, yes," I tell her simply, and then I place the bill in her hand and roll her fingers up and over the wad of money…not letting go of her. "Just take it. In case you need it, in case you need a place to stay…" Inside my head, I'm thinking, *This is so stupid, what are we doing, this is a once-in-a-lifetime, across-worlds meeting, and we're throwing it all away*, but I know we're not throwing it away. We've met. We've made love. We've found out that, all along, our dream person existed. If we go farther down this path, if we learn to love each other more deeply, we're going to break our hearts far past mending.

"You can come here anytime you need to," I say quickly, gulping down air. She glances at me, surprised, her eyes a little wide.

"But…the whole point of this," she tells me, waving her hand between us, "is to…make the break clean." She says it almost apologetically, holding my gaze with her bright blue eyes. "If the break is messy…" She trails off, her jaw clenched.

"Once, a long time ago," I say, and I'm inhaling deeply, my pulse erratic. "Um…there was this girl. That I knew," I say, stumbling over the lie. "And she was… She was homeless. She didn't have anyplace to go. And she would have done anything to find a place to stay with someone she trusted, but she didn't have anyone. And that was…really hard for her." I swallow. "So, because of her, in honor of her, I always make sure that everyone I care about knows that they have a place to go. Should they need it."

Charaxus watches me carefully, her eyes hooded, her expression guarded. I know she's caught me in the lie, but she doesn't know what's the truth, and there's no time to tell her. And I don't want to tell her. I can't bear the thought of telling her something so sad, so dark…so shameful.

"All right, yes," she says, and she stands straight, lifting her chin. "Then I guess…this is goodbye?"

We stare at one another, and this parting feels wrong. *So wrong.* But what can we do? Charaxus has to go back.

"Goodbye, Charaxus," I say, blinking back my tears. But they leak out, anyway, tracing shining paths down my cheeks.

Charaxus nods, her jaw tense, a flicker of uncertainty dimming her blue eyes, and she's going to say something else…but she doesn't. Instead, she straightens, pushing her hips off of the kitchen island, stretching a little languidly, like a big cat might, before she inclines her head, glancing at the center of the island…

To the little goldfish bowl that's sitting there on the counter.

I stare at it, blinking. The bowl is almost impossible to see since a pizza box lid is set on top of it, but she reaches over, removing the lid, leaning her elbows on the counter.

All of this started with a goldfish.

This woman from my dreams, standing right in front of me...I never would have found her, never would have saved her life, if it hadn't been for this goldfish.

What's that saying about the butterfly effect? How, with a simple flutter of a butterfly's wings, a tremendous hurricane can be created?

Yeah...my butterfly is a goldfish.

Charaxus clears her throat, glancing sidelong at me as she curls her shoulders forward, bending at the waist, her elbows firmly planted on the counter. She nods toward the goldfish bowl. "This little creature said that you left the house last night because of him." She's glancing sidelong at me. "You left to get him food because you felt sorry for him—is that true?"

I blink. Okay, is Charaxus implying that...she can speak *Goldfish?* But is it really that weird, considering the fact she came from another world, that she's a *knight* from another world, and that she can do magic?

Yeah, not so much.

"So, you can talk to goldfish," I say calmly, and despite the tears gathering at the corners of my eyes, I smile a little.

"I can speak to all animals," says Charaxus with a wave of her hand, as if that's nothing remarkable. "It's a trait of my people. A gift."

"Sure," I say with a little shrug. Because...why not?

"Anyway," she says, sniffing a little, and I can tell she's struggling with her emotions but masking them mightily. She stiffens a little, suddenly very formal: "The goldfish said that it was very kind of you. And, without him, I would not have been saved by you." She holds out her hand to me. "So…here."

And she hands me a bottle of fish food.

The bottle is bright yellow, and the top of the food canister is covered with a thick layer of dust, and beneath that dust is the unmistakable, clearly-from-the-late-seventies price tag of Wiggs, our corner store.

I glance up at her, my eyes as round as saucers. "How did you get this…" But then I'm shaking my head. "Wait, no, don't tell me."

Charaxus is smiling softly at me, her eyes narrowed with fondness. Then she takes a step forward, and she curls her fingers gently around my right elbow. She leans down toward me, and my breathing intensifies, my heart rate skyrocketing as she presses her lips against my right earlobe. Her mouth, her breath, is so warm, and this close, I can smell her cinnamon, the scent of her skin, and it kills me. It *kills* me how much I want her, how much I can't believe this is happening… How much I hate letting her go.

"Magic," she whispers, her voice low, throaty, a growl, and then she leans back, an expression of deep regret on her face before she carefully masks it again. "I brought that food here with magic. I displaced one of these," she says, holding up the wad of twenties, "for that canister of food. Was that enough money for the exchange?"

I glance at the price tag on the top of the bottle; it reads "$0.95."

"Yeah," I tell her with a soft sigh. "That should cover it."

"Feed the fish. He is very hungry," murmurs Charaxus. And then, again, she looks like she's going to say something else, but she doesn't. She nods vaguely, and she's stepping forward, brushing her mouth against the corner of mine.

"Take the katana, okay?" I tell her, catching her gaze. I carried it downstairs with me, and now I'm presenting it to her, gripping the hilt. Her fingers drift over mine as she takes the katana's sheath from my hand, and she nods gravely.

"I am so glad to have met you," she whispers to me, tears leaking out of the corners of my eyes as she kisses me once more. So I close my eyes, my body shuddering at her touch, beneath her soft, chaste kiss, because I can't bear to see her, can hardly breathe. My entire being is crying out that this is wrong, that she shouldn't leave…

I keep my eyes closed as she steps away from me. As I hear her pick up the canvas bag of armor.

I love you, I think, but I'm frozen—I can't speak the words.

I keep my eyes closed as I hear her boots cross the floor.

I love you, my soul screams.

I keep my eyes closed as she opens the door.

I love you.

I keep my eyes closed as she shuts the door.

I only open my eyes when Charaxus is gone. Disappeared, like she never was here at all.

I hold the bottle of goldfish food in my hand, and I stare down at it, trying to see it through my tears.

My heart isn't breaking.

It's too shattered to break.

Chapter 9: When the Battle's Lost and Won

"I've made a terrible mistake."

Cecile glances up at me in surprise, her white hair a little askew in its bun, tendrils dangling down around her face. There's quite a lot of blue paint in her hair, offsetting its whiteness. Her glasses are perched on the top of her nose, and there's a little blue paint on the lenses, too, smudged across the glass.

It looks like she's been painting for hours: I notice a new canvas on her easel, and it's boasting a gorgeous, evocative, dreamy seascape (with wings all over it, because Cecile's work is a little surreal). She seems tired, exhausted. I stand in the doorway, twisting my hands in front of me, and I hate that I'm bringing this to her when she looks so worn…but I don't know what else to do.

My heart hurts so much that the pain is vacillating toward numbness.

"I'm so sorry to bother you, Cecile," I say, choking around the words as the tears stream over my cheeks, dripping off of my chin. I wipe them away quickly with the back of my hand, self-conscious as I sniff a little and give her a watery smile. "I can come back, maybe after you've rested. Did you get any sleep last night, or did you paint the whole night through?

Actually, you know what? Don't even worry about it. I'll talk to you later." I mutter all of this at once, as if everything I said was one long, mumbled syllable, without a single breath between the words, and I'm already backing up, ready to shut the door behind me.

"You get in here right now, young lady," Cecile tells me firmly, her mouth forming a thin, hard line: she's wearing her no-nonsense expression, and I know better than to argue. Cecile is still perched on her painting stool—I've *never* done my painting while seated on a stool, and I have no idea how anyone would think it's comfortable for such long periods of time, but Cecile's always laughed and said it's simply the way she's always done it, and she can't imagine painting any other way. She's leaning forward on her stool now, dipping her brushes in her water pot as I step inside, shutting the door behind me. My knees wobble beneath me, weak.

"Now, what's the matter? You look like you've seen a ghost," Cecile tells me, getting up and wiping her hands on her apron. Light blue smears from her palms, blending with the other colors on the once-white apron. I've always loved looking at that apron, seeing the history of Cecile's work in the colors merging there. She paints primarily in blue hues, and it's exquisite to see all of those shades of blue, millions of different shades...

"No, I haven't seen a ghost," I whisper, my mouth so dry that it's hard to force the words out. I cross the room quickly, sit down on the futon. The couch is covered with saris, and I sink back into the silky softness, drawing my knees up toward my chest.

"Come on, my dear. What's happened?" asks Cecile, crossing over to the rickety table that holds her percolator and box of dollar-store brand tea.

The minute she turns the kettle on and draws out the tea packets, the soft scent of herbs permeates the room, and I'm a little comforted by it.

"All right," says Cecile, after she fills the percolator with water from the tap in her bathroom and plugs it in. She comes to sit beside me, and she watches me, one white brow raised, her head tilted to the side. "Tell me what's bothering you, doll."

"Last night was..." I begin, staring down at my hands, clasped tightly in my lap. I try again: "Something...really weird...happened." I look at Cecile, and her expression is perfectly neutral. She's good at this, drawing out what people need to say, listening as attentively as a saint. It's one of the reasons I love her so much.

And it's one of the reasons that I have always trusted her so deeply.

Still, I don't know what I was thinking coming to her with this. If I tell Cecile the truth, she might not believe me. Oh, she'd be awesome about it, of course, let me down gently, murmuring something about bad dreams. She'd say that, yes, I may have brought a woman here last night, but she most definitely was not from another world.

Cecile waits, her hooded eyes glittering.

Then she says, "I know that something odd happened last night, my dear. Something...not quite of this world changed things."

I stare at her, dumbfounded.

"What?" I ask weakly.

"There was a storm." Cecile glances sidelong at the percolator; it's starting to make a bubbling sound. "Just a second, doll. The tea's on," she says with a soft smile, and then she's up and striding toward the little table. "Would you like one lump or two?"

"Two," I whisper, shocked by the normality of her question, given the circumstances, but then I'm standing, spreading my hands. "Cecile, please tell me *exactly* what you're saying, because...because right now, I need things put in really simple, logical terms." I rake my hand back through my hair as I breathe out.

Cecile lifts her antique sugar tongs and takes the lid off of her sugar bowl. She told me once that the bowl was her mother's; it has a delicate rose pattern along the side. She takes two lumps of sugar out of the bowl and sets them in the center of the white teacup before splashing hot water over the bag.

"I told you there was magic in the world, sweetie," she says, and her eyes are twinkling as she hands me the teacup and saucer. She winks. "And last night, it happened, didn't it? Here. *Magic.*"

"*How* do you know that?" I sit down and lean against the futon as I hold the teacup gingerly in front of me, staring at Cecile.

She shrugs, sitting down beside me and lifting her own teacup to her lips. She blows gently on the surface. "Magic is afoot, my dear," she tells me, her mouth turning up at the corners. "Delicious magic. That is *exactly* what is happening, and you know it, despite your pragmatic, 'tarot cards are bullshit' nonsense," she says with a hearty chuckle.

I frown. "Well, tarot cards *are* bullshit—"

"My darling girl." Her eyes are dark, though her words are soft, full of fondness. I breathe out, watching her. "All of the times I have read for you, and you still don't believe? Even when I read the truth?"

"It's...just that you know too much about me,"

I protest, though my voice has softened. "You know *everything* about me. You're the only one who does."

"But think about that, Mara," says Cecile, and her tone is a little different now. There's pain in her gaze as she takes my hand, squeezing it. "I have been there for you, haven't I?"

"Always," I tell her, and suddenly, my eyes are swimming with tears. "When no one else was there…you were. But that doesn't mean that tarot readings are real," I persist, wiping the tears away from my eyes, forbidding them to fall.

Cecile holds my gaze, her eyes calm.

"I knew about you, dear heart, didn't I?" she murmurs, her head tilted to the side. "I knew about you."

I close my eyes, resting the saucer in my lap so that I can grip the teacup with shaking hands.

"I know you did," I whisper, and though I have tried to push everything down, to keep a lid on my past, on my pain…darkness can't stay hidden forever. There will be times when your scars throb so painfully that you can't ignore them anymore.

I close my eyes, and I remember.

Everything rushes back, and all at once. It's as if a dam has broken, and the angry river of memories roars over me, dragging me down into the rapids of darkness.

I've just turned eighteen. For most people, it's a momentous birthday, one full of happiness and good memories.

But…not for me.

It's going to be the worst day of my life.

I'm standing in my bedroom, staring at my reflection in

the mirror. My palms are sweaty; I wipe them on my jeans. Real attractive, *I think to myself, gulping down air as I slide a tendril of hair behind my ear and gaze at my reflection with wide eyes.*

I invited Kim over for the afternoon. It's my birthday, and my parents aren't doing anything for it—why would they? I stare at my reflection, trying to remind myself that I don't care that they forgot. Again.

But of course I care.

When my friends say that their parents hate them, they're just being dramatic. Most parents love their kids—that's how human beings are wired. But sometimes there are aberrations in nature. A bear kills her cubs and eats them. A stallion rips his foal's throat open.

Sometimes there are deviations.

Like my parents.

I've often wondered whether my parents ever loved me at all. Maybe when I was born, too tiny to find fault, too helpless to actively hate. Maybe. But I'm not really sure. I have a feeling that, even as a baby, there was something about me that they found unlovable.

The put-downs started when I was pretty young. The "you'll never be good enoughs" morphed quickly into "I wish you'd never been borns." It was hard to endure, but life got even worse once they started beating me.

I gaze at my reflection, at the bruise around my right eye that I tried to hide with concealer this morning. I reach up, wincing, as I press a finger to it, smudging the concealer from that small bit of tender, black-and-blue skin.

I don't know why they hit me. That's the worst part. My mother's wailed a few times that she wishes she'd had a son, instead. But is that reason enough to hate her own daughter?

I don't know.

Sometimes, people are just cruel.

Sometimes, you're born to the wrong parents.

For a long time, I doubted that I should have been born at all.

That sounds dark. And, for a long time, it was.

Until Kim.

Kim has been my best friend for the last few years of school. Since the beginning of ninth grade, actually. She's a pretty brunette girl, a full foot shorter than me. She describes herself as a firecracker, and she is. Kim has a temper; she's feisty as all hell. She loves soccer and ice cream...and she's the most loyal person you'll ever meet.

She knows I'm gay. She's always been there for me, even after I told her about the dream I keep having, about the woman in the water. Kim is such a good person—the best person I've ever known.

I stare at my reflection in the mirror, eyes wide as I consider the truth of why I wanted Kim here today. Not just because she's my best friend and this is my eighteenth birthday. Not just because I wanted someone to celebrate this day with.

It's because I...I think I'm falling for her.

No—I already have.

That's stupid, right? It's honestly the stupidest thing I could ever do in my stupid life. Headline: gay girl falls for straight best friend who can never love her. This is my life, my life that I'm about to profoundly mess up by loving someone out of reach.

I can never be with her. She's straight; I'm not. And that disconnect is tragic.

The tragedy of the whole damn thing makes a twisted sort of sense, though. It fits in with the rest of my sorry existence. Being born to parents who wanted a son instead of a daughter, who hate me because I'm not a boy. Having dreams about that gorgeous mystery woman since I was a kid, a woman who doesn't exist but who I love all the same. The dream is especially tragic, because at least, someday soon, I'll escape my parents' hate, leave this house forever. But I'll never find my dream woman, because she isn't real. And I can never truly love Kim, because she could never love me back.

It's almost summer, and after this last summer together, Kim and I are going to part ways. She's going to NYU; I'm heading to UCLA. Colleges on opposite sides of the country. In a few short months, our lives are going to change so much. We're going to change so much…

I pick up the compact of powder concealer and try to cover my bruise better, but when I stare into my eyes in the mirror, there's a flicker there. A flicker of doubt.

I'm wondering if I should just hold my tongue.

Not tell Kim that I'm crushing on her.

Problem is, I've been feeling for a long time that this secret is too big to keep inside. Besides, it's tough to hide a secret from my best friend. And this secret…it's massive. Voicing it could change everything.

I watch my reflection pale at the mere thought of telling her. My heart is drumming against my ribs.

Then I lift my chin, eyes flashing.

Resolve courses through me.

Yeah. She needs to know.

And…and if I manage to tell her tonight, if I don't chicken out, then Kim can decide what she wants to do next. She can figure out whether she wants to remain my friend or not. She can figure out if this knowledge, my crush on her, my thinking— at eighteen—that I'm falling in love with her, irrevocably alters our friendship.

I pat the concealer puff against my bruised skin, and I flinch. God, it hurts. You'd think I'd be used to this by now. I mean, this shiner isn't the worst of the bruises and breaks my parents have given me over the years. But, for some reason— maybe because it's my birthday—it's bothering me a whole hell of *a lot more.*

And someone noticed this time.

My gym teacher pulled me aside this morning, her brow furrowed in concern as she lowered her voice, asked me what had happened to get me a black eye. I lied, told her I'd fallen down the stairs. I panicked—it was the first thing I could think of— and even to myself, it sounded like the stupidest lie. A flat-out lie. I've been covering for my parents since I was a little girl. You would think I'd have had a better excuse on the tip of my tongue. But my gym teacher caught me off guard. Her expression was so kind, so pitying as she stared down at me, her hand gentle on my upper arm, like my bone might break beneath the weight of her fingers. That look of pity on her face filled me with a deep, consuming horror. With dread.

I was so worried that she'd see through my lie, and finally, finally find me out.

I know—thanks to Oprah—that it's common for abuse victims to feel ashamed of their abuse, and to feel protective of their abusers. It's this dangerous pattern, but what can I do? My parents threaten me to keep me quiet. My mother tells me over and over again that if I ever tell anyone that she hurts me, that my father hurts me, I'll be laughed at. No one will believe me.

Besides, she says, they're only trying to shape me into a better person.

Growing up, Mom told me all these horror stories about orphanages and the foster care system. I believed I'd be worse off in an orphanage—starving, bloody, filthy, alone. Orphanages are like dungeons, she said. Some kids don't ever make it out alive.

Better the devil you know, right?

I guess my gym teacher believed me, despite my fumbling excuse. She told me go to see the nurse, and that was that.

But Kim?

For a long time now, Kim has sensed that there's

something wrong with my home life. She never buys my bullshit excuses about why I'm late coming to her house, or why I'm limping, or why there were black-and-blue handprints on my arms one day after my father grabbed me. I see her watching me carefully, see her brain working things out. She's never even been to my place. We meet at the bowling alley and the library, at the park and at the diner.

I know that, if she's ever around my parents for even a minute or two, she'll pick up on the truth right away. Kim isn't stupid. She's the smartest person I know.

Obviously, I've never told my parents that I'm gay. That knowledge would just give them more ammunition to use against me. Part of me wonders if they'd send me to one of those gay conversion camps. They'd never want to be associated with something as profoundly "wrong" as a lesbian daughter.

I hope they'll just never find out, not ever.

They don't deserve to know.

Yeah...my life is all sorts of messed up.

I've managed to hide my abuse from my best friend for years. I've never let her step over the threshold of my house.

But now, tonight, that's going to change.

Tonight, Kim's coming to my house for my birthday.

And it's terrifying. But I'm ready.

My parents don't remember—or care—that it's my birthday, and, as luck would have it, they've gone out to dinner. "Gone to dinner" is code for "staying at the bar until it closes." Which is fine by me. By the time they come back, so drunk that they should never, ever have been allowed to get behind the wheel of a car, Kim will be long gone, and if they wake me up and beat me in their drunken stupors…well, my birthday will already be over. Technically, it will have been a mostly good day.

I can live with that.

I'm eighteen. I've already graduated. I need to get a shitty summer job, and then I need to go to college, get the hell out *of Dodge and never look back. I have full scholarships. Once I save up enough money to afford the security deposit on an apartment or the first semester of a dorm, I'll be set. I can live on ramen. I don't need luxuries.*

I'll do anything *to get out from under my parents' roof. I will work my ass off in the blistering heat. Whatever it takes.*

I am almost *free.*

And that almost-freedom is making me a little reckless.

This morning, on the way to school, I watched a butterfly land on a flower along the edge of the sidewalk, and I knew that it might be the only present I'd get, seeing this gorgeous creature up close. I wanted to grab my sketchbook and draw it right away. When I stared at that butterfly, I was filled with inspiration to paint.

I've been painting a lot lately because it soothes me, makes me feel something like happiness. My parents—with all of their anger and their bitter, jagged words—can't take that away from me. I should probably study business at college, something practical, but what I really want to do, what I want to do with my whole heart…is study art.

It's crazy, right? There's that joke that if you major in the arts, you're guaranteed to end up flipping burgers. But I don't believe that's true. My aunt Sandra went to college for creative writing, and she's an author now. Yeah, she has to work a second job, but she makes a nice living with her books.

I know I'm not a half-bad painter. I've gotten my art into sandwich shops and cafes here in town, and a couple of my paintings have even sold. I haven't told my parents about that, because they'd want a cut of the money, payment for "allowing" me to live in their house.

There's this hope rising inside of me, and it's pretty fierce. I want to be an artist. Right now, I'm tentatively going to major in computing. But the reason I chose UCLA is because of their art program.

Suddenly, I hear the doorbell ring, the tinny sound echoing through the empty house.

My heart in my throat, I race downstairs to open the door.

Kim's there.

She's got her platform sneakers on, her jeans tight at the hips, a peasant blouse baggy around her curves. The shirt is low cut enough to reveal the creamy tops of her breasts. I'm embarrassed that I notice that. I love everything about Kim—her heart, her humor, her loyalty and kindness and courage. But I love how she looks, too, and I'm eighteen, never been kissed. Stupid Jeffrey McKinley doesn't count; he copped a feel and kissed me without my permission at summer camp when I was thirteen. I punched him in the face.

Kim grins at me; she's hiding a helium balloon behind her back. Why she's holding it behind her back is beyond me, because it's pretty obvious that there's a bright pink balloon floating above her head. It has a princess crown on it, with the words "Birthday Princess" printed on the cardboard. I laugh, pointing at it, and she laughs, too, hugging me before handing me the balloon.

"I saw it, and it made me laugh so hard that I snorted Coke out of my nose, so I knew I had to get it for you." She moves into the foyer, looking around with wide eyes. "Wow. So this is where you live. Honestly, after all this time, I was kind of wondering if you were Batman or something, and lived in the Batcave, and that's why you had to keep it so secret."

I flush, twisting the balloon's ribbon around my fingers. "Nah. My folks have just been remodeling a lot," I say, wincing at the half-assed lie. "Do you like it?"

My parents have money, and they love to show off, so they never settle for less than the best. The foyer has a ridiculously expensive marble floor.

Kim nods, shoving her hands into her jeans pockets,

rocking her shoulders forward as she glances sidelong at me. "It's a'right," she says with a little smile. "But I really want to see your bedroom. I have a present to give you."

Tugging the balloon behind me like I'm five years old, I lead the way, and we ascend the staircase together. We're comfortable enough with each other that we don't have to fill the silence with chatter. Kim wasn't in school today—she had a doctor's appointment—so we should have a lot to talk about since we last saw each other. But I'm too nervous to talk... And, anyway, I can tell that Kim is plotting something. She has a mischievous smile on her face, brown eyes twinkling.

When we get into my bedroom, I close the door behind me. My palms are so sweaty. I let the balloon go, and it drifts up to the ceiling, gently bobbing, the ribbon dangling down over my shoulder.

"Very nice, very nice," says Kim, glancing around the room. She bounces on her heels, and I realize that her hand is, again, hidden behind her back.

She's biting her lip.

Wait—is she nervous?

Okay, now I'm a hell of a lot more nervous than I was before.

What surprise does she have planned?

Kim steps forward, and a strange expression sweeps over her features. She's looking at me like she pities me. As if I'm...pathetic.

"Mara, I'm really sorry," she says, though she doesn't look sorry. Her brows furrow together, and she wipes one hand on her thigh.

I hear the front door open and close downstairs.

My heart is pounding inside of me. Oh, no. Shit. Shit. *My parents are home, and there is no way that they should already be home unless something has gone terribly, terribly wrong. Maybe Mom got one of her migraines, and Dad had to take her* home, which will mean that Kim is going to have to meet my parents, and this whole damn thing is going to come crashing down around my head.

But I can hear footsteps now, and there are definitely more than two people climbing the staircase.

Heart skipping a beat, I blink, opening my bedroom door just a crack, raising a finger to Kim. Just a moment. I just have to see who's out in the hallway...

But it is my parents.

And...someone else.

I try to swallow, but my mouth has gone dry.

Jonah. He's been my youth pastor ever since I was a kid. My parents are pretty devout born-agains, and Jonah runs the youth group at our church.

What the hell is he doing here?

My father heads for my door, his eyes steely. I can feel my throat closing up. What's happening?

Kim's hand rests on my shoulder then, and it's so reassuring, so comforting that I turn toward her, needing her. Needing a friend more than anything, as my mother and father and youth pastor stare at me, their faces grim.

But Kim gives me that pitying look again, her mouth downturning at the corners. "I'm sorry, Mara." She pats my shoulder. "It's for your own good."

For.

Your.

Own.

Good.

I gape at Kim, my best friend, the only person in the world who knows I'm gay, and then my father is coming in, and mom and Jonah come in behind him, and all three nod to Kim.

As if they know her.

"What...what's going on?" I back up, my calves brushing against the bed.

There's nowhere to run.

"*Mara, I think you know what this is about,*" *says Jonah, and his face is pitying, too, as he clasps his Bible in front of him. Why did he bring a Bible? He looks like that priest from* The Exorcist—*so serious, stoic. But he's not a priest; he's a youth pastor.*

Why is he here?

"*No, I have no idea what's going on. Is this...is this about my birthday?*" *I ask desperately, hoping against hope. Maybe this is some weird, pathetic attempt at a birthday party. Are my parents actually trying to do something nice for me?*

No.

Not even close.

"*Mara, Kim has told us that you are a homosexual. That you have homosexual desires,*" *says Jonah, and his eyes take on a cool, hard cast. "So your parents have called me to take you to Camp Savior.*"

Camp Savior.

A gay conversion camp. Oh, my God.

I swallow around the dry lump in my throat, but I suddenly feel like I can't breathe. I stare at Kim, at Kim, the only person in the world who knew, the only person in the world I trusted enough to keep my secret.

She looks a little guilty as she stands there in my parents' shadow. But she doesn't say a word. She doesn't even look at me, only glances aside, out the window.

"*Kim told us, sweetie,*" *says my mother, the hard edge in her tone making the word "sweetie" sound like an expletive. "You're going to Camp Savior. Right now.*"

My heart is pounding against my rib cage. I'm staring at the four people gathered around me, looking at me as if I'm a freak of nature, a thing to be punished, pitied, remade.

And something inside of me just snaps.

"*No,*" *I whisper, my heart hammering so hard that*

there are stars blinking at the corners of my vision. I feel dizzy, lightheaded, as I stare at my mother, and for a brief moment, storm clouds flash behind her gaze. But she recovers quickly.

"What did you say?" she demands, her words so icy that they sting my ears.

I lick my lips, stand up a little straighter, legs shaking. I hope my long skirt hides the worst of my trembling. "No," I repeat, hands balling into fists. "I'm eighteen," I say, reveling in that word, having waited for this moment my entire life. "You can't make me go to gay conversion camp," I tell them. The truth. "There's nothing wrong with me," I add, my words so soft that I can barely hear them myself.

But I've said them.

And, finally, I believe them.

There's nothing wrong with me.

I take a step forward, pulse thundering, and I say it again, just one more time: "There's nothing wrong with me."

My whole life, I've believed what my parents told me. That I was less than. That I was deserving of their anger and their harm.

But I'm not. I'm not. I don't know how I know that. Maybe it's desperation. Maybe it's the fight-or-flight instinct, or something primal inside of me trying to stay alive.

Regardless, this truth fills me, fuels me.

There's nothing wrong with me.

"We thought you might say that, sweetheart," says Dad then, calling me a nickname he's never spoken before in his life. He hardly even uses my name. Mostly, he just calls me "worthless."

"Which is why," he goes on, clearing his throat, "we brought Pastor Jonah here. He's going to help us mediate this situation."

"We really want you to go, Mara," says Kim, and when I meet her eyes, there's a flicker of sadness there. "For your own *good."*

"*For my own good,*" *I repeat, the words falling, wooden, from my mouth.* "*No,*" *I say, and my voice is starting to rise, but I don't care.* "*I don't think it's for my own good. I think it's for my parents' good, who don't want to have a lesbian for a daughter.*"

"*We don't* have *a lesbian for a daughter,*" *my mother snarls.* "*We have a daughter who's confused and deviant, who needs to be fixed.*"

"*I don't* need to be fixed." *I push my shoulders back, curling my hands into fists.* "*I'm fine.*"

"*Mara,*" *says Jonah, using the cajoling tone he resorts to when he's begging the congregation for donations,* "*your parents know what's best for you.*"

I gape at him. I think about the concealer hiding my black eye. I think about the time my parents took me to the ER—because they were worried that the broken bone in my arm might turn gangrenous, not because they cared that I was in pain. I told the doctor that I'd tripped, and he believed me.

"*No, they don't,*" *I say firmly, quietly.*

They're the truest words I've ever spoken.

"*Mara, if you don't come with me to Camp Savior,*" *says Jonah, and again that maddening look of pity flits across his face,* "*your parents say that they'll have no choice but to disown you.*"

"*You'll have to leave,*" *my mother adds quickly, as if I'm too stupid to understand what Jonah meant.*

My parents are kicking me out of my home.

They want me to leave. Now. If I don't agree to get "fixed."

I stand motionless in my bedroom, with all of my familiar things around me. My paintings hanging on the walls. My old desk, scribbled on, painted on. My winged horse treasure box on my bedside table. This little room has held me since I was small, sheltered me as I sobbed, alone.

My parents stand before me, two people who have scarred me irrevocably, who never wanted me in the first place. My best friend stands before me, the girl I trusted with a soul-deep secret, only to now be betrayed.

How could I have ever imagined I loved her? How could I have trusted someone who could do this to me?

And there's Jonah. The guy who's preached about how homosexuality can be overcome. I only remember him talking about it once: he said that being gay is a choice. I was about thirteen at the time, and I knew he was wrong.

I'm gay, and that's just an essential part of my being. Unchangeable. Immutable. Essential.

"I'm not going," I whisper.

And it's the first decision of the rest of my life.

My father huffs, regarding me with glinting, unfeeling eyes. "You have twenty minutes to pack your things and get out," he says simply, and then he turns on his heel, leaving the room just as quickly as he entered it. My mother doesn't even look at me. She follows after my father, a small smile playing over her lips.

Jonah tries again. He steps forward, gripping his Bible tightly. I don't think he's ever been told no about conversion camp before. "Mara, you can't be serious. Think about what you're doing—"

"I only have twenty minutes," I tell him, my voice hoarse. "Please leave."

And, surprisingly, he does. He walks out of the room...

And I'm left alone with Kim.

"You told them." I look at her, squint at her, realizing that, after all of this time, I never really knew her at all.

She's staring back at me, her hands shoved deep into her pockets. "I care about you, Mara," she says softly. "Being gay… Man, you know how wrong that is. Don't you?"

A tear streaks over my cheek. "Just go."

Shoulders hunched forward, she walks out of my room, closing the door gently behind her.

I have twenty minutes—well, nineteen now—to gather up the remnants of my life that are precious to me before I leave my childhood home forever.

I'm going to be homeless, I'm going to be homeless, I'm going to be homeless *loops in my head as I stumble around my room, trying to stuff as much as I can into my battered suitcase. I've never gone on a trip with my parents, though they've taken plenty of trips without me. I found this suitcase on the roadside on trash day; I liked how vintage it looked. Baby blue, hard-case shell. It looks like something from the fifties, when women wore pretty dresses and went on great adventures in convertibles.*

I fill the suitcase with clothes. With a few favorite books. With my toiletries, my hands shaking as I press them into the case. I grab the money from beneath my mattress, the money I made on my artwork. The treasure box from my childhood with the winged horse on it.

And then I pick up the suitcase, glancing around the bedroom.

I leave everything else behind.

I walk down the staircase. Kim is already gone, but I can hear my parents and Jonah arguing in the kitchen. With a hard lump in my throat, I step into the kitchen, set the suitcase down on the floor. I look at my parents, and they fall silent. They stare at me, and I stare back at them.

This moment is crystallized: I'm waiting for my parents to say something to change all of this. Hoping, desperately, that—somehow—my whole life has been some sort of bad dream. That maybe I actually do *have parents who love me, who want the best for me.*

"Get out," my father says.

My mother turns so that her back is facing me as she takes a sip from her martini glass.

Only Jonah meets my gaze, his mouth opening and closing repeatedly, as if he's in shock.

I turn on my heel, I pick up my suitcase, and I walk out of my home forever.

I don't look back.

Chapter 10: Across the Universe

I stare at Cecile, unseeing, as the memory of that night washes over me in a single, cutting instant. My eyes prick with unshed tears, and I try to take deep, even breaths, but I'm panting with anxiety.

"I found you near Elmwood Avenue," murmurs Cecile, holding my gaze, squeezing my hand gently. "Six weeks after your parents kicked you out. You'd been living on the streets because you didn't want to use the money you had for a hotel room, for an apartment. You wanted to go to UCLA, and you knew you'd need your savings to get there."

I watch her carefully, still trying to gain control of my breathing. I don't remember much of those six weeks. Hardly anything, really. I remember stopping in the local YMCA to take a shower. I remember eating food from dumpsters. I remember getting sick, so sick, on the garbage cheeseburger that had been out in the open air for too long. I've blocked most of those memories out, probably for good reason.

"You walked up to me," I whisper, my voice breaking. "You asked me if I had a place to go. And I lied, told you I did, because I was worried you were a cop or something."

Cecile chuckles, glancing down at herself. She's always dressed like a glamorous hippie, and only a scared kid could mistake her for a cop: Cecile with her white hair in a pretty updo; flowery handmade skirt so long that it trailed on the ground like a queen's train.

But I *was* a scared kid. Newly eighteen. Homeless because her parents kicked her out for being something that she couldn't change.

I was so afraid—every moment. But Cecile gentled the terror in me that I would never be able to trust anyone again. Cecile saved me in more ways than I could ever articulate.

"And the rest, as they say, is history." Cecile squeezes my hand again, before letting me go. "I had a house in California. I took you to UCLA. I put you in contact with the right people."

"And I became the artist I'd always dreamed of being," I murmur to Cecile, gazing at her fondly. "You were there when no one else in the whole world cared about me." My eyes flood with tears. "You believed in me. For some reason, you picked me up out of the gutter and loved me unconditionally."

"But that's the easy part, doll. You're very easy to love." She pats my thigh affectionately before standing, stretching, her hands at the small of her back. She picks up her empty teacup. "I saw the diamond that you were, and I just gave you a little shine."

I inhale. "But...do you ever think about what would have happened if you *hadn't* found me?" I ask her, the familiar fear pressing down like a weight on my chest.

"No," says Cecile, "because I did find you. It's a waste of time to consider 'what ifs.'"

I stand up, and I start to pace, restless. "But if you *hadn't* found me that day," I go on, because of course *I've* thought about it, far too many times to count, "I would have stayed homeless. I would have had no way to get out to UCLA, way on the other side of the country. I could never, ever have afforded the bus *and* an apartment. I would have just stayed here in Buffalo. I'd probably have started working low-paying jobs, because it's all I would have been able to get. Maybe I would have started taking drugs. Maybe I would have ended up in a really dark, bad place. Maybe...maybe..." I gulp down air. "Maybe I wouldn't even be here anymore."

Cecile shifts uncomfortably, her eyes bright.

I swallow hard. "I don't know the paths *that* Mara took, the Mara you *didn't* find. I don't know what happened to her, the horrific life she ended up leading. But it scares me, Cecile—that I was that close."

She sets the china down, saucer and teacup clinking softly on the old table, before stepping forward and taking my hands. "I know you don't believe in fate, my darling girl. But it was fate that led me to you that day. *Fate*, the unavoidable, inescapable force," she murmurs fervently. "I knew you before I met you. I knew you were going to be like a daughter to me. That I'd love you with all of my heart, and that you'd fill the emptiness I had in my life...that I never knew how to fill.

"That's because it was *yours* to fill, with a love that is profound, the kind a daughter has for a mother. I gained the daughter I never had, you gained the mother you never had, and it all worked out because it was meant to," she says simply, certainly. "That's how love works, Mara. A perfect give and a perfect take." She gazes at me shrewdly now. "And what happened last night, my dear—that was fate, too."

"Cecile...the woman I brought home last night? Charaxus? She says she's from another *world*. She did... She did *magic*. Right in front of me. I feel like I don't understand anything anymore—"

"Mara." She searches my face. "A scientist cannot tell us how a person knows what another is thinking, or how, across time and space, two souls find one another. They can't tell us why a body is lighter after it passes. They can't tell us...so many things.

"You've been hurt in the past," she whispers, her eyes shining with tears. "But you need to see, you need to understand, that some things can*not* be explained. Some things just happen, are *meant* to happen. You and Charaxus found one another, and that is as it should be. Don't throw that gift away. You are never going to find it again."

I stand there, shaking—physically, emotionally.

You are never going to find it again.

Oh, my God...

"What did I do? Cecile." I grip her arm. "Cecile, what did I *do*? I told Charaxus that she should go. That...that I...we..." A tear, hot as boiling water, falls from my eye.

Then, I take a deep breath and sit back down on the futon.

And I tell Cecile the story of last night.

She listens intently. Occasionally, she asks a question, but mostly, Cecile just listens, because that's what Cecile does. When I'm done, she considers all I've told her thoughtfully, nodding. She doesn't seem to doubt a word of it. Of course, Cecile has never doubted me for as long as we've known one another. She takes everything that I say at face value, believing me utterly. That's...priceless.

"I did a tarot reading last night, you know. That's how I knew that she had come for you, your dream woman. Well, that and the storm," she says, inclining her head toward the window in her room. "Don't you know that storms bring magic?" There's no hint of teasing in her tone. "Storms are so powerful that they just can't help it. Magic naturally rises whenever a major storm breaks."

I think about this... Considering the events of last night, I am, frankly, open to believing anything is possible. Sighing, I regard Cecile with a pained expression. "All I know is that I've made the biggest mistake of my life. I..." Tears sting my eyes, blinding me. "I let her *go*."

"You were afraid," says Cecile, and her words are so soft. "You were afraid, and sometimes we can't think clearly when we're afraid. But you've done nothing irreparable, Mara."

"Haven't I?" I stare around Cecile's room with glazed eyes. "How can you know that? I have no idea how to find her. She left...two hours ago," I say, after glancing at the clock on the table by the door. "She could be anywhere by now."

"Do you honestly believe, Mara, that after crossing worlds to find one another, it would be impossible to find each other again—in the same *city*? My dear," she murmurs, giving me a warm smile, "I know it's hard for you, but try to have a little faith."

I look at Cecile, this woman who, *magically*, found me when I needed her most. And I realize that, throughout my life, I've been through some terrible things. But a lot of good things have happened to me, too.

Maybe…just maybe…

I shake my head, fear rearing up inside of my chest. "I don't know how to do that—have faith."

Cecile draws in a breath, as if she's about to tell me something, but instead, she rises, angling her head toward the door...listening. Then Cecile turns back to me with a sense of urgency, as if we're running out of time.

"Everyone has faith in something," she promises. "You have faith that the sun will rise. That gravity will prevent you from floating away. That there are terribly cruel people in this world and also very, very good people, too.

"For your whole life, my dear, Charaxus came to you in dreams. Last night, she came to you in real life. And she'll come to you again, because she must, because you two share a connection that the laws of nature must obey. Just believe in her, sweetheart. She *will* come back to you."

My fingers brush against the gold pendant at my throat, the pendant that has so many bad memories attached to it. My parents gave it to me; it's one of the only gifts they *ever* gave me.

And I wear it for all of the wrong reasons. Its existence makes me unhappy, reminds me of things I'd rather forget. I grimace now, fingers closing around the pendant, gathering my thoughts, about to respond to Cecile...

But then there's a knock at the door, a dull sound that echoes off of the metal walls. Cecile smiles, laying her finger across her nose as she winks at me, before crossing the room. She already knew someone was coming, even though there were no sounds from the hallway. Sometimes I wonder if Cecile, herself, is made of magic.

She's always known things, always had this uncanny sixth sense.

But as I stand, as Cecile opens the door to Toby, who's dressed to the nines in a plaid suit, Rod standing behind him in cut-off shorts and a t-shirt, holding a six-pack of beer, I wonder about what Cecile said. I wonder if Charaxus and I really do have a chance at happiness.

"We've got to get going now to snag a good spot by the stage," says Rod, checking his watch.

Then Toby and Rod both notice me, and their eyebrows lift. I've been crying; my face is probably a ruddy mess. I sniff a little, running my fingers over my eyes, self-conscious.

"Hey, Mara. Where's that hot lady from last night?" Toby asks, his voice soft, almost tender. "Are you...okay?"

"Charaxus is out right now, Toby—but she'll be back," Cecile states, answering for me, before glancing back over her shoulder. "Toby's right, doll. It's the opening night for *Macbeth*, and we don't want to be late for Miyoko's performance."

"Yeah... Of course." I stand up, tucking an errant curl behind my ear.

"Let's get going!" Toby says with a wide grin.

Chapter 11: Screw Your Courage to the Sticking Place

Nothing ever goes quite according to plan in the Ceres, and while Iris and Emily swore they'd meet up with us at Delaware Park, where the outdoor stage is set up, Cecile has to get changed…and I should put on something prettier, too. I obey glumly as Cecile shoos Rod, Toby, and me out of her room.

"I'll be quick," she promises. "We'll meet down in the common area, all right?"

"Yeah," I tell her quietly.

Then Toby grips my elbow, and he's leaning down toward me with a little grimace, adjusting his plaid bow tie. "Okay, you're *definitely* not dressed up enough for the *theater*," he observes dramatically. Rod is about to protest—he's wearing a t-shirt and jeans, after all—but Toby waves his hand, dismissing the opinion of his boyfriend, and all but drags me down the hallway, toward my bedroom.

"Now, I *know* there is something *seriously* wrong," he insists, after he's shut my bedroom door in his boyfriend's face. "Sweetheart," he calls to Rod, "just go downstairs and play Candy Crush on your phone for a minute! We need some time to ourselves!"

I hear Rod grumbling, but he, apparently, complies.

"Okay, *spill*," Toby demands, turning back to me, his hands on his hips, his mouth drawn into a thin line.

"Toby…" I stare at him, shaking my head. "You wouldn't believe me even if I told you."

"Fine. You don't have to tell your brother-in-arms anything you don't want to." He sniffs, as if his feelings are hurt, but then he holds up his hand. "However, I *do* remember your coming into our bedroom earlier and borrowing some of my clothes. So? Were you doing some sexy role-playing that required men's sweatpants?" He waggles his eyebrows, smirking, and I punch him in the arm—hard. But I guess it's not as hard as normal, because his joking subsides, and Toby stares at me with an expression of quiet expectation.

"Look, I need to change." I open my wardrobe, riffling through my summery dresses. But Toby catches my arm, spinning me back around a little more theatrically than necessary—but this *is* Toby, after all.

"I'll just weasel it out of Iris if you don't tell me yourself."

"Iris doesn't know anything about this."

His mouth falls open in shock. "Okay, now you *have* to tell me."

But I shake my head stubbornly—until he gives me the puppy-dog face.

Sammie, sprawled on my bedroom floor, is *also* giving me a puppy-dog face, but that's because Sammie is actually a dog and just has soulful eyes. And because I haven't fed him his vitamin treats yet today. I drag the box of treats out of the back of my closet and pop open the top of the box. Sammie trots over, his big claws scraping on the floor, and he sits down patiently, his big tail sweeping back and forth.

The thing is, we're pretty open with each other in the Ceres. Few things remain secrets for long. So as I toss Sammie a few dog biscuits, I begin to tell Toby the story of last night—abridged.

And, because Toby has been to a few Burning Man festivals and genuinely insists he was Elvis Presley in a past life, he believes my story, no questions asked.

"*Why* did you let her *go?*" Toby moans, slumping down onto my bed with his arms flung above his head.

I'm digging through my closet now, intent on finding my favorite black maxi dress, but at his question, I freeze in place, gripping the closet doors with white-knuckled hands.

I know why I let her go.

I let her go because, like Cecile said, I was afraid.

I *know* that. I know that in my bones.

I was afraid of experiencing something wonderful.

I was afraid of love, because love hurts. And my feelings for Charaxus are too strong; they make me feel vulnerable, my heart exposed...

I start to cry. Not loudly. I try not to make a sound. I only curve forward, sink down to the floor.

"I was so stupid." Quiet, quiet sobs rock my body; my heart feels as if it's been stabbed.

Toby leaps off of the bed and races across the room, wrapping his long, lanky arms around me, squeezing me with a profound gentleness that only makes me cry harder. "Oh, honey," he murmurs, as I hiccup sobs against his shoulder. "You know you're gonna find Charaxus again." He sounds fully convinced.

"God, this is the stupidest thing I've ever done."

Toby snorts at that, moving his hand in soothing circles over my back. "I'd like to point out that the *stupidest* thing you've ever done was try to walk that tightrope on Delaware after you got drunk at the Summer Solstice party last year." I can hear the grin in his voice.

Sighing heavily, I lean away from him, smiling a little in spite of myself. Toby always knows how to make me smile. "Yeah, and I got *halfway* across," I say defensively, but he's already gesturing up to the ceiling.

"And if I hadn't hooked that safety harness on you? They'd still be mopping you off of the pavement, young lady." After a few moments of mock sternness, his expression softens. "So, yeah, this is *not* the stupidest thing you've ever done. Because this? This is *fixable*," he tells me sagely.

I draw in a deep breath; my lungs ache.

Why do Cecile and Toby seem so certain that I'm going to see her again, and it's so difficult for me to fathom it? I feel as if I've made an irreversible mistake. But maybe that's it: I *always* believe that my mistakes are irreversible, that what I've done can't ever be repaired.

But the people who love me...they think I can fix anything.

I wish I had that kind of faith in myself.

Toby rises and offers a hand to me, helping me rise to my feet. "You've got this," he promises, opening the bottom drawer of my dresser and dragging out the black maxi dress that I was searching for. "And *voila*."

"How did you know—" I begin, but he holds

up a hand.

"Because you always wear black to plays—*and* I borrowed this dress for my drag performance last weekend." He shrugs his shoulders sheepishly. "Sorry, boo."

I pretend to groan. "Just *ask* me next time, you jerk." I move quickly into the bathroom, closing the door behind me. For sanity's sake, I need to stop thinking about Charaxus. I clear my throat, peel off my clothes, and toss them into a little pile. "Did you speak to Miyoko before she left?" I ask as I dive into the dress. God, we're going to be so *late* if I don't hurry. I can already hear Cecile's voice in the common area; she's ready to go, which means *I'm* the one holding us all up.

"So, here's the thing. We kind of have multiple crisises going on in the Ceres right now," Toby begins conversationally. "Wait—would that be 'crisises" or, like, 'criseese'? What's the plural of 'crisis'?"

"Don't ask me. I'm an artist," I smile, smoothing the dress over my hips.

"We'll go with 'crisises,'" he says flippantly.

I examine my hair in the mirror, and, judging it too messy to salvage, I attempt to pull it into a ponytail.

"Anyhoo," says Toby from the other side of the door, "Miyoko's *super* nervous. Before she headed out this afternoon, she was blathering on about how *Macbeth* is the most infamous Shakespeare play, and everyone's worried that something awful is going to happen on opening night. Like, something *tragic*. Have you ever done any research about the curse of *Macbeth*? Because she was telling me all of the stuff that's gone awry during performances over the centuries, and, seriously, Mara, that's some spooky shit."

I sigh, forcing a bobby pin into my hair. "There's no such thing as curses, Toby."

"Ha! Says the woman in love with a chick from another planet," he laughs. "I mean, how can you be so *myopic*?" he snorts.

I stare at my reflection, biting my lower lip.

Toby's right. But...it's hard to change your worldview in a day. I've always been the Scully to the rest of the world's Mulder. I would be the one on *Scooby-Doo* telling the gang that, no, a monster had nothing to do with the disturbance; it was just some idiot in a mask.

I just thought I knew how the universe operates. Up until yesterday, I'd been able to fit my experiences into neatly labeled boxes. But now... My boxes are overturned, and all of my hard-earned observations are blowing out the window.

And that's impossibly strange.

I open the bathroom door, and Toby's standing on the other side, his plaid-clad arms crossed over his chest, his brow raised triumphantly.

"You have the thinky face on," he points out. "What are you thinking about?"

"I think we're going to be late. And Miyoko really needs our support tonight. And there *are* no such things as curses." I hold up my hand before he can protest. *"But*...if enough people get nervous, then there's a *possibility* that something will go wrong. So we need to be there to support her. Let's go."

We all pile into my car (Sammie, too; there are all sorts of dogs getting their culture on at Shakespeare in the Park performances), and we head out onto the 190 toward Delaware Park. But as I drive along the water's edge and glance out at Lake Erie, my heart rises up into my throat.

There, along the horizon, over the water, is a dark cloud bank that flickers with ominous lightning.

Shakespeare in Delaware Park has been going on for thirty years now, and I've been to many of their summer productions. The troupe has a pretty strict rain-out policy: if it starts raining, they wait a little while to see if the sky clears up, but if there's a downpour, they cancel that night's performance.

The organization wants to do right by the actors—performing in the middle of a storm just isn't safe—so I understand, but I also know that Miyoko, along with the rest of the company, will be sorely disappointed if the first performance of *Macbeth* gets rained out.

I pull into an open parking space along Lincoln Parkway, and we all tumble out of my Beetle, stretching and then unloading the trunk. The stage is set up along the lake in Delaware Park, and it gets chilly at night, so we grab some blankets, pillows, and the lovely dinner picnic that Cecile packed earlier this afternoon. Rod and Cecile carry the picnic basket between them, and Toby and I struggle with the heaps of blankets and pillows. With Sammie's leash looped around my wrist, I follow my friends toward the hill.

It's imperative to arrive early on an opening night, because the people of Buffalo love these performances. The plays are free, after all, so a lot of cash-strapped students come, along with families and couples.

As we crest over the lip of the hill, we all, as a group, sigh.

It's five minutes until showtime…and the entire hill is full with spectators. We're going to have to spread our blankets along the treeline to the left, or out in no-man's land on the right, where we might (might, *might*) catch a glimpse of a performer...occasionally.

"This is crap," sighs Toby, voicing what we're all probably thinking.

"But it can't be helped," Cecile says brightly. "Let's just pick a spot, kids, get set up. I don't think Emily and Iris are here yet—"

"*Hey, guys!*" someone screams at the top of her lungs.

And there, right in front of center stage, is Emily. And she's lying spread-eagled on the grass, covering as much of the lawn as she physically can.

Cecile laughs, and we make our way down the hill, dropping our blankets around Emily, who grins at us cheekily before getting up.

It'll be a tight squeeze, but we've got the best seats on the lawn.

"You saved the day, darling," says Cecile, brushing a kiss upon Emily's cheek as Em flutters her eyelashes and deepens her grin.

"Hey, I went back to check on Miyoko, like, an hour ago. She's got a bad case of the nerves. Somebody else needs to see her before the performance starts and, like, give her a really tight hug...or maybe some weed."

Cecile gazes at Emily with raised eyebrows, and Emily shrugs, grinning.

"Hey, it'd relax her."

"Yes, but she needs all of her wits about her." Cecile purses her lips, and then she glances at me. "Mara, would you do the honors while we set up the picnic? Go tell her we're all wishing her luck." Cecile takes Sammie's leash from my hand and points down to the blanket; Sammie curls up companionably between Toby and Rod, who were about to make out. Rod laughs, tousling Sammie's ears, and then he feeds my dog a cracker, which Sammie munches on happily.

"Yeah, sure," I say, wandering back toward the trailer where all of the actors are currently waiting for the show to begin. I knock on the door, and an intern comes running at me, waving her arms, prepared to tell me that I'm not allowed back here, but Miyoko opens the door and pulls me up the last few steps, right into the trailer.

"Oh, my God," she whispers to me, her eyes wide, her lower lip quivering. "Mara, I have such a bad feeling!"

I look past Miyoko's shoulder to take in the rest of the inhabitants of the trailer. Miyoko has been in several productions with different theater companies here in Buffalo, and I've visited her backstage at most of them. And backstage, right before a performance, there's this atmosphere that you come to expect. The actors are high on adrenaline, and they go through their pre-show rituals—warming up, doing stretches, dancing and singing together; some crack jokes. There's always an air of joyous expectation, despite the nervous energy pumping through the performers' systems.

But here, tonight, it feels...different. Oh, the nervous energy is present, all right, but the actors are sitting in silent, tight-knit groups, or leaning alone against the walls, brooding.

No one, absolutely *no one,* is talking. And, to be honest, being surrounded by a bunch of normally extroverted, effervescent actors who have fallen as silent as the grave is a little unnerving.

"What's the matter?" I ask Miyoko, but she

shakes her head, puts her finger in front of her lips, and then she pushes me back out the door, following at my heels, though she has to go sideways to get down the steps in her hoop skirt. She shuts the door behind her, and then she glances up at the full hill anxiously.

"Big crowd?" she asks, folding her arms in front of herself.

I nod, mystified. "Why is everyone acting like they're at a funeral in there?" I gesture back toward the trailer. "Did something happen?"

"No! It's because of the *curse*," she whispers, her eyes as round as saucers. And because Miyoko is a really, *really* good actor, her pronunciation of the word *curse* sends a chill up my spine.

"There wasn't supposed to be rain tonight," she goes on, her chin quivering, "and there's *still* no report from any station that there's going to be a storm—but did you *see* what's brewing over the lake?"

"It's summer. Storms just...happen in the summer," I tell her in my most soothing tone, but she shakes her head so adamantly that some strands escape her perfect coiffure.

"We *all* feel it, Mara. Something really bad is about to go down."

She speaks with so much conviction that I can't help but wonder if she might be right. Stranger things have happened, after all...

Don't think about Charaxus.

I cross my arms over my chest, clear my throat.

"Mara, I'm scared."

"Listen, it's going to be fine." I gather Miyoko into a tight embrace, and she rests her chin on my shoulder for several moments, hugging me back.

"But what if it's not?"

I take a deep breath, drawing back from her and forcing a tight smile. "It's going to be *fine*," I repeat, feeling my heart rate skyrocket as my thoughts wander, again, to Charaxus...wondering if I'll ever see her again.

No, I *don't* know if anything's ever going to be fine again.

But I realize, as I gaze into Miyoko's anxious eyes, that maybe, just maybe, I do have some hope.

Hope is this intangible, fragile thing. I've often pushed it away from me, through pain, through grief. But somehow, tonight, as I soothe my friend, as I mull over the conversations of the day, a tiny seed of hope unfurls in the deepest, darkest, saddest parts of my heart.

"I believe in you," I tell Miyoko, which is perfectly true: I may not always believe in myself or have the most optimistic view of my life, but I sure as hell believe in my loved ones and their abilities to triumph. They are, each and every one of them, amazing, bright, passionate people, and Miyoko is going to be fantastic tonight. She's going to *shine* in one of the most powerful roles that Shakespeare ever wrote for a woman.

I take a step back, holding Miyoko out at arm's length. "You're a phenomenal actress," I tell her, as her jaw tightens and her chin trembles. "You've *got* this. Everything's going to be okay."

And that's when my dog starts barking.

Chapter 12: Only You

Any proud puppy parent can recognize his or her dog's bark, even in a crowd. And right now, I can hear Sammie—in his loud, deep baritone—barking his head off. "Crap—I've got to go," I tell Miyoko, stepping forward and giving her another hug before turning back toward the hill. "No more worrying, okay?"

"Okay," she smiles weakly, though the expression on her face tells me she's still anxious about the performance.

I blow her a kiss before racing back to the hill; I find the blanket where everyone's sitting—Iris has joined the group now—and Cecile hands me Sammie's leash with bewilderment in her eyes.

"He just won't sit still," she says, shaking her head. "Do you want to take him for a walk? Maybe he needs a potty break."

"Maybe he wants a hot dog," Toby suggests with a wide grin.

"I don't know..." I regard my restless dog worriedly. He isn't barking anymore, but he's panting hard, little bits of drool pooling from his tongue. Sammie doesn't normally act like this, even in a populated setting. He loves being around people.

I bend toward him, and he peers up at me with wide brown eyes—and then barks in my face.

It's an insistent bark. An urgent one.

"Okay, buddy, come on," I tell him, tugging on the leash and turning to edge out of the crowd, aiming for the top of the hill, where the park spreads out before us. And—if need be—there *is* a hot dog vendor up here. Toby was right: Sammie *really* likes hot dogs.

I notice right away that Sammie is acting strangely: he isn't sniffing the ground, and he's ignoring all of the people milling about, getting programs from the interns or buying t-shirts from the merchandise stand. Instead, his nose is thrust up into the air, and my gentle, docile dog is sniffing the wind...a little like a wolf.

The hairs on the back of my neck rise, because Sammie was acting out of character last night, too...when he pulled me toward the river—and Charaxus.

"What is it, baby?" I ask him, sinking down by his side. I want, so badly, for him to be tracking Charaxus... But when he dips his nose to the grass, pulls me toward a sapling, and lifts his leg, I sigh, hope disintegrating.

He just had to pee. None of this has anything to do with Charaxus.

"Hey, Mara?"

I'm so lost in my grief that it takes a moment for the guy's voice to register. Finally, I blink, shifting my gaze, and there, standing next to me, is Stan.

Stan and I have been friends for years. He's one of Buffalo's homeless; it was something that we bonded over when we first met. I was volunteering with Food Not Bombs every week, and whenever Stan showed up, he was always cheerful, despite his circumstances, and he gave the best hugs.

Stan's bisexual and the happiest guy you'd ever want to meet. Cecile has offered him a space in the Ceres, should he ever need it, but he likes to stick to himself, though he's spent a couple of nights in our grain elevator during the city's worst snowstorms.

Stan does a lot of odd jobs around Buffalo, but he loves making jewelry best of all. He used to be in the service, has PTSD, and he's told me that making jewelry really soothes him. He finds bits of broken glass, gravel, odd beads, and he strings them together on fishing line, or unravels thrown-away clothes for string. Everything he makes is dramatic and unique; I own a couple of his bracelets and wear them often.

"Hey, Stan!" I say, offering him a big grin and a quick embrace. He smells like cigarettes and Nag Champa. When I back away, he smiles at me, too. "Are you here for Shakespeare?" I ask with a wink, and he laughs at me, shaking his head as if I just asked him if he's the President.

"Hell, no. That bullshit's for yuppies," he says pleasantly, then opens up his cigar box and holds it out to me. "Hey, do you want to see what I have tonight?"

I gaze down at all of the different necklaces, bracelets and earrings that he carries around in his cigar box, the lot of them hopelessly tangled. I loop Sammie's leash on my wrist and start poking through the box, still feeling preoccupied and uneasy about, well, a lot of stuff, when my fingers brush up against a sharp edge.

"Ow," I mutter, then blink. And blink again.

Something inside of that cigar box is…glowing?

I move aside the tangle of necklaces, the threads and beads and natural fibers all twisted together, and there, on the very bottom of the cigar box…

My heart skips a beat.

Okay, I shouldn't leap to conclusions. I shouldn't assume that what I'm seeing is…

Could it be?

It's difficult for me to believe that *I* would find the shard. Charaxus' shard.. The means for her to return home.

But this piece of glass—raw and sharp—isn't behaving like a normal piece of glass. It's illuminated from within. Stan has done his best to wire-wrap it carefully, in order to dull the edges, but he left the long tip uncovered, and that's the part that pricked my finger.

There's a tiny cut on my fingertip; a drop of blood wells up.

I peer at Stan, stricken speechless. Can *he* see that the shard is glowing? Stan is standing beside me wearing one of his ear-to-ear smiles, acting as if everything is completely normal.

"Um…where did you get this piece, in particular, Stan—do you remember?" I ask him, acting nonchalant as I detangle the necklace from the others and dangle it in front of him. The shard of glass twinkles in the warm light of the setting sun.

He squints at it, his head tilted to one side as he tries to remember. "I'm sorry, Mara. I don't really know," he tells me with a shrug. "Why? Do you like that one?"

"Yeah." I rest the pendant on my palm, watching the light flicker over its surface, coalescing over the glass as if it's a magical object…which, I realize, my heart hammering…it *is*. Shit. *Shit*. I need to buy this from Stan, and—more importantly—I need to find Charaxus and give it to her.

The hairs on the back of my neck stand on end as the realization sinks in that Charaxus' brother, Charix, is also looking for this shard. I assume that he has magical abilities, like Charaxus, and wonder if he can sense when the shard glows. I wonder if it's calling to him right now...

I'm in over my head; I don't know how any of this works—but first thing's first.

"Okay," I say, offering Stan a small smile. "How much?"

"For you, Mara?" he asks, considering. "Eh— what would you give for it?"

Anything.

I take a deep breath, pat my empty pockets. A thin sheen of sweat breaks out over my face because I didn't bring my purse with me to Shakespeare in the Park. I was too preoccupied... I forgot it at home, with my wallet stuck inside of it.

I stare at Stan, stricken.

I can't ask him to just give it to me. The only way that Stan earns money (aside from sporadic odd jobs) is through the sales of his jewelry. But I don't have any cash to give him. I'm too panicked, worried that Charix might be on his way, might leap out from the bushes and slit poor Stan's throat in order to get the shard...

I need this shard, but I have nothing to give him in exchange.

Then I notice Stan's gaze lingering on the pendant at my neck.

"Oh," I whisper, feeling my face pale as I lift my hand, pressing my thumb and forefinger to the gold pendant.

It's gold—real gold. If Stan pawns it, he might

get twenty bucks, maybe even more, but the pendant he's selling to me is worth more than that, and I know it. It's Charaxus' ticket home, and that makes it priceless.

But this gold pendant it's all I have to trade.

I press my thumb against the back of the pendant so hard, I know it's leaving an imprint on my skin. I've held onto this stupid pendant for all of these years in this terrible, vain attempt to hold onto some part of my parents. Which is ridiculous, I know. Some small part of me has always hoped that they'd come back for me, that they would realize their error, realize that they love their gay daughter.

But I know they don't. Some parents just don't love their children, are anomalies of nature.

Mom and Dad are never going to be part of my life, and I've got to let them go; I've got to give up this last piece of them, in order to get the shard.

It's almost poetic, but it's still gut-wrenchingly hard to reach up, to undo the clasp at the back of my neck, to let the pendant fall into my palm. I hold it, dangling it from my fingers, the embedded diamond flashing in the dying light.

"I'll trade you?" My voice cracks. I clear my throat as I hold my hand out to Stan, the pendant whirling in the air as it hangs from its thin gold chain.

I watch the pendant, and I think of all of the pain and resentment I still hold inside because of my parents. God knows I've tried to let it go over the years, but it's been hard. They were my *parents*. And they betrayed me in every possible way.

Cecile's right.

I need to let it go. I need to let all of it go.

And the best way to do that is to give Stan the

pendant.

He frowns as he watches the necklace, his gaze flicking from the pendant back to my face. His grizzled jaw works back and forth, as if he's trying to figure out what to do. "I dunno, Mara," he says, sounding uncomfortable. "I'd feel pretty weird taking that from you. You always wear it."

"It's not my favorite," I say, and it's the truth. I *hate* this pendant. I hate how—when I look at myself in the mirror—I'm reminded of my parents. I hate that I haven't been able to free myself from the past.

I'm not stupid. I know that the pain will be part of me for the rest of my life, that getting rid of this pendant isn't going to heal the scars in my heart. But holding onto the pendant has symbolized my inability to move on.

I hold out the necklace, and when Stan hesitantly offers his hand, I let the thing fall into his palm.

"You take it, Stan—is it enough for the trade?" I ask, rocking back on my heels, gathering up the slack in Sammie's leash as Sammie sits beside me, thumping his tail as he gazes happily at Stan—who has been known to, on occasion, give Sammie treats.

Stan nods, holding out the shard to me; I take it from him with trembling fingers. Then I hiss out in pain when my fingers graze the glass: it's much too hot against my skin. What the hell?

I try to mask my surprise, mustering up a small smile. "Thank you, Stan," I mumble to him quietly, and then I'm turning away, pulse racing, as I stare down at the pendant in my palm.

Wait—was that a trick of the setting sun? But I turn again, toward the copse of trees nearest to me, and there it is again.

If I'm facing forward, pointed toward the rose garden and the Abraham Lincoln statue (Abe as a young guy, book spread in his lap), the shard doesn't glow as brightly. But when I turn to the side, toward the woods and the lake…it shines like a flashlight.

"You take care of yourself, Mara," Stan says, his voice sounding uncertain, and I glance over my shoulder: he looks worried about me.

"I will," I promise him, and then Sammie and I walk down the hill but away from the crowd in front of the stage; the play is about to begin. The music has changed from the generic, light classical they put on beforehand to the more robust soundtrack they composed specifically for the production.

The shard glows white-hot in my hand, brighter, brighter still. As if it's pointing me in a particular direction…

I have to follow it.

Recorded thunder rolls over the stage: the three witches are about to begin *Macbeth*. The first witch is whispering, her microphone crackling with creepiness as I duck down one of the jogging paths, into the woods along the lake, "When shall we three meet again, in thunder, lightning, or in rain?"

And then Sammie and I slip between the trees, and the noise from the stage fades.

Delaware Park is well maintained, expertly designed and groomed, so there aren't a lot of heavily wooded areas here, but there are enough that teenagers in the city love to hide in the trees to make out and smoke weed. The scent of pot hangs heavily in the air as Sammie and I creep along.

We pass a gaggle of teenagers who whisper

among themselves, one of the boys hiding a joint behind his back, and I cast them a sideways smile, shaking my head, as if to say, "Don't worry. I won't call the cops." They look pretty relieved.

Deeper into the woods we go. It would be gorgeous here if it weren't for the graffitied tree trunks and the beer bottles littering the ground. But, to be honest, I hardly notice those things as I tread steadily, the shard glowing ever brighter in my hand...

There's a rustling sound to my left.

I pause for a moment, my heart beating hard. I know the park is crowded right now, but my senses are on overdrive. Something moved in that dense thicket over there—more kids getting high?

Sammie's ears have perked up, and he lifts his nose to the air.

Then my dog begins to growl.

It's a low, deep, resonant sound that starts in his chest, and it really creeps me out. I watch him with anxiety, and then I glance down at the shard in my hand. None of the kids back there commented on the glowing thing I was holding, and neither did Stan, so I can only assume that other people can't see the light. What does that mean? As I wonder, turning to face the enormous thicket, the shard starts to burn even brighter.

I bite my lip, staring at the mess of nature. I'm not sure how to get in there, but that's the way the shard is telling me to go.

For one long moment, I wonder if I'm stark, raving mad. The shard is "telling" me to go into those bushes? Have I lost my grip on reality?

But how else can I explain any of this?

Maybe Cecile is right. Maybe there *are* no

coincidences; maybe some things are fated, meant to be.

I'm standing there on the twilit path in the woods in Delaware Park, holding onto a shard that shines in my hand. The thing is, I don't know for certain that this is the shard Charaxus was looking for, but it *feels* as if it is…and that's really weird for me. I've never felt anything mystical in my life…

Aside from the dreams I had about Charaxus. Those always seemed magical.

I push away my misgivings, draw in a deep breath, and tug Sammie toward the bushes. He gives me a , "You've got to be kidding me, Mom," expression as I push the leafy branches aside, tugging my big dog after me. "Sorry, buddy."

The branches snag at my hair, tangle in my clothes. I hear the hem of my dress tear, but I push on, deeper and deeper into what I'm starting to think of as a hedge. The shard glows like a star in my palm, whiting out my vision when I stare directly at it.

Now Sammie takes the lead, dragging me along, his leash taut and digging into my wrist. Since he's shorter than me, he can move through the less-dense areas more easily.

"Buddy, slow down," I say, but he doesn't let up; instead, he pulls even harder. I put my arm in front of my face to protect my eyes—

And then there are, suddenly, no more thorns, no more branches.

Lowering my arm, I stand a little straighter and glance around me. We're in a clearing, though it's not much of a clearing. The central tree is larger than the rest, probably a hundred years old. An oak tree. Like the other trees on the path beyond these bushes, this trunk is graffitied with some unrecognizable symbols in blue spray paint.

And Charaxus is tied to the tree with rope.

She's standing straight, the rope tight—too tight—around her shoulders and her waist, her hips, her thighs and calves; her arms are pinioned at her sides. She's staring at me with a shocked expression, silent—because rope is looped around her mouth, too. Her forehead is sweaty and creased, as if she's panicked, or in excruciatingly pain.

I gape at her, heart rising in my throat, horror moving through me...but the horror is quickly replaced by potent, powerful rage. I drag Sammie toward her, holding the shard in my hand as I examine the rope that's cutting into her mouth, affixing her head against the tree.

Charaxus' too-blue eyes look startled, urgent, haunted. I take in the blood dripping down from the sides of her mouth, painting her chin with garish red streaks.

A muffled sound comes from Charaxus' throat, then: she's trying to tell me something.

Suddenly, Sammie snarls, the fur on the back of his neck bristling as he spins around and stares at something behind us...

Sick with dread, I turn.

There's a man standing at the edge of the hedge, filling the space I made when I pushed through the bushes. He's wearing the same type of armor Charaxus wore when I found her in the river: black, heavy-looking, with spikes on the shoulders. But there are more spikes on his armor, the kind of spikes you might put on something that you're trying to warn people not to touch. He has spikes on his chest-piece, along the lower-arm guards, even on each one of his knees and the toes of his metal-plated boots. He's wearing a helmet with a long nose guard, and several spikes jut out of the helmet, too.

His skin is as pale as milk, and he's staring at me with narrowed brown eyes, his face twisted into a terrible grimace. There's a sword in his hand, pointed right at me. A sword with a black hilt and a wickedly glinting blade.

Shit.

I gulp down air, take a step backward, tugging Sammie with me. I wasn't prepared for this. Well, no one could be prepared for this, but...I can't think, can only reflect that here and now may be my last moment in this life. I'm going to die. This guy is going to kill me. Obviously. He doesn't look like the type of person who asks questions first.

The only advantage I have is the shard, still glittering in my hand. I hold it up to him, gripping it like a blade.

His dark eyes trail over my hand, and he's already laughing, as if this is the most hilarious sight he's seen in days...but then he stops short: he just realized what I'm holding.

His shrewd gaze travels up to my eyes again, and this time, a cunning expression crosses his face.

I think I just gave him an extra reason to kill me.

Oh, no.

Oh, *no.*

I shove Sammie behind me, because I'll be damned if this guy harms a *hair* on my dog's head. I still hold the shard out, as if it can somehow protect me, because I'm not going to leave. I've got to stand my ground, even if my knees are shaking, even if I feel like the earth is going to crumble beneath my feet.

I've got to be brave. For Charaxus.

I take a deep breath, and I lift my chin.

"What the fuck did you do to her?" I ask, my voice low, gruff.

The man, unsurprisingly, says nothing in response. Instead, he takes a few nonchalant steps toward me, as if he's walking down the aisle of the grocery store, looking for the bakery section. He turns his sword in easy circles, the hilt moving back and forth in his palm comfortably; he seems a little bored by the prospect of killing me.

Fear, cold as ice, trickles along my spine.

I'm going to die, but I have to save Charaxus first. She's worse off than me right now. And I've got to get Sammie out of here, get him somewhere safe… But even if I *could* elude this guy, are there other armored men with him? What if they're scouting all over the park? What if the people I care about are in danger, too?

I lift the shard higher, at the level of my heart, in a false show of bravado. "Let her go," I growl—or try to, but my words are the kind of trembling, high-pitched crap that might come out of a twelve-year-old boy's mouth when he's going through his voice change.

Of course, the man laughs at me. Well, he doesn't just laugh: he tips his head back, closes his eyes, and roars with amusement at my expense.

I'm no expert on combat or anything, but I *have* taken a couple of self-defense classes. And right now?

It's a golden opportunity.

The guy is laughing at me, carelessly distracted. I lick my dry lips. I don't have time to wonder whether his armor is thick, to wonder whether the chink I'm seeing, between his breast-plate and his abdomen-plate, has anything beneath it to shield him…

I just go for it.

I'm not a violent person. I've never done anything like this before. But when there's a sword-wielding guy threatening you, bound and determined to kill you and the woman you love (*and* your dog), this great big ball of anger fills you up. You know you're the only thing standing between your loved ones and certain death—and that's an indescribable motivator.

As I move toward the guy, holding the shard in my sweat-slick hand, snarling, my teeth bared, I think about Charaxus.

I love her.

I've loved her my whole life, unconditionally. She doesn't have to love me back. She doesn't have to do anything. She just has to be. I know she exists now. And that means everything.

And I'm not going to let this guy touch her.

The clearing is quite small, and the guy had already taken a few steps toward me, so it's only a matter of one, two, three steps, and then the shard is through the chink in his armor: it sinks into soft leather there, and beneath the leather, into flesh and bone.

The shard is long, and it punctures deep.

I gasp, startled by what I've done. I make eye contract with the guy—who stares at me, his face puzzled, his brows furrowed as if he's trying to figure something out, like a hard equation. But then I'm flying through the air, and I realize that the butt of his blade went into my stomach, and I'm falling against the trunk of a tree, the small of my back cracking so hard that the air is knocked out of my lungs.

I topple to the ground, gasping.

The man looks at the shard still protruding from his stomach, and he sighs, holding it gently between leather-clad thumb and forefinger. He hisses out in pain, but then he's wiping the bloody shard on the leather underside of his forearm, looping the chain over his belt.

There's a small amount of blood leaking from his abdomen...but that's it. When he whirls toward me with hatred on his face, I admit that I was pretty stupid to think that such a small injury could distract the guy from his quest. As I stare up at him from the leaf-littered ground, still trying to catch my breath, I realize this is it.

My last moment.

I brace myself. My body tenses up, and as he comes closer, I find my eyes focusing not on my assassin but, rather, just past him.

On Charaxus.

Her sky-blue eyes are full of pain, but there's also rage creasing her features... And as I hold her gaze, as the armored man takes the last step toward me, Charaxus' features soften. She looks at me, her eyes brimming with tears, with an expression of deep and profound love.

And that's enough. I know that she loves me, even though she can't say it.

I tense as the killer lifts the sword over his head, prepared to deliver a blow that's likely to slice my head off. I refuse to look at him; besides, icy fear freezes my muscles. I don't want to die, nobody wants to die, and I had *so much* to live for. This is horrifying, horrifying—will Sammie be safe? I can't see him; where did he go? Will Charaxus live? Will she ever get back home?

I blink at Charaxus, and a small measure of peace moves through me at the sight of her. I mouth the words: "I love you," and I hold her gaze, and I wait for the pain.

God, I hope there's something after this. I hope it's not just darkness. I hope I've been wrong all this time, that there's something to that nonsense about souls.

For the first time in my life, I hope there's a better place. I hope I'll have the chance to see Charaxus again.

I hope.

I can hardly breathe as the sword extends over my head, as it starts to streak down—

Sammie.

I had dropped Sammie's leash when I was plunging the shard into the man's stomach. I was hoping against hope that he would run away, find everyone back on the hill, stay safe.

But that's not what Sammie had in mind.

I hear the growl before I see my dog leaping into the air. And it's a barbaric growl, the kind that makes your instincts kick in, that makes your breath come short and fast. I break my gaze with Charaxus, and I'm watching in horror as Sammie flies, hurtling himself across the empty space between him and the armored man.

Sammie's going straight for the guy's throat.

I don't know how my dog knows that all of that armor is too tough for his teeth to sink into. Maybe he doesn't know; maybe he just realizes that a human's throat is a vulnerable place. I think every dog owner secretly believes that, if they got into a life-threatening situation, their loyal dog would come to their defense.

But Sammie is just a big, lovable goofball. There isn't a mean bone in his body...

Still, his teeth hit their mark and connect with the guy's neck. At the same time, the necklace loosens on the man's belt, and the shard falls, glittering, to the ground.

I crawl quickly, gasping, sobbing, scrabbling through the overgrown grass at my feet, searching for the shard. I find it, but my fingers also connect with something else.

Shit.

Yes.

Oh, my God...

The katana.

Whoever attacked Charaxus must have taken the katana away from her and just dropped it into the brush, like a piece of garbage. My fingers close around the familiar hilt, and I turn around on my knees, holding the katana up in front of me like a shield.

Sammie and the man are still locked in battle: my dog is growling, so low and rumbling that it sounds a little like thunder...

No, that *is* thunder, a peel of it rumbling along the horizon far away. I glance up, at the flicker of lightning that dances in the sky, and then I'm tripping to my feet, gripping the shard in one hand and the katana in the other.

Sammie's jaws are locked around the armored guy's throat, and the guy bangs Sammie up against a tree, trying to dislodge him. It doesn't work; Sammie stays put, so the guy slams him against the tree again, prying his jaws apart with strong, leather-gloved hands.

Sammie springs down to the ground and then darts forward, trying to bite the guy's leg, but he misses, because the man whirls around suddenly, coming for me, Sammie angry on his heels.

Okay. Final showdown.

There's Sammie, this guy, and me with the katana, and one of us has to die in order to end this nightmare. It's not going to be Sammie—I'll be damned if I let this son of a bitch hurt my dog—so it's either the man or me.

One of us is going to die.

One of us is going to die.

And as the guy barrels down on me, I stiffen my muscles, praying that somewhere in the back of my head is the knowledge from those self-defense classes that I can't fully remember…

He lunges, his sword angling toward me with the certainty of a head-on collision. I sidestep him, not because I remembered how to sidestep an attacker, but because, under pressure, that handy not-wanting-to-die instinct really *does* take over your body, even if you're in shock over what's happening…which I am.

I think the man assumed he was delivering my death blow, so he keeps barreling forward with the momentum, trying to pull up, trying to turn and swipe his sword across my middle…

And when he pivots, when he puts on the brakes…that's when Sammie catches up with him.

My dog rises onto his back legs and attacks the guy's jugular. Sammie's earlier bite had already injured him there, and now Sammie zeroes in on the same place, as if it's a bull's-eye.

I stumble forward, heart skittering in my chest as I watch Sammie dangling in midair. The man is tall, and Sammie's tall, too, when he stands up on his back legs, but the guy wrenches his neck away, causing

Sammie to swing through the air...

And that's when he brings the hilt down, between Sammie's shoulder blades.

My dog yelps, but he holds on, his jaws still gripping the man's throat as I realize the armored guy is about to sweep the blade of the sword down, right onto—or into—Sammie.

"Leave my dog alone, you asshole!" I scream, the words bubbling up from someplace bright and burning deep inside of me, and I swing the katana toward the seam in the armor where the chest plate and the abdomen plate connect.

The katana isn't a *real* katana (it's too cheap to even be called a katana, probably), and it's not especially sharp, but with enough force, something that's *sort* of sharp suddenly becomes really, *really* sharp.

I'm not aiming that well, but I don't have to. Because the guy is arching away from me, the gap in the armor, revealing the leather shirt beneath, plenty wide enough for the katana to sink in—and it does. The katana slides through the leather and his skin and hits his ribs with a sickening *thud* that I feel in my own bones.

I jerk the katana back, and the blade is sliding over his flesh at the exact same time that he's pulling away from *me*, and everything moves so quickly: I'm standing there, the katana dripping blood to the ground, the armored guy standing a few feet back, staring at me with this incredulous expression on his face, gripping the hole I just made in his body, and we both watch one another for a long, surreal moment, panting.

I feel as if the world has slowed, as if I'm moving through water... The armored man, gasping, circles me slowly, Sammie growling beside me, his shoulder pressed tight against my leg. I want to sink my fingers into his fur, want to tell him it's okay…but I know it's not okay, and so does my dog. We move together, the guy's expression shifting from one of shock to one of utter loathing.

He's so pissed, he's going to slice me open.

I lift the katana, and my hands aren't shaking anymore. Suddenly, I realize that my back is to Charaxus.

Charaxus. The reason I'm doing all of this.

Her.

I love her. I can't let her die. She's given me hope when I was hopeless, her dream the only constant in my life. When I was desperate and deeply alone, she was always there, if only in my dreams.

It was enough then to keep me going. It was enough to keep me trying to survive, to keep me *wanting* to survive, even during the darkest days.

So now, as my dog leans against my leg, loyal and loving, willing to fight for me no matter the cost, his heart so big and pure that it leaves me breathless—I make myself a vow.

I'm not going to die. Charaxus is not going to die. And Sammie is going to live to be a hundred and two (in dog years).

I face the man, whose neck and abdomen are streaming with blood, as he lifts his sword, gathering his strength, ugly thoughts distorting his face, twisting it into a cruel grimace.

He thrusts his sword forward. I sidestep it, twisting the katana up. The guy's strong and relentless, and when his sword bangs down onto the katana's blade, I feel the force of it travel into my nerves, my shoulders screaming from the strain.

This can't go on forever. *I* won't be able to take this forever.

From somewhere deep inside of me, something starts to rise. I parry the blade again with sheer, dumb luck (I am *not* a sword fighter; hell, I wield a *paintbrush*), and I decide that this is it. This is where I hope that sheer, dumb luck will see me through this.

My katana is still vibrating from his blow, and as the guy prepares for the final chop of his sword, ready to kill me and end this fight...I step forward, *toward* him.

And I push the shard, still wrapped tightly in my palm, *so* tightly that my palm is bleeding, into the hole I made in his stomach.

He groans, and his knees buckle. He's starting to fall forward, and his sword is descending, too. There's no time to move away; I'm hopelessly entangled with his limbs, and I can't let go of the shard...

This heat begins to pulse through my shoulder. I don't understand what it is, but it's instant, lancing...

I twist as I tear the shard out of his stomach.

Then I turn and glance at my shoulder.

Oh.

Oh.

There's so much blood.

I stumble toward Charaxus. I'm starting to see white dots at the corners of my vision. Half-blind, I use the shard on the rope that binds her hands.

Sammie's at my feet, quiet now, only panting. I'm trying to saw so hard through the rope that I don't realize I'm falling against Charaxus. The rope snaps away from the tree, and everything moves slowly as I stumble backward.

I didn't think he'd get me with his sword. I was doing so well, was so close...

I fall, lie on the ground, stare up at the sky through the tree's branches. From somewhere far away, I hear my name, and Sammie is licking my face, but I can hardly feel it.

"I love you," I tell Charaxus, a whisper. It felt important to say that. So important. It's my deepest truth.

All my life, I loved her. And now, in death, I love her, too.

I'm not afraid, I realize, closing my eyes.

I just hope I get to see her again.

I'll love her endlessly. Always.

Always.

Chapter 13: In that Heart Courage to Make Love Known

I can't see anything, only darkness, but I can still feel. I can feel the hopelessness of loss, the deep cavern of regret, swallowing me whole.

I don't want to die. I have too much to live for.

I want to keep painting. There are so many things I want to paint.

I have friends, people who love me.

I have her.

I want to live.

I want to live so badly that the longing starts to thrum through me, but there's nothing for me to fight against anymore. There's only me, and the feelings rising inside of me, like petals unfurling around a rose.

I'm alone now.

Gradually, I become aware that the sensation of loss is growing bigger, wider...or is it the loss? I don't know; I can't tell. Whatever this is, it's painful, and it's large, and it's tugging at me, pulling me, and there's nothing I can hold onto in this empty space...

So I go. I move forward.

Into more darkness.

And then...

I'm staring up at something, kind of like someone would stare up at a drive-in movie screen, their head tilted back to watch the moving images. But I'm not in front of a drive-in screen, not exactly…

Everything's strange: I don't know what I'm seeing. There isn't really a screen, because what I'm experiencing is bigger than me. Bigger than…everything.

I stare, and I try to focus.

There's a little girl. That's the first thing I make out.

She's small, maybe five years old, and she has long black hair that curls in waves over her back. She's pale. Incredibly pale.

I watch the girl lift her head, watch her wipe a bit of blood off of her chin with her sleeve, pain wrinkling her features.

Charaxus.

Somehow, I'm seeing Charaxus as a child.

"*Again*," someone commands in a low growl, and the little girl picks up a wooden sword. I realize now that she's wearing black leather armor, but no metal pieces. The guy across from her is holding up a wooden sword, too.

The side of her face is starting to puff up, her lip bleeding, blood leaking out of her nose. But she doesn't cry, doesn't pause. She positions herself, holding the sword at shoulder height.

The man comes toward her. He's three times her size, and when he brings down his sword, he holds nothing back. The sword strikes the back of her head, and she falls immediately, crumpling to the ground.

I see blood leaking through her hair. The cut on her scalp is bleeding profusely. But the guy lifts the wooden sword again. He's about to bring it down to the small of her back.

I know, *know*, it'll break her spine if it connects.

And it does connect. I hear the excruciating *crack* of her bones.

Her spine breaks, but the little girl lies there, and she doesn't make a *sound*. She's still conscious; I can see her face contorting into a terrible grimace, a gaping moan of…complete silence.

"Take her away," says the man standing above her, tossing the wooden sword beside her head, spitting down to the ground, right beside her.

Two men scurry forward, their heads bowed. When the man steps away from them, I notice a dark crown on his head, pushed back from his face.

Is he a king?

The little girl is carried away, and though the men carrying her are being as gentle as they can, one at her shoulders, the other at her feet, her face remains stuck in that contorted grimace. They take her through stone corridors, lanterns guttering along the walls, until they reach a whitewashed room. They lay her down on a bed, and then they disappear, fading into the background.

A woman, clad in white, approaches the bed and the little girl lying there, who seems to be incapable of moving. Is her spine severed? I stare in horror at the little girl, at the tears silently leaking out of the corners of her blue eyes.

The woman has jet black hair, just like the girl's, and her skin is pale, too, but there are curving tattoos moving up from her wrists, fading into her arms, the color of smoke.

"Be still, lovely girl," the woman says quietly, smoothing Charaxus' hair away from her forehead. Then the woman stands, pressing her palm to the top of the girl's head.

Light radiates from the woman, flowing down her arm, over her hand, pulsing: bright light that washes over the girl's body, spiraling until it sinks down into the bed beneath her and disappears.

Charaxus sits up, wincing, her hands at the small of her back.

"Why must this happen?" asks the woman then, crouching in front of Charaxus, preventing her from rising off of the bed. She rests her hands on Charaxus' knees, and she gazes up into the girl's face, her own expression perplexed, concerned. "He shouldn't do this to you."

"It is I who let this happen," says the little girl solemnly, gazing at the woman with unflinching blue eyes. "It is my fault. I must get better. Then father cannot break me."

The woman stands, folding her arms in front of her as the sick realization of what Charaxus just said sinks deeply into me.

The man who just broke her back…

That was her *father?*

What the *fuck?*

"You are too small and too young, sweetling," the woman soothes her, voice gentle. "*No* one your age is as skilled as you are. No one is as hardened or as graceful with the blade. That is enough. You must stop this foolishness. Stop asking your father to fight you. You cannot win. You are yet too small."

Charaxus gazes up at the woman, her long lashes dark against her skin. "Healer Alanna," says Charaxus then, so serious, "it was kind of you to heal me. Thank you. I am sorry you must. I will try to do better next time."

"Sweetling," says the woman, Alanna, reaching out and gripping the little girl's arm as she pushes off from the bed, standing on the stone floor and grimacing a little as she stretches.

Charaxus meets the woman's gaze, but she doesn't say anything, and—after a long moment of silence—Alanna drops Charaxus' arm.

"Sweetling," she repeats, and her voice is soft, quiet, "you must know that your father may kill you one day. You may be hurt so badly that the men will be unable to bring you to me in time for healing. And I don't think," she says, her jaw tightening, "that your father will be remorseful. You know he is a very hard man."

"Yes," says Charaxus, her voice thin. She shifts her gaze, staring straight ahead as she lifts her chin. She's so small, and in the soft light of the lanterns placed around the room, she appears very fragile, with her large eyes and white skin.

She bows low to Alanna. "Thank you, healer," the little girl says again, drawing in a deep breath. "I promise to do better next time."

"You shouldn't have to do better, Charaxus." Tears threaten to spill from the healer's eyes. But she blinks them back, folding her hands in front of her as she inclines her head toward Charaxus. "Stay safe, princess," she whispers with a long sigh.

Charaxus nods, and—limping—she leaves the room.

The image in front of me starts to warp, and I see many things all at once. Charaxus growing up, slowly but surely. Pain, so much pain, so much struggling and trying and falling down and getting back up again.

So much blood. So many broken bones, broken over and over again. The healer, Alanna, weeping as she heals Charaxus; I lose count how many times. She probably does, too.

It's a blur of sadness and despair, the hundreds of times that Charaxus faces off against her own father.

Now I see Charaxus on the back of a black horse. She's riding steadily along a path through the woods, and Charaxus looks more like the woman I know now—though younger, a teenager, maybe. Her face is already hardened, the frown lines well refined, but there's a softness to her eyes that hasn't been taken away yet.

It's fall: the leaves on the trees drift around her and her horse. There are mountains in the background, soaring above the trees, their austere, gray facades ascending toward the equally gray storm clouds brooding on the edge of the sky. I think Charaxus is high up on the slope of a mountain, actually, and—in the distance—nearly at the summit of one of the tallest mountains, steep and slick with snow, is a grim, gray castle with squat turrets. It looks pretty damn inhospitable. And cold. The place looks incredibly cold.

Charaxus' horse skids on the mud as they turn a corner, the hooves kicking up earth as it thunders along—but then Charaxus is pulling up fast, hard, the reins taut in her hand as she frowns, staring at the path ahead.

There are ten horses at the edge of the woods, mounted by riders wearing black armor just like hers.

The horse in the lead bears the only man without a helmet, and he grins as he stares across the distance between himself and Charaxus.

A few things occur to me all at once: That's not a *nice* grin. A bit deranged, actually. And...wow. He looks shockingly similar to Charaxus. This could only be her younger brother.

"Ho, sister!" calls Charix.

My gut reaction to this guy is that he talks and acts like a colossal asshole. I have instant revulsion for him. He pulls his own horse up short, and the horse's breath is coming out of its nose, fogging the air. It's a cold morning. "Where are you going?" he asks, his voice so haughty that it's nausea-inducing.

Charaxus says nothing, only gazes at the group of men guardedly, reaching forward and patting her horse's neck with a gloved hand, trying to calm it. The horse snorts, pawing the ground with a mighty hoof. There's tension crackling in the air as the siblings stare at one another.

"I heard father bested you again today," says Charix, rising up in his stirrups and standing in his saddle as he gazes smugly at his sister. "You fight him once a moon now. There's truly nothing more pathetic."

Charaxus, still, says nothing. She gazes between her horse's ears, her jaw set, her bright blue eyes flashing.

Charix glances back at his men, all of them shifting uncomfortably in their saddles, watching the one-sided exchange. The helmet of the man nearest to him boasts *five* spikes, as opposed to the three on the others' heads. I suppose that must mean this man is more important. A country that denotes rank with ugly-looking spikes... Not a place I'm eager to visit.

Five Spikes leans forward a little, clearing his throat. "Lord, the dignitaries from Vella will be arriving before the sun sets. We must go back to prepare for them."

Charix frowns, and his eyes are as dead as a doll's. "If the dignitaries came from Vella to see me, they will not mind waiting, will they?" he says almost sweetly to the man, who blanches but remains in place, his arm resting on the pommel of his saddle.

"Lord, dignitaries make—"

The man was bracing himself, and I suddenly understand why, because Charix reaches out, and as casually as you flick a mosquito from your arm, he brings his closed fist against the side of the man's helmet. The sound of the impact is deafening in the quiet of the woods. Somehow, the man stays in his saddle, but he bows low over his horse's withers and backs his horse up, away from Charix.

"They will wait," says Charix, with a wicked smile, before he turns back to confront his sister.

"Careful, brother," says Charaxus then, her voice that familiar, low growl. "Dignitaries kept waiting are more likely to start wars."

"War, sister?" Charix cocks his head and rises up in his stirrups again, his face taking on an even more sinister smile. "*War*," he murmurs, licking his lips, "is what I *live* for."

Charaxus shakes her head a little, and she urges her horse forward. I watch in shock as she squeezes her legs, giving her horse its head to start walking *toward* the group of men and not away from them.

This makes the guy that Charix clobbered nervous, obviously nervous; he leans toward Charix again, his voice pitched low. "Lord, we must return to the castle."

Charix turns in his saddle with a small shrug. "I

haven't gotten my training in today," he says to the man, rolling his shoulders back. "It'll be a fine warm-up for me to spar with my sister."

Charaxus flicks her gaze to her brother, and—much closer now, close enough that the horses are only a few feet apart—stops, sitting down in the saddle.

"How many times have I beaten you since the snows melted, sister?" asks Charix, grinning grotesquely. "And, pray tell, how many times have you beaten *me*?"

"I've not beaten you yet," says Charaxus, her voice steady. "But I will."

Something flickers across Charix's face: it comes and goes as quickly as a bird diving from the sky, and I almost miss it.

It's rage. Pure, incandescent rage.

And it seems vastly out of proportion. Charaxus answered him simply. Elegantly. *I've not beaten you yet, but I will.* Yet, for some reason, that string of words fired up his anger.

He's drawing his sword over his shoulder in one smooth, sweeping motion. The horse beneath him starts to dance in place, sweat breaking out on its glossy black neck as it tosses its head.

For Charaxus' part, she does nothing. Her sword remains where it is, in her scabbard, and she doesn't take her hands from her reins.

"Let me pass, brother," she says, flicking her gaze to him now, her bright blue eyes as steady as a star. "I have no quarrel with you."

"That's the problem, *Charaxus*," he snarls, spitting out her name like a curse. "I have a problem with *you*. It should have been just *me*. Just *me*," he bellows, beating his chest piece with a closed fist, the leather smacking against the metal. The rest of his men wince, and the man closest to him—Five Spikes— glances from Charix to Charaxus in a state of near panic.

Apparently the royal kids aren't supposed to be fighting like this.

But nothing is going to stop Charix. He goads his horse forward, scooping up the reins and swinging the sword in a rather clumsy arc toward Charaxus.

All Charaxus has to do to evade that sword is lean forward a little over her horse's neck, and she does, effortlessly, squeezing her right calf against her horse's belly, causing the horse to trot sideways, away from Charix.

It's easy to see that Charix has brute strength— and, I'm guessing, he's the type who doesn't always fight fair. But as I watch the two of them squaring off, both on horseback, I wonder why Charix has a history of beating her...

And then I see the other men drawing their swords. They edge their horses closer to Charaxus.

Oh.

That's how he does it.

Ten against one.

Those are impossible odds, even on the best of days, for the best of warriors.

Charaxus' neck stiffens, and her gaze flicks to the side, surveying the men gathering around her. She glares at her brother again, and her jaw sets. Hard.

And Charaxus reaches over her shoulder. With a *shing* of metal against metal, the blade leaves her sheath, the hilt held lightly, gracefully, in her leather-clad hand as she turns the weapon in the air, each movement effortless, the metal glittering in the afternoon's overcast light.

"Come fight me, brother," says Charaxus, holding her head high—but the words sound weary.

Within a matter of moments, Charix's men have overpowered Charaxus. She fought well—she was a maelstrom—but there's only so much you can do to stave off ten armed men before you're dragged off of your horse, before you're held back by your arms—your sword removed—and your brother stands before you, gloating.

Charix looks sickeningly smug, his lips pursed as he watches his sister, standing with quiet dignity between two men, her head still held high. A single drop of blood oozes from the cut he made on her mouth, tracing its way down her chin.

She didn't make a sound when his hilt struck her jaw. She bore the pain silently, like she does now, staring straight ahead, her blue eyes shining dangerously.

"Ah, but you're not defeated yet, I see," says Charix, throwing his sword into the ground, blade first. The sword sticks up, quivering from the force of his arm. He turns to the one man who remains mounted, the man with the five spikes on his helmet, his second in command.

"Oslo," says Charix almost companionably, grinning at the guy. "Can you come here? I require your services. As the wolf, if you please."

Oslo shifts uncomfortably, but he obeys.

I watch him dismount; I watch him say something soft to his horse. And then he takes off his helmet, placing it on the ground, and the metal pieces of his armor fall away...

And Oslo, dizzyingly fast, transforms into a

wolf.

Oh, my *God*.

He's a large gray wolf, and maybe I'd be a little more shocked about the werewolves-are-real thing if I hadn't already witnessed magic and come to realize that there are other worlds out there that I didn't know existed.

Still, it's pretty strange (and that's an understatement) to see his hands become massive paws, his hair grow long and gray. And then a mournful howl fills the air. A howl so sad, so aching, that it physically hurts to hear it.

"Now," says Charix, rocking back on his boot heels, folding his arms in front of him after gesturing to his sister, held tight by his men. "You must be hungry, my dear friend," says Charix, and he grins with more teeth than a wolf probably possesses. "So, feast."

I watch in horror.

Charix is telling that guy—that guy who transformed into a *wolf*—to maul his sister.

I remember what Alanna said to Charaxus: someday, there might come a time when Charaxus was so injured that her wounds would be beyond healing.

And then I remember Charaxus telling me that she doesn't like dogs, remember the deeply uncomfortable look on her face as she stepped back from Sammie. Sammie, who's just as big as a wolf, who looks a little like a wolf...if you squint.

Grief floods through me as the wolf pads forward, as he crouches, snarling, and springs toward Charaxus—Charaxus who is held, defenseless, an offering to a beast.

But Charaxus is not helpless, after all. And she is no offering. One moment, she's pinioned between the two men, and the next, she's wrenching free of their grip, rolling forward, grasping her sword from the ground. She holds the hilt tightly, and then she's turning, the blade shimmering in the air…

She points her sword at the wolf, but she faces Charix, her bright blue eyes full of menace. "Call him off, Charix," she spits, blood dripping from her chin. "*Now.*"

But Charix does no such thing. He raises a brow, as if somewhat intrigued by this development, but that's all he does.

The wolf, Oslo, snarls, snapping his jaws. And Charaxus does not move, though I can tell her body wanted to take a step back.

Finally, the wolf lunges.

And Charaxus brings up her sword.

It's sudden, bloody, and brutal, the way that the wolf is killed, and while Charaxus is standing there, blood pooling on the end of her sword, her face blank, unreadable, eyes wide, Charix stares at the remains of his second in command.

That's when Charix picks up the blade that he stuck into the ground. He snarls just as angrily as the wolf, and he's whirling, dancing with the sword, savagely advancing on his sister.

Charaxus gazes at him wearily, but there's a sharp shine to her eyes. She lifts up her blood-soaked blade, and then the two siblings are fighting hard, metal clanging against metal, the rest of his men watching, unable or unwilling to step in and aid their leader.

That's why what happens next is so surprising. Surprising and seemingly impossible, considering the fact Charix has pushed Charaxus up against the dead wolf's body, her boots sliding in the blood on the forest floor. Charaxus slips, but she uses it to kick Charix's feet out from under him, side-swiping them with her boot.

Her chest heaving for breath, she rises over him on her knees, her blade pointed at his throat as he lies, flat on the ground, his sword out of reach.

Charaxus has *won*.

Her brother glares at her with such hatred in his eyes, hatred that, I'm guessing, has been there all of their lives. He has always hated her, every moment.

Charix hates almost everything.

But he hates his sister the most.

I watch as Charaxus stares down the blade of her sword, and—in that moment—I feel everything that she's feeling. The pain and despair, the inability to understand why her brother has always despised her. Furo, their country, is patriarchal, and her brother will ascend to the throne when her father is gone. She has never posed a threat to him, and yet, from an early age, she knew that he loathed her, loathed the sight of her, and she could never grasp why.

Her parents were endlessly hard on her. Her father fought her daily, trying to make her stronger, always wondering whether she was too weak to survive in Furo, wondering whether she was too weak to be his daughter. She learned that she had to fight in order to survive. She learned that she had to be *brutal* to survive.

And she's tired of it. She's so tired of it. Tired of the blood spilled, of the rampant hatred and negativity seething inside every person within Furo's borders. Those from Furo pride themselves on being better than everyone else—tougher, braver, more bloodthirsty.

That's nothing to be proud of, she thinks. And

anger is not the same thing as bravery.

Charaxus steps away from her brother. She wipes the blade of her sword on her leather-clad arm, and she leaps up onto her horse. She turns the horse's head, the reins gripped a little too tightly in her hands. The horse pulls at the bit, and Charaxus leans forward in the saddle, urging her mount on.

Charix stands, spitting blood down onto the forest path. They both know that this is a turning point, a moment that will forever alter their lives.

"I'm leaving," Charaxus tells her brother. And he doesn't say a thing in response. He wipes the back of his arm over his mouth, and he spits again as Charaxus coaxes her horse down the path at a stiff gallop, the horse's hooves pounding, each step drawing Charaxus farther away from a place that has never loved her, a family that has never loved her, a brother who has always loathed her.

Away. She's leaving. She's finally *leaving*.

And she does not look back.

I watch this, releasing a breath I didn't realize I'd been holding, and then the picture warps again.

I see flashing scenes: the moment that Charaxus rode into Arktos City. She had listened to her parents speak derisively of Arktos all of her life, so she couldn't *wait* to journey there one day. But she had imagined it as a very different place: full of kind, compassionate women who would immediately accept her.

And while it's apparent that the women here are kind to one another, they have no room in their hearts for a child of Furo, the country they openly despise, that they've warred with in the past. There hasn't been a war with Furo in years, but hatred burns long, and it's hard to extinguish the fires of prejudice.

Charaxus moves through her life in a haze of pain. She joins the Knight Academy, and she is the best, but none of her fellow knights embrace her. They are a sisterhood, a passionate sisterhood, loyal to one another in every respect, but they shun Charaxus because she is from Furo.

I take in all of this in the blink of an eye, and in the blink of an eye, I feel all of Charaxus' heartache, this deep need to belong…while knowing she never will.

And, each night, she dreams. She dreams of a woman with wavy red-gold hair, the hair of a lioness, with a sideways smile, with paint on her fingertips, on her nose. Charaxus is in the water with her, the stars shining on the surface, creating the illusion that they are floating not in water but in space. Together.

She dreams of this woman, and though everything in her life urges her to give up hope…

She doesn't.

Charaxus never gives up hope.

Because of me.

Chapter 14: Come What Come May

I'm cold. The coldness is tingly, numbing, a little like peppermint, and encompassing my entire body.

Suddenly, I gasp, opening my eyes, and I swallow a little water. It tastes like algae—that's the first thing I notice—and I'm spitting it out, but that tiny motion makes a bright fire ignite in my shoulder, and then I'm blinking, gasping, moaning, because my shoulder is burning, burning, ablaze…

Fire… Why do I think everything's on fire—my skin, my bones, my muscles, inside and out?

Wait, no. Not fire.

Light.

I blink, and I realize that everything I am is brightness: everything surrounding me is brightness, my body going supernova… I must be in the middle of a star, but I'm not burning anymore. The star isn't hot, only light. And I'm not in any pain.

Someone is gazing down at me, someone very close. I stare up at Charaxus, Charaxus who is holding me in her arms, who is staring down at me with tears in her eyes, tears that remain unshed until she catches my gaze, holds it. And then, one by one, silver tears stream from her ice blue eyes, trace themselves over her cheeks. And she holds me closely, carefully, cradling me with profound tenderness as I take deep, even breaths and try to figure out why I'm not dead.

I thought I was dead.

What…just happened?

I don't know, can't possibly know, so I whisper to her, "Charaxus...did I die?"

She gazes at me in surprise, and she laughs a little, a low, throaty laugh. She sounds so deeply relieved that tears spring to the corners of my eyes. I breathe out, and breathing is easy, even though I know it shouldn't be. The sword sliced through my shoulder, invaded my lungs. There was so much power behind that strike.

"What's happening?" I whisper to Charaxus, who is glowing with light. She looks like an angel, light streaming from her face, her pale skin almost translucent.

"I don't know. I brought you to the water to wash your wound," says Charaxus, and her words come out choked. I watch her face, watch the anguish that crosses over it before she gazes into my eyes and her face reverts to tranquillity once more. "I brought you into the water," she whispers, "and light came up when I healed you. Like it did when I healed myself last night."

Last night.

Was it really only last night that we met?

No.

Because we've known each other our whole lives, bringing one another hope, faith, courage when we, alone, had none.

I stare up at Charaxus, my arms loose around her neck, and I feel it, feel it beginning in my toes and filling me like water fills a vessel, warm and right and everlasting.

Love.

I love her. My whole life I've been searching for her, and I found her. I finally found her.

The light pulses around us, as bright as the heart of a star, and I rise up, lift my chin, my mouth finding hers easily. I close my eyes, the sensation of the kiss moving through me, the warmth of her mouth, the softness of her lips—God, how soft they are... The heat of them suffuses me with a profound sense of surety. Yes. I am alive. Yes. She is alive. Yes. We are together.

I'm cold, I realize suddenly, because I'm in the water. A fish brushes past my foot, and I open my eyes, glancing around me. Charaxus is holding me in her arms, one arm nestled beneath my knees, the other around my back and shoulder, and I'm buoyant, floating in the middle of a pool of light.

It's so surreal: I gaze at Charaxus, at that calm, beautiful smile, and I feel, in that moment, as if every puzzle piece of my life has finally fallen into place. Every loose end that's ever troubled me, every moment of pain and pleasure, has finally come around full circle.

Because, as Charaxus supports me in the water, as I stare up at the light surrounding her, I realize this is it.

This is *the* moment.

This is *the* dream I've been having my whole life. We're living it. Right now.

It's actually *happening*.

I...can't begin to tell you how *weird* that thought is.

I think the realization is dawning upon Charaxus, too, as she watches me. Once she senses that I can hold myself up, she lets my legs float down into the water. We both tread quietly, our arms hovering on the surface, our legs moving in the darkness below. Light still radiates around us, washing over our skin.

"Is this real?" I whisper, and she nods once, twice, her mouth set into a soft line, her blue eyes sparkling with stars.

"This is it," she says, her head tilted to one side as she examines my expression. Her gaze softens, and her lips turn up at the corners. She moves closer, her breasts pressing against mine, one arm wrapping tightly, securely, around my waist.

I breathe out slowly, glancing back toward the land. We're not that far out, and there's no one else around. There are usually joggers who come by, and from here, I can see the Scajaquada Expressway, its cars flashing past. The lull of the night traffic is soft, almost like a lullaby.

We're together. Alone.

Alive.

Relief floods through me, along with the acceptance that this is the moment we've both dreamed of. It feels as if a ritual is about to be performed, like a wedding or a ceremony, something that will change our lives forever, and the weight of that is strange, but there's a lightness, too: knowing that we have no idea what's going to happen after this.

That's true of every moment in life, and I've been fine with that fact up until now.

I push away from Charaxus a little, swimming backward with a little kick, glancing down at my shoulder "You healed my wound?" I ask her, and she nods, her eyes darkening as she watches me.

"Well," I say, searching for the right words.

This is such an important time. The gravity of the situation is compounded by the fact that—after losing one another in the rush of the world—we found each other again. My mistake wasn't permanent.

Charaxus watches me, her chest rising and falling in the water. She's still wearing the clothes I gave her this morning, Toby's shirt, the sweatpants underneath.

And here's the thing about our dream: we weren't wearing *anything* in the water.

I think she realizes that at the exact same moment that I do, because she's laughing as I reach the shallows, as I shimmy out of the sopping-wet black dress, tossing it onto the shore.

Outside of this moment, there is so much waiting for us. Outside of this moment, there is the weight of the armored man's death. My dog, Sammie, waits for us on the shore, wagging his tail and panting at me as I peel my bra off, too, and my panties, tossing the water-logged garments on top of my dripping dress. I ruffle his ears, getting Sammie's head all wet, and then I wade back into the water, the chill sluicing over my legs until I'm deep enough to swim back out to Charaxus.

The light that had been glowing around us has subsided, and all that's left is the moon and countless stars.

I take a deep breath, and I gaze at Charaxus. My hands are on top of the water, and I move them back and forth as Charaxus comes closer to me, wrapping an arm around my waist again. I shiver at her heat, as her body bumps gently against mine.

"You're still dressed," I tell her with a small smile, and she's chuckling, lifting the shirt over her head, bobbing low as she wrestles with it. I'm laughing, too—maybe some of it is shock. A *lot* of it is relief. But we're both weak with laughter as I help Charaxus out of her clothes, and then we toss them into the shallows.

We fall into solemn silence now as we watch one another—waiting, watching…breathing.

"I love you." I'm breathless, swallowing, so nervous suddenly. I've told my friends that I loved them before. I've told Cecile. But I've never told anyone else, because it was never true. I've never loved anyone, not like this.

And Charaxus lifts her chin. She fixes me in her beautiful blue sights. And she draws closer to me, letting herself drop into the water, letting her chin submerge, her eyes flashing, her lips level with the surface.

"I know," she murmurs, and she drifts closer, her long black mane streaking out into the water behind her like night descending onto the earth. "And I love you," she murmurs; her arms come around me. I'm holding her up in the water, then, as her legs wrap around me, too.

She kisses my neck, her mouth so hot against my cold skin. The stars twinkle overhead, and her hair is submerged in the water. I see that the stars are caught up in her dark strands…

I gasp as her teeth find my skin, as her long fingers trail down the front of my body, as they move over me. We're both so aware of the fact that this moment has been foretold, and that—within it—we are limitless. It feels like we're dancing in the water, a dance we've practiced for our entire lives.

A dance that has the power to change us both.

"Wait," I whisper to her, and I'm not laughing now; neither of us are.

Charaxus waits. She rises higher, her hair dripping down on either side of her face, the stars reflected in the glossy black depths of it. I cock my head, reach up with my wet hand and trace my palm over her cheek. She closes her eyes, breathes out, and she moves her face into my hand.

"When I was little," I tell her, and emotions rise in me, potent and painful, and I finally let them. I swallow, and I hold her gaze, and she holds mine, her brow furrowing gently with sympathy. "When I was little," I repeat, lifting my chin, "this was my only safe space. This dream."

"Me, too," Charaxus whispers.

We're silent for a long moment. The stars overhead move quietly, and the world spins, and the moment stretches out, sustaining us both.

"My parents kicked me out of the house for being gay," I say then, and the words are soft, but that doesn't make the truth of them any less hard. "For loving women," I say then, searching her face. "I was eighteen. It was my eighteenth birthday. They told me to leave. I was homeless."

Pain floods Charaxus' features. Anger follows soon afterward, but the pain remains, and when she gathers me into her arms, I press my cheek against her shoulder and try my best not to weep.

But I cry. I cry for the little girl I was, hoping and praying that my parents would love me—knowing that they could not. I cry for the teenager who was pushed out into the streets because of who she was, something she couldn't change, a part of her that went deeper than her bones. I cry for the teenager who lived on the streets, who was helped by kind people, yes, but who still went through horrors...

I cry for the girl who was so, so alone.

Alone...except for my dreams.

"I'm here," Charaxus tells me then, and I feel those words deeply. The heat of her skin pressed against mine, the pulse of her heartbeat, the warmth of her body, her caress, her kiss, her mouth soft against the top of my head—I feel everything, but most of all, I feel those words: *I'm here.*

She's here.

"I'm sorry." She holds me close, cradling me so tenderly, and I hold her, too, grip her tightly. We float in the water together. "I'm sorry," she repeats, and she clears her voice, keeps talking. "They should have loved you for who you were," she says. "They didn't deserve you. But I'm sorry."

Tears pour down my cheeks. All of the pain, all of the sadness, seems to be pouring out of me, too, rolling away with each tear. The warmth of her, the tenderness and compassion of her...it's healing.

"I'm not like this," says Charaxus then, and she moves away from me just a little so that she can gaze into my face. Her jaw is working—she's searching for the right words—and she clears her throat, too, her voice coming out strained. "I'm not like...this," she says, and she breathes out. "At least, not around others. I am... I am formal. Perhaps...unkind. Sharp," she says, grimacing around the word. "I left my father's kingdom when I was a young woman. I traveled to Arktos, where I joined the Knight Academy. But they did not care for a woman from Furo joining their ranks. They shunned me."

"I know," I say. "I saw."

Her dark brows rise, perplexed.

"I don't know *how* I saw it, but when I was unconscious, I saw your past. I saw you fighting your father. And your brother." I swallow, heart aching, as horror flits across her face.

"You…saw?" she whispers.

And then the horror is replaced by shame.

I know shame. Shame can strangle you. Shame nestles inside of you so deeply, you begin to wonder whether your whole being is essentially worthless. Whether you are wholly unlovable.

I cup Charaxus' cheeks. "No," I whisper then, and the word is firm. "Please…please understand that everything that happened to you—it was wrong. Just as my parents should have loved me," I growl to her fiercely, "your parents should have loved *you*. You were just a little girl, and you were put through hell."

"I see it in your eyes," she whispers back. "You have suffered, too."

"Our suffering was different," I tell her, voice shaking. "But we both suffered, yes. And we can't go back in time, and we can't erase our scars. They are embedded in us too deeply."

Charaxus watches me carefully, her blue gaze pained.

"But you are beautiful," I tell her. "You are *beautiful,* and your scars do not define you. Your courage does."

Charaxus breathes out. And when she speaks to me then, her voice is small. "I am not courageous."

"You're here." I draw her to me, I wrap my arms tightly around her, and I hold her close. "You survived it," I whisper into her ear. "You survived all of it. And *that* makes you courageous."

When Charaxus meets my gaze now, there are tears in her eyes, but her jaw is tense. "Then you must know that you are courageous, too."

My heart flutters inside of me.

I've never felt courageous. Not when I stood on the streets, wondering where I was going to sleep that night.

But Charaxus wouldn't lie; I listen to her. And then I say, "We both are." And she nods solemnly.

We float together in the water, our limbs moving quietly. The stars spin overhead, and beneath them, we exist in a moment that's stolen from time, a moment that is built inside of our hearts. Eventually, Charaxus backs away from me, and she lifts her right hand out of the water. She brushes the hair back from her face, and then she unloops the cord that's tight around her wrist, dangling it from her fingers.

She holds the shard's necklace out to me, the moonlight reflecting brightly off of the sharp little mirror.

"One last thing is missing," says Charaxus softly, and her lips turn up at the corners, though her eyes are so sad. We both know that this dream is ending, that we'll have to confront the real world soon.

I tilt my head. "What's missing?"

"The star at your throat," she murmurs, and then she's reaching up, tying the necklace around my neck, her warm fingers lingering against my skin.

The shard winks brightly against my chest; I reach up, pressing my thumb and forefinger to it, breathing out slowly.

In the dream, Charaxus always saw *this* pendant. Not the one I traded to Stan. I lift my eyes, hold her gaze.

This is impossible. *She* is impossible.

But she's here, nevertheless.

"Charaxus," I whisper, my tongue tasting the syllables.

Something hangs in the air around us, something heavy. Suddenly, I feel as if I'm gasping for air. I don't want to let this moment go, don't want to let her go…

"Charaxus—"

Then the world takes us back, devouring us in one bite.

Because a scream ripples across the water.

And it's coming from the Shakespeare in the Park stage.

Chapter 15: Blood Will Have Blood

Lightning flickers as Charaxus and I move in the water, looking in the direction of the stage. We can't see the stage, but now we hear an uproar from the crowd, dozens of voices raised in surprise—or panic.

"We've got to go," I whisper to Charaxus, and there's a tremor in my voice. I see pain etched on her face, too: neither of us wants to leave this moment.

But we must.

We hold hands as we ascend out of the water, staggering as the buoyancy of the lake is replaced by the gravity of land. Charaxus helps me up onto the beach, and then we're throwing on our dripping-wet clothes as quickly as we can, Sammie whining unhappily at my feet, thumping his tail with hope as he gazes at me with big brown eyes, clearly worried. There's something ominous hanging in the air; I think all of us can feel it.

"It's okay, buddy," I whisper to him, grabbing his leash, though I have no idea if it's okay or not.

After Charaxus picks up the katana from the ground, we break into a trot, aiming for the stage. And as we get closer, I hear a man's voice raised in anger… The voice sounds a little familiar, and when I glance at Charaxus, see the tension in her muscles, the anger flashing in her eyes, I know where I heard that voice before.

It belongs to Charix. Her brother.

"Charaxus," he bellows, the sound echoing on the loudspeakers. The people in the crowd have fallen silent now, deathly silent. We haven't rounded the corner of the path, can't yet see the audience. The stillness of the night is strange. It's almost as if the play is continuing, though we know it's not.

"Charaxus!" Charix bellows again, and I can hear metal clanging against metal. "Come out and face me! I know you are here!"

It's the last part that makes me bristle, gets under my skin, because Charix doesn't sound angry; he sounds *smug*.

Charaxus shakes her head at me, lifts her hand, fingers curling around my shoulder gently as she coaxes me to pause. We've reached the back of the stage, and now I can see audience members fanned out around the front of the stage, seated on blankets—some of them standing—their hands raised to their mouths. They all look quietly horrified as they stare at something onstage with wide, worried eyes.

Anguished, Charaxus says, "You must stay here, Mara." Her blue eyes search my face, her expression grim.

"I'm not letting you go out there alone."

She works her jaw, preparing to say something else, but she finally sighs, as if she realizes that it's futile to argue. She takes the cord that the shard is dangling from around my neck, and she lifts it up, peeling back the top of my sopping wet dress. She lets the shard dangle down between the cloth and my skin, then, and she lets go.

"Don't let him see this," she murmurs, and I nod, swallowing.

And then, hand in hand, we walk around the

stage.

The first thing I notice is that there are several people on the stage who shouldn't be there. They stand out starkly because they're all wearing black armor, armor like Charaxus wore, like the guy in the woods wore. They have their helmet face plates lowered, and they're spread out in a semicircle around the man standing in the middle of the stage.

That's Charix.

I remember him from the dream/vision/whatever-the-hell-that-was, when I thought I had died. He's similar in height and bone structure to Charaxus: high cheekbones, noble nose. But that's where the similarities end. Because Charaxus' eyes are bright blue, and Charix's are dark, and while her eyes can be soft and kind, there's nothing but cruelty in Charix's gaze.

It's obvious, just by looking at him, that this guy is an asshole, and I think everyone in the crowd can sense that. He's standing in the dead center of his men—his knights, I'm assuming. They have their swords drawn, and they're staring out into the crowd, probably searching for Charaxus.

But Charix has more leverage than just haughty demands.

Because Charix is gripping tightly to Miyoko.

She's standing there in front of him in her Lady Macbeth dress, and though he's twisted her arm behind her back, her face isn't contorted in pain. Instead, she looks pissed. Her back is snug against his front, and his sword is raised, positioned at her throat.

When he sees us moving around from the back of the stage, his shrewd eyes narrow. He isn't looking at Charaxus, though; he's looking at me. I hold my head high, and despite the fact that my whole body is trembling, I keep up with Charaxus' pace. We must look so strange: dripping wet, our long hair draping around our faces.

Heart hammering, I catch Miyoko's gaze. She looks beautiful, defiant, and the anger doesn't leave her face as she looks at me...but there's a flicker of something that only I would notice, and only because I've known her for so long.

She's putting on a tough front, as she tends to do—but she's afraid.

Shit. The curse. The curse of the opening night of *Macbeth*.

Yeah, I'd guess that being held at sword-point by an evil guy from another world qualifies as something going wrong.

"Charix, let the woman go," says Charaxus then, holding up the katana. She moves her fingers easily from the hilt to the blade, and she offers the weapon to Charix. It's a gesture of goodwill, of surrender—he's too far away to actually take the blade—but that doesn't stop him from tightening his grip on Miyoko and pressing his own sword harder against her throat.

"I know you have it, sister," says Charix, growling out the words. "Give me the portal key."

Portal key? Is that what this shard is? I can feel the weight of the pendant against my breastbone, and I take a deep breath, squeezing Charaxus' hand.

"What's the plan here?" I whisper to her softly. She flicks her gaze to me and shrugs infinitesimally.

Oh, great.

No plan, then.

That...can't be good.

"Brother, let the woman go," Charaxus repeats, and her voice is sterner now. Everyone in the audience is watching us, is watching the stage; no one stirs or makes a sound.

God, I really hope someone dialed 911. That would throw a wrench into Charix's plans. I mean, police with guns against a deranged guy with a sword—how hard would it be to defeat him?

Oh, wait.

I forgot about magic.

And that's exactly what Charix uses now. He reaches out, and despite the distance between himself and his sister, he pulls the katana out of her grasp. The katana swings through the air, end over end, to embed itself, blade first, into the wooden stage, the hilt quivering back and forth as it settles.

"Give me the portal key," says Charix, his head to the side. "You will die, of course, sister, but I might spare this woman. And that one," he says, and his evil gaze flicks from Charaxus…to me.

When I say "evil" gaze, you have to understand, this guy looks completely unhinged. Like he kills a dozen people before breakfast, and hopes he gets a new torture machine for Christmas. He looks like what actors *hope* to look like when they're filming a new serial killer movie.

Yeah, he's got the evil thing down pat.

Charix presses his blade against Miyoko's neck, and a tiny, hairline cut appears. Miyoko doesn't react, not even a little—she's pretty badass—but I can tell by the stiffening of her back that the wound really hurts, and was more than a little upsetting to her. Beside me, Charaxus tenses; she knows that we have to get Miyoko away from him sooner rather than later.

Then I'm stepping forward, clearing my throat.

"We have the shard," I say, and I lift my chin. "The portal key. Let her go, and we'll give it to you. We're unarmed," I say, gripping Sammie's leash tighter as my dog growls.

"Do you think me a fool?" asks Charix. He cocks his head to the side and smiles the smile of a guy who's about to eat an entire pizza and enjoy the hell out of it. "Give me the shard now, *or* I'll slice her throat now."

And he tightens his grip on his sword.

Heart in my throat, I reach up, yanking the cord around my neck, breaking it. I lift the shard, the glass glowing in the stage lights. I don't say anything. I simply hold the shard out and take a step forward. Sammie glances up at me, and he whines once, twice, before following behind.

I can see Cecile in the audience, Toby and Rod and Emily, Iris. They're all staring at me, horrified, but they don't intervene as I ascend the steps leading onto the stage. Behind me, I feel Charaxus' powerful presence, but she hasn't moved, has raised her hands in the air, level with her shoulders, a gesture of surrender.

"Let her go," I tell Charix quietly, calmly, holding out the shard to him.

Charaxus didn't have a plan, and I certainly don't have one, either. I just know that I need to get Miyoko away from this asshole *stat*.

I peer out at everyone from the Ceres because I notice a movement among them, and it draws my eyes.

Charix isn't moving. He's gazing at the shard in my hand, and his eyes are narrowing, zeroing in. But Toby...Toby's standing up on the blanket. He's shaking—I can see that he's shaking—and he's lifting something up.

"Hey, asshole!" he shouts then.

Charix looks—of course he'd answer to "asshole"—and then Toby grins at him, the kind of grin that he used to give the boys in the clubs before he settled down with Rod: fetching and adorable.

"Strike a pose!" he shouts, and he lifts up his phone, the thing he was holding in his hand, and he takes a picture.

His phone's flash goes off.

A few things happen at once. I realize that I have a small window of opportunity. I realize that Charix is probably not going to let go of Miyoko unless she's dead. And I realize that Charaxus is far behind me; I'm the only one who can do this.

I drop Sammie's leash, and I leap forward. I hit Miyoko square in the stomach with my shoulder, and it's enough to dislodge her from Charix's grasp. For his part, Charix is blinking rapidly, unsettled—for half a heartbeat.

Miyoko moves quickly, so quickly that you'd never imagine she was wearing a heavy costume. She flies off of the stage and onto the blanket, into Cecile's arms.

But I don't get away fast enough.

Charix recovers from the flash, and even though Toby is still taking pictures, Charix grabs me, pinioning my arms behind my back at the exact same moment that someone from the crowd—Cecile, I realize—is grabbing Sammie's leash so that he can't go after any of the knights himself.

Thank God. My dog is safe.

But me?

Not so much.

I stand there with Charix pressed behind me, and all I feel is utter revulsion. He's not like his sister at all. He's enjoying the fact that this *hurts,* the way he's pulling my arms behind my back. I don't make a sound, because I'm not going to give this bastard any sort of satisfaction. Not even when he holds his sword against my neck, as he did with Miyoko. Guess he's a one-trick pony when it comes to restraining hostages.

He looks out at Charaxus, Charaxus who is standing there in the middle of the crowd, her face pale as she lowers her hands to her sides, her mouth open just a little as she stares at me in Charix's arms.

Her brother takes the shard from my hand, tossing it to one of his lackeys.

The guy catches it, and that's it.

Charix has the shard.

And…he has me.

I gulp down air, meeting Charaxus' gaze. She hasn't removed her eyes from me, though she has schooled her features to be blank, serene.

"Well, sister," says Charix, and by his tone, I can tell that he's smiling. "Who is *this* pretty thing?" he asks, enunciating each word. He sniffs at my hair, like a wolf sniffs its prey.

"Brother," says Charaxus carefully, "be warned." Her hands are curled into fists now, and she's taken a step forward.

I can *feel* Charix's grin deepen. He laughs, a low, deep rumble, the kind of laugh a poker player makes when he's about to reveal his perfect hand. He tightens the sword at my throat. "She dies," he says, as casually as if he's commenting on the weather. "Be clear, Charaxus." He spits out her name as though it's the most vile expletive. "She dies because you love her."

And it's obvious—obvious as Charaxus takes another step forward, as she locks eyes with me—that, yes, Charaxus loves me.

And Charix hates her. So he hates anything that she loves.

He's going to kill me.

It seems obscene to die in front of so many people. I hope that my death won't traumatize the kids in the audience (or, you know, the adults). At least Miyoko is safe.

I lock eyes with Charaxus, tense, and I struggle against Charix's hold on my arms, even though it hurts, my shoulders screaming in protest, my wrists crying out in agony. I'm not going to go down without a fight. I'm not going to stand here like a lamb led to slaughter.

Then, just like that, my odds shift: Charaxus takes two running leaps, and she's standing right beside me. She pulls out the katana from the stage, and she hits her brother on the face with the butt of the weapon—*hard*.

I'm shocked that he wasn't expecting this. Maybe he was paying too much attention to me and my struggles. I wrest my arms out of his grasp and leap off the stage; Cecile and Toby and Rod and Iris and Emily gather me into an enormous group hug.

And before us, on the stage, Charaxus and Charix square off against one another.

"Sir," says one of the armored men, stepping forward. He's got the shard, and he's holding it up to Charix, clearing his throat nervously. "Sir, we should go. We don't have to fight this traitor."

Traitor, because she left a country that had no use for her. *Traitor,* because she wanted to go someplace where she felt like she belonged.

Charaxus is no traitor.

Her *family* betrayed her.

"Better run home, brother," she says, and she hefts the katana with a small smile. "Wouldn't want your sister to best you. Again."

Charix is snarling. Was it really just yesterday that Charaxus and Charix were fighting one another, right before she appeared in the Buffalo River? That battle may have been left unfinished, but in truth, it's been unfinished for all of their lives.

Charaxus and Charix have been engaged in a lifelong fight, wrestling with their destinies, their inheritance, their fate.

As brother and sister begin to circle one another, stepping artfully, expertly, it's clear that Charaxus does not hate him. There's pain in her eyes as she studies him, as she follows each move that he makes. I doubt that Charaxus is capable of hating anyone. I know I'm biased, but after everything that Charix has put her through…she really ought to hate him. And she doesn't.

Charix steps forward now, and he makes the first move, lunging at her with his sword.

From somewhere far away, I hear sirens…

God, the cops *are* coming. This is going to be awfully hard to explain. But if they arrive in time, maybe no blood will be shed. Maybe—

No. Charix leaps forward, and with a single flick of his wrist, he draws blood from Charaxus' cheek, a thin slice across her cheekbone bleeding brightly onto her pale skin.

She doesn't flinch, simply keeps up her pace, gracefully placing one foot beside the other as she moves across the stage, the katana held to the side, its blade flashing.

Cecile grips my hands, and I risk a glance away from the fight to meet her eyes.

"Mara," she whispers to me, squeezing my palms. She doesn't say anything else, just holds me tightly, as we watch what's happening on the stage.

I've never felt so helpless in my life.

Charaxus doesn't *need* me up there—my presence would only cause more problems for her—but it's awful to stay down here, watching her swordfight her brother.

This isn't a warm-up or a practice.

This is a matter of life and death.

It's Charaxus who steps forward just then, raising the katana. The thing isn't very sharp, and I'm sure she knows this. There can be nothing elegant in the way she thrusts forward if she expects to draw blood: she must be direct, concise in her swing. And she is. It's still graceful, the way the blade shimmers through the air as she darts forward, as fast as light.

But, of course, Charix grew up cheating; there isn't a world in which he would fight fair. As Charaxus aims for her brother, the katana before her, Charix's men rush in from the sides and surround her. She has to change her trajectory, swinging the blade in a wide arc to fend off the armored men.

Her blade whizzes through the air, whistling sharply, but it only keeps the men at bay. Charaxus steps back, away from her brother, her bare heels at the very edge of the stage as Charix lifts his chin, his eyes flashing triumphantly.

"You always lose," he says then, cocking his head. "That's what you do. You lose, dear sister." The *dear* is spat out, and then he does spit, his spittle landing on the floor of the stage, right beside Charaxus' feet.

But Charaxus doesn't rise to his childish bait.

I watch her move, her long legs lean, flexing; she's a predator, hunting a man who mirrors her, though there's such a difference in their fighting styles.

I remember seeing Charaxus as a child, falling again and again beneath her father's sword—and rising again and again.

As I watch Charix take a step back, wielding his sword like a club, I wonder what his early life was like. I only glimpsed it when I saw Charaxus' past. I wonder how much training he underwent? I wonder how many privileges he enjoyed, simply for being the son his father wanted?

As I watch Charaxus stalk him over the stage, twisting the cheap katana in front in her hands, I know that I'm watching poetry in motion when I look at her.

And Charix can mimic, sure, but he's no match for Charaxus, not in hand-to-hand combat.

They both know it.

"Get her," commands Charix then, lifting up his sword in a shielding gesture, the blade in front of his face. The men rush around Charaxus, ready to disarm her.

"No!" I shout, as Charix takes the shard from his underling. He peers down at the necklace, and then he glances up at Charaxus with a snarl.

"We're leaving this pathetic world," he says, glancing around at all of us with disdain, as if he doesn't have the time of day for Earth. And the feeling is mutual. But as Charix's men close in around Charaxus, I realize that this is the end. Charaxus is going back to Agrotera...with this *asshole*.

There are too many of them, only one of her.

They'll surely kill her if I don't do something to stop them.

Thunder rumbles, and lightning flickers overhead, a spider web of light. The sky been threatening rain all evening, and now the clouds are swollen with rain; they want to release a deluge…but they're waiting.

I remember what Cecile told me earlier today—that storms and magic go hand in hand.

Charaxus stands on the stage, Charix's goons surrounding her, and she looks at me. Her long black hair—already drying—is swept over her shoulder; her t-shirt and sweatpants are soggy, practically falling off of her long, lean body, the muscles in her stomach, in her arms, clearly visible as she lifts the katana, as she gazes over her shoulder at me, her bright blue eyes quiet, calm, resolute.

She's beautiful. She's amazing. She's everything I've ever dreamed of—*literally*.

And I'll be *damned* if I'm letting her get away.

Not like this.

Not by force.

No.

I press Sammie's leash into Cecile's hand, and then I'm climbing onto the stage. My heart is in my throat; I'm utterly defenseless. I have no weapons, and when Charaxus turns to see what I'm doing, there's searing pain in her eyes. She was happy to know that I was safe, and now I'm not, because I've done something stupid: I'm on the stage with Charix and his men, and that means that horrible things could happen to me.

But I'm not going to stand by and do nothing. I can't.

I'm not going to leave her to suffer alone.

Charix laughs at the sight of me. It's not even a big laugh, only a small, amused chuckle. He knows I don't pose any threat. But Charix's men have stopped rushing Charaxus; they've turned, watching their leader, waiting for his command.

I step beside Charaxus, stand with her, glancing up at her.

"What are you doing? Why did you come up here?" she asks quietly, her katana still raised. "You could be hurt, Mara," she tells me, and her voice is so tender that I reach out and rest my fingers on her arm, cherishing the heat of her skin.

I draw in a deep breath. "I won't lose you—not like this." I offer her a small smile, taking another deep breath and lifting my chin. "You're not alone."

She stares at me, blue eyes wide, her lips slightly parted. "What...did you say?"

"You are not alone." I curl my fingers around her arm. Love crests through me, like a wave rising up, covering the shore. I love her, and—in this moment—nothing else matters.

Just her.

Just us.

As I grip her arm, I feel it before I see it: this great pulse of love that moves through me... But what's weird is that it's not just love. It's *light*, light like the light we experienced in the hospital, light like what happened at the lake, washing over the both of us. Light so bright that my eyes are dazzled; I use my free hand to try to shield my eyes. But the light is coming from everywhere, and even when I close my eyes, I see it.

"What's happening?" I ask Charaxus, and I feel

her hand on my forearm.

She draws me to her, places her chin on the top of my head, holding me close. The warmth of her body radiates through me, and as I wrap my arms around her waist, I hear another *crack* of thunder overhead.

The sky erupts.

One moment, the clouds are full, laden with water, black and brooding far, far overhead, blotting out the stars and moon. And the next, lightning seems to slash them open, pouring water down onto the world below. The stage lights flicker and go out as the power surges and then gets completely cut off; we're all plunged into darkness.

But...there's still light, the light that spirals around Charaxus and me.

Light that's emanating from the shard in Charix's goon's hand.

Charaxus holds me close, and as the light spirals around us, I close my eyes tightly. I think about what happened in the hospital, how she asked me to lend her my energy. I don't have any idea how this works, or even if that's what is happening now...but it feels right to try, so that's what I do. I concentrate hard on all of the places Charaxus is touching me, and I imagine my energy like light, pouring out of me and into her.

I imagine us blending together, merging.

Even though we don't have the shard in our hands, it begins to glow brighter. It ascends up into the air, a little like the star did when Charaxus created magic for me, and then it begins to twirl gently, bobbing up and down, as if it's floating on a river.

Rain pours over us in buckets, the water oddly warm. But everything else seems to fade away as I stare up at Charaxus, meeting her intense gaze.

I feel whole as the light pulses around us. Not devoid of scars—because I will always have scars—and not devoid of pain…but filled entirely with love. My anger and my hardness gently washes away as Charaxus holds me close, as she bends her beautiful face to mine, as she tenderly brushes her mouth against my cheek.

I am filled with love, and through love, I'm made whole.

From somewhere far away—but what is actually close by—I hear a roar of rage. As if he's plodding through quicksand, Charix is trying to make his way across the stage to reach us. He has his sword raised over his head.

But, suddenly, he's motionless.

The light strobes, and I feel more and more of my own energy feeding into Charaxus.

"Is this magic?" I whisper, looking around us at the rain, at the light that's turning the raindrops into prisms.

"Yes," Charaxus whispers back, and we watch as the shard moves through the air until it's as high as Charaxus' head, and then it spins much faster. "It's…it's happening. The shard is responding to us. To both of us," Charaxus murmurs, peering down at me. "I'm going home."

And she should sound relieved, euphoric. She is, after all, going *home*. Home is where everyone wants to go, to be. All roads lead there, and so much of our hearts belong where we hang our hats.

But as I stare up at her, I realize that things have shifted for me.

Because home is no longer a place.

It's her.

She's my home.

And she's leaving.

"How will I…" I swallow my tears, and I grip her tightly, feeling her heartbeat beneath my fingertips, feeling the pulse in her skin and knowing I'm no longer the same. It's been twenty-four hours, this romance…but it was a lifetime in the making.

And I'm changed forever because of it.

"Please," I whisper to her, as the shard drops a line of light to the ground, as the line begins to expand into a wide circle, as it begins to pull on Charix's men, dragging them through the portal. "Please find me," I tell her, tears streaming down my cheeks as I feel Charaxus' feet edging across the wood, the portal pulling her away.

"I will find you," she promises, her hand gripping me so tightly, her fingers strong, insistent, as she searches my gaze. "I am not lost…wherever I am. I must always come home," she whispers, her voice catching. "I must always come home to you."

"I love you," I tell her, but Charix's bellow of rage drowns out my words. He's being pulled through the portal. And so is Charaxus.

"I love you!" I tell her again, and I say it again and again and again as she's drawn away from me, her fingers slipping through mine. She holds my gaze, doesn't ever glance away, until she's drawn through the ring of light.

They're all gone.

Charaxus is gone.

The shard of glass stops glowing and falls to the stage floor with a dull clatter.

It's just a broken bit of glass.

I drop to my knees, sobbing, as the rain pours over me.

Chapter 16: Not Lost

Cecile steps back from the painting and glances at me, one brow raised. "Is it straight, doll?"

I chuckle, shaking my head. "Why are you asking the lesbian?"

"Oh, right. Toby, is this straight enough—oh, what am I thinking?" Cecile laughs. Behind us, Toby snickers and draws Rod in for a kiss.

I press my hands to my small of my back and stretch. The Burchfield Penney museum is hosting my first art show, and a lot of volunteers showed up to help me hang my paintings. Tonight's the grand opening, and I needed to hang the last few canvases, so, of course, everyone from the Ceres stepped up to assist me. And, of course, there's pizza in store for all of us. They don't call me the pizza queen for nothing.

Speaking of which… I gaze down at my phone before sliding it back into my jeans pocket. "I've got to go pick up the 'za," I tell everyone, and they nod, though Iris dances over, doing a pirouette in front of me in her purple-and-black tutu—which is, she informed me earlier, her painting-hanging uniform.

"Hey, before you peace out, where do you want the last canvas?" she asks.

I glance back at the only framed painting still leaning against a support column, and I take a deep breath.

It's been months now, but it still feels so tender, this healing scar over my heart. I haven't stopped believing in her. And I never will.

"That's the focal piece," I tell Iris, and I offer her a soft smile. "It's what the whole show is based on: 'She was the storm.'"

It's the painting that I did of Charaxus when she was with me in my bedroom. She's naked, holding a sword, and though that sounds like an '80s-era fantasy poster...it doesn't look the way you might imagine it.

Remember the storms, the electricity, the colors, the blues, the purples, all of it merging together into stars, galaxies, the subtle suggestion of the most perfect female form...

The painting is alive. And it's what won me the art show.

Every time I see it, it makes my heart break just a little more.

"So the central wall, Iris—but it can wait until I come back. I'll only be gone a few minutes," I tell her, pocketing my car keys. I head toward the back door of the gallery, and when I hit the pavement, I draw in a deep breath, trying to ground and center myself. Trying to find...what? I'm not sure. Something to help me get through the night.

Most days, I'm okay. I keep up with my normal routine because I'm holding onto Charaxus' promise. I've got to keep living, even if it feels impossibly hard.

I know she's trying to find me. And I'm trying to find her, too.

I reach up, closing my fingers around the shard at my neck. I wear it every day, never, ever take it off. Sometimes I think I glimpse light shining from the surface of the glass, but it's always explainable: just a reflection of overhead light, or the light of a star.

There was something electric inside of me while Charaxus and I were together. The magic we made was big, explosive. But without her, I can't make the shard do anything.

All I can do is wait. And I hate waiting.

I walk toward my car in the parking lot. The sun is setting behind Buff State's planetarium, and it's painting the sky with extraordinary jewel tones. As I lean against the side of my car, I bury my hands in my pockets. My fingers itch to paint that sky.

The Burchfield Penney is right beside Delaware Park, where the big showdown with Charix happened a few months ago. As I climb into my Beetle and turn on the engine, I have a sudden urge to drive by the park. Despite all of the traumatic things that went down there—the dead knight in the woods (whose body mysteriously vanished); the hostage situation and all of the police interviews I had to give—I still have only fond memories for that place. For that lake.

I grip the steering wheel and consider. It couldn't hurt just to drive by. It's autumn, so the rose garden is dead, but there might be one or two roses still in bloom, and, anyway, Hoyt Lake looks so beautiful at twilight…

It doesn't take much to convince myself of the detour. Because I'm a ridiculous romantic, I park my car on Lincoln Parkway again, and I walk to the rose garden, because I want to see if there are any roses left.

Of course there aren't. It's been too cold lately. I run my finger across one of the dying leaves and sigh. Winter is coming up fast on autumn's heels.

I walk down the steps of the casino, toward the lakefront, my hands deep in my pockets. Everything is so still and quiet. When I reach the sidewalk in front of the water, I draw in a deep breath, inhaling, staring out at the water...

And I stop breathing.

Everything stops, actually: the blood in my veins, the birdcalls from overhead, the soft breeze that was drifting over my skin... It all *stops*, because the world itself stops spinning.

Rising out of the water like a dark-haired mermaid, skin as pale as snow...

She's here. She's back.

Charaxus.

She ascends the steps leading out of the water like an armored goddess, lake water sluicing from beneath her armored plates. I fly toward her as if I have wings, my arms flung around her, and I kiss her fiercely, kiss her like I've been longing to kiss her all of these months...

I kiss her as if no time has passed at all.

She's holding me so tightly that I may be in danger of bruised ribs, but I *love* it, love the way she's holding me, as if she's never going to let go.

Not this time.

"You've got to stop appearing in water," I tease her, breathless when we break apart. There are tears streaming down my face, and I'm really in no great emotional space to be joking, but I can't help it. "I mean, your armor could have weighed you down, and then I'd have to rescue you again..."

"You'll always rescue me," she says, a soft smile curving her lips, "and I'll always rescue you. That's the way it was meant to be. We'll save each other. And find each other. How have you been, beloved?" she asks me, and then she's sinking to her knees, her arms around my middle as she buries her face between my breasts, inhaling me deeply. I'm wearing a t-shirt and jeans, really not sexy at all. I've been hanging artwork all day. But when she breathes me in, my heart rises inside of me, and I cup her cheeks with my hands, tilting her beautiful face up toward mine.

"I've been missing you," I whisper to her, tears falling from my eyes. "What took you so long?"

"I had to come to you across worlds, beloved. I'm sorry for the delay." There are tears in her eyes, too, as she stands, lifting me up by the waist, my legs sliding effortlessly over her hips, her hands on my ass as I kiss her again—fiercely.

There's a storm flickering on the very edge of the horizon as my dark and stormy knight holds me against her, love and lust sparking from her eyes. Her cool hand slips beneath my t-shirt.

"Shouldn't we go home for this?" I ask, grinning, dipping my head back and exposing my neck to her. She kisses it, licking it, her mouth like fire against me.

"I'm already home," she growls, as my hands catch in her beautiful black hair.

There are a few stars twinkling overhead, but they're soon swallowed up by the storm as Charaxus and I run for the trees in the woods, laughing until we find cover, divesting one another of armor, t-shirt, boots, sneakers.

We fall into the familiar, timeworn patterns of each other, reveling in our dream come true.

The End

The next book in the Knight Legends series is out now!

Search for **"Forever and a Knight**, Bridget Essex" wherever you buy your books!

Author's Note

A question that every author gets asked at some point in their writing career is, "Are you anything like your characters?" The answer is different for every author, of course. Some say, "My characters are nothing like me," while others admit, "There's a little bit of me in every character I write."

In my case, the latter is true.

Like me, Holly, the protagonist of *A Knight to Remember,* collects unicorns. Elizabeth from *The Protector* plays violin, like I do. Josie from *Forever and a Knight* lost someone close to her and wrestled with that pain; so did I.

And, like Mara in the book you just read, when I was eighteen, I became homeless for being gay.

Mara and I dealt with that pain differently, and the circumstances around our becoming homeless weren't the same, though some details that I endured were purposefully put into this story. I was told that I had to leave in a very short amount of time, and—like Mara—I struggled to figure out what I should possibly take with me. What, of my life, was precious enough to stuff into a duffel bag. I didn't know where to go, where to sleep, where I was going to get food, and it was surreal, standing outside, gripping the strap of that duffel bag, not knowing.

Feeling so alone that my heart shattered.

My story is sadly, heartbreakingly, not unique. Up to forty percent of our homeless youth in America identify as being somewhere on the LGBTQ spectrum. Forty percent. That's not just a number; that's an epidemic.

But it goes so much deeper than that. Because if you, beloved reader, identify as being on the LGBTQ spectrum, too, you have suffered in your own ways. You have been hurt, like Mara, for being something you cannot change.

Maybe, like me, you have been so lonely, so heartbreakingly lonely, wishing someone understood you. Maybe like me, you ached for love. Maybe, like me, you endured physical abuse, hiding the bruises; or maybe, like me, you knew the deep pain of betrayal by someone who should have loved you, but instead, took away the safe space of your home, and—with it—the innocence of your trust.

I wrote this story as a love letter to the girl I once was, but I also wrote this story as a love letter to you. To you, the person who has been bullied and beaten down. To you, the person who was hurt and harmed for being different. To you, the person who has ached because of love, whose heart was so badly broken, you wondered if you'd ever be able to put all the pieces back together. You have suffered, yes. You have felt deep pain.

But you have not stopped being beautiful.

I, too, have been broken by others. I have suffered for being a lesbian. I have suffered for love. And I have found in the depths of my heart a courage that kept me rising. Because becoming homeless did not mean that I was unlovable. Because being hurt did not mean that I wasn't worthy of love.

Because my suffering did not make me worthless.

And neither did yours.

You are strong. You are courageous. You are beautiful.

Every day that you have survived, every day that you have lived, you embody a dignity and strength that this world needs so much.

Thank you for being. The world needs you.

And your story is important.

Your story is essential.

All my love,
Bridget Essex
June 2016

Made in the USA
San Bernardino, CA
29 November 2016